About the Author

Lindsey Erith was born in Reigate, survived a girl's public
school and severe health problems before achieving a graphics
diploma. Portrait work developed her interest in character and
likeness. Writing is an escape from mobility restrictions,
opening the window on a central character who the audience
will wish to follow. Her life was transformed when her husband,
record producer John Boyden, married her on Valentine's Day,
discovered her novel and gave her the encouragement to submit
it. It was accepted by the first publisher to see it, who also took
her jacket design.

Wanton Troopers

Lindsey Erith

Wanton Troopers

Illustrations by Lindsey Erith

Olympia Publishers
London

www.olympiapublishers.com
OLYMPIA PAPERBACK EDITION

A CIP catalogue record for this title is
available from the British Library.

ISBN: 978-1-80439-913-2

This is a work of fiction.
Names, characters, places and incidents originate from the writer's
imagination. Any resemblance to actual persons, living or dead, is
purely coincidental.

First Published in 2024

Olympia Publishers
Tallis House
2 Tallis Street
London
EC4Y 0AB

Printed in Great Britain

Dedication

For John Boyden, my husband and (non-fiction) romance.

The wanton troopers riding by
Have shot my faun and it will die.

"Hugh Malahide"

Chapter I

Hugh Malahide's visit to his venerable uncle came when he could snatch it in the ebbing of the conflict, unhappy King's man he, in the stormy, cloud-wracked autumn of 1645.

He had half expected warmth at last and blessings, had them stored up as miser's gain. But he had already been upstaged. The tableau that greeted him was not of upflung arms and welcome, but of a medical emergency in front of him, centred on a writhing, groaning heap of bloodied old clothes there on the floor of his uncle's hallway.

For a moment, he feared his uncle had succumbed to his shadow and his footfall as if to reproach him for getting so entangled in the conflict as to delay his coming. Delay was hard, at ninety.

His footsteps, first resolute, faltered. In the dark hallway his eyes adjusted. It was not his uncle, thankfully. That antique was visible in his clumsy wheeled chair, aged to a skeleton, peering at Hugh's outline darkening the doorway.

"You're come, then."

"Half my men deserted, at the last sorry tidings. This we call Taking Winter Quarters." But this year, the old joke failed him. For the first time, he knew nothing could rally them back.

He had leisure forced upon him and not chosen to go home.

The injured man made an "Aaagh" sound as if repudiating him.

"Here's one who didn't reach his billet. We have a soldier

injured up the road, bit of a scurry, he's looking for Fentiman's."

"The enemy, then."

The hurt man made every attempt at this to shake his head, say Nay, but only managed to mouth the word and fall back. Hugh stepped forward to look at him. The maidservants drew back like scared hens before him – do I look so terrible? – leaving a handsome old beldame holding the hurt soldier. A child, thumb in mouth, and a sporting dog peeped nose by moist nose over the bench behind.

Perhaps the habit of authority carried sway. Or Hugh was the only able-bodied man in the room.

"… pair of troopers dragged him up on a hurdle…"

"There's a bullet in him," squeaked one of the servants, "bled a deal, he has."

He was soaking wet, as well. His arrival could only have preceded Hugh's by minutes. Hugh was wet, too, but this was no time to notice. Lightning irradiated the scene again with its too-bright light. In the ominous space before the martial roll of thunder Hugh bent down. "King's man, like myself?"

The wretch nodded, saying, "F—ff."

"Fentiman?"

Hugh could comprehend yes, yes, and the look of urgency in the man's eyes.

But Fentiman was the name of the man down the hill, who rode a horse of the Parliamentary colour, wasn't it? The man who was a thorn in flesh of his uncle's ageing, impoverished Royalist hide.

Old man though he was, Uncle Josiah's wits still ticked. And chimed, as he peered at the casualty, as a picture came to him of a boy's likeness to fit against the white mask going. "Ff—ff" still, like a kettle.

"You're Tom, aren't you?" asked Josiah.

"Tom Fentiman."

"This is the one they disinherited," he hissed penetratingly to his nephew, both wishing and failing to spare the sufferer.

"He'd better have the nearest surgeon, and quickly," stated Hugh.

"We've dispatched the troopers who brought him here," answered the older woman in a contralto. Hugh knew her tone with tint of foreign climes, Luisa, the housekeeper. How could he forget Luisa?

"They need to chase up the barber surgeon," trumpeted Josiah, abandoning the whisper, "they'll have a task, where in three parishes he'll be. Nor may they try too hard. Give a hand, Hugh, there's a fire in the kitchen."

There were two struggles, first to get the prone soldier to the warmth of the kitchen, then to roll the old gentleman in his wheeled chair in the wake of the first procession. Hugh pushing and trundling moved the chariot up the hallway. He left clods of earth behind his unscraped boots. All formalities of arrival, all explanations, had been superseded by the crisis.

He trod the boards in a different calamity to the one in which he lately had been performing, and snatched at it: anything to distance himself. His uncle hissed anew. "Never thought to see Tom Fentiman again! Last time he was whistling home with the fish he'd hooked out of my stream over his shoulder. Not a care in the world." He raised a claw hand upholstered in wasted vellum to shield what he had to say, "This is the plot from a tragedy. If that proud reptile Fentiman the Great were Capulet and this poor boy, Juliet, Juliet that would wed the royal cause, see you Hugh, then we all have a part in this play. If the poor boy is like to die, for all my opinion of the father, he ought to know the state of his child."

"A chance to reconcile."

"Aye."

"Mayhap this Tom's purpose was to reach his own gate."

"Aye. The soldiers were afraid to drag him further, hurt as he is."

"Preventing the homecoming."

"A poor hunted beast," said the old man.

"Will the family soften? You said they sundered."

"They must have the chance."

Hugh had seen death aplenty, seen the pull of home and kin. He'd seen division; yes, even reconciliation leaping divided loyalties.

"He's bad," wept the little servant girl, tears welling. She applied the hem of her apron to her eyes.

Hugh saw she spoke truth. A doctor was most urgently required and in any case the father should be fetched.

"I'll go, if you've no man to send," he told his uncle.

"I'd be obliged," growled Josiah, gruff because his spirit was lasting better than his old carcass and he hated not being able to dash out himself.

So Hugh still clinging wetly in his shirt and buff coat and breeches did not get them off and the towel down he'd been anticipating, but trod more clods back down the kitchen again, felt physical reluctance at quitting the temporary warmth and haven, paused.

"Get the horse doctor, if he hath any skill, and quickly."

Poor Tom Fentiman. Hugh had seen too many die.

Three days before, it could have been himself in Tom's place, sagging by a stranger's fire. He shivered a little and flinched as he stepped back into the rain.

He should have come before, he was shocked to see his uncle failing. "Alas, that I must send you in my stead…" The old man's apology still wailed on the stormy wind as he rode away.

Well, he at least could go, mounted on the barn-door cart horse, his own mare being spent. The farm horse, the one who had the inspiration to be dead lame the day the soldiers swept up horses and sound the week after (so the urchin informed him, heaving the gate in the mud pool left by the pouring rain).

Hugh slunk into his cloak, candlesnuffed. The chance-comer was going forth to beard the Turk at the – not Golden Horn, but Fentimans.

Something new to think about, a new little course of action, took hold of Hugh, a lifeline. He would involve himself in this errand as if it mattered to him, because for half an hour it would remove the great disaster, offer an alternative to the ache, the brooding, even from confessing how matters stood to his uncle.

The King was beaten: so Hugh was beaten too. Mere disaster had not caused him to throw his hand in; but King Charles had revoked Rupert's Commission, and Hugh was Rupert's man.

So he plunged headlong into a different world, for an afternoon, and see in what stead it would stand him.

He set himself to muse upon the likely humour of the local Turk he was a-visiting.

What have we here? He reined in his cart horse.

His musings deserted him like the King's tattered army.

There had been an accident in the hollow where the stream ran high after the storm. The water was spanned by a broken coach, gone in sideways at the ford, one wheel off, another ticking round like the church clock. On the bank, a struggle of slips and hoof marks, a thrown down spoilt cloak, two chests and an upended cask marked stormwrack in their wake.

The carriage horses' crescent and skid hoofmarks cut a morass where their struggles had ended with broken or cut traces. The travellers had gone on. Hugh urged his charger knee deep to make the crossing, holding his booted toes up out of the water. He was stuck by the incongruity of a coach party upon autumn roads in warfare. "This isn't a baggage train, not booty, but a private journey, by Heaven," he told himself. And heading, unerringly, for Fentiman's.

Had the Turk himself only just arrived?

But no, what had he been told? "Luckily for the young man, his father is here. Scarce a month up from London. Wouldn't risk the roads until King's men got cleared away." Thus had Josiah snorted, adding. "Bold as brass now, of course," in a derogatory tone.

Fentiman's great guests had found no protection from the Almighty's flood at the ford. They would be arriving draggletailed. Pursued by the faintly ludicrous single enemy, he, Hugh Malahide, King's man riding a borrowed cart horse.

How would Fentiman take Hugh's tidings that business more urgent then junketings with his Parliamentary friends had called upon him? Did the Puritan conscience even permit junketing with friends? These people, who could fast o'er Christmas...

Rain inserted itself between Hugh's collar and neck. He heartily hoped a word in the ear of the elder Fentiman could speedily be over and done with, so he could dry himself off back by his uncle's fire. This had been the scenario he'd been painting before all this happened.

Let the father and son say their greetings or farewells, whichever way the wound would go.

Here were bronze-tinted trees behind the Fentiman house

darkening the approach with their dripping fan-vaulting. He swung off the broad beam of his mount, looped the reins and advanced on foot, making less ado than were the knot of people complaining their way into the back doorway of a gloomy brick and flint house. They looked like recalcitrant sheep in charge of an apologetic sheepdog; a servant in collie's black and white followed behind them as if wagging his anxious tail.

"Do ye come in, sirs and lady, come in! such bad fortune, but the luck no harm done. Master's been that anxious waiting, you'd not believe. Here we be, safe an' sound, soon fetch the baggage up—"

"Bad enough," bleated a voice.

"I've wrenched my knee…"

It was not old friends, deduced Hugh, getting interested. There was too much apology in the one tone, too much acerbity in the other. Still, the upset was to be laid at the door of the elements, which were beyond the control even of this Fentiman.

Stern Parliamentarians, who looked everywhere for the Will, Hand and Sword of the Almighty, might feel it more personally than mere Cavaliers when he visited a thunderstorm upon them. Hugh smiled at the thought, his first smile in days.

The muddy bat's-wing cape of the last in the group flapped through the entrance, leaving Hugh in the sights of the worried servant who rushed up to him.

"Oh, sir, not hurt? Praise be… please to come indoors and recover yourself."

"Not hurt in the slightest," replied Hugh Malahide, thinking if he was accepted as another of the visitors arriving via the ducking in the ford, then this served him rather well.

It occurred to him he must get the ear of Master Fentiman privately. He trod the cobbles and used the bootscraper, he was

19

in the door. Fentiman's disinherited boy lay three parts dead two miles away. Better a climb down of attitudes before the servants knew. Or these guests.

Probably Fentiman was less black than he'd been painted. His uncle did call geese, geese, and swans, swans – and which men on hearing a stranger derided, will not look for hidden qualities?

Thus thought Hugh, reasonably hopeful he could bring out the father's heart.

In the passageway a serving maid with the face of a cross kitten (ginger, with white tucker under her chin) was struggling off with wet cloaks. She gave Hugh a look but did not offer to take the muddy cloak he wore.

"What a fuss," she muttered flouncing off and managing to sway her hips for his benefit. Hugh repressed amusement. She must think visitors worth her waggle.

He felt obscurely she was right about the fuss. Less should be made over an upset coach in wartime than in halcyon, easy times. It was a pleasure jaunt, presumably, and he could see no corpses, only that he had now come up against the heels of the newcomers. They were living, up on their feet, and they were Parliamentarians. A dowager was beating at mud and grass where she had evidently sat down on the banks of the shipwreck. She was tutting at the underling making attempts to brush her down like a horse.

A haughty fellow began to speak, "We surely don't want to endure this reception straight off? Do we?"

"He hath it lined up in there."

"Then, we'll have to cut it short."

There was a swing round as they beheld Hugh. Eyes swept him. "Well, fellow, have you caught the carriage horses?"

"Yes, sir," replied Hugh promptly. "Soon rounded them up, no trouble." Perhaps someone had. So far he felt like a successful bigamist: deceiving both parties.

"Bid that girl fetch a sewing woman, fellow," ordered the cool young man with gimlet blue eyes – Curious, thought Hugh, that the Puritans hadn't forbidden blue eyes.

"Don't just stand there."

"Certainly, sir." Hugh could see this black crow's feathers were costly, with a sleeve ripped in the accident. He strode confidently out of the wrong door in his urge to appear at home, found himself in a different passageway with tapestries, featuring Job, mainly, with comforters. This passageway had a further door, which was stopped by a heavy figure with his eye to the chink, who stepped back guiltily at Hugh's entry, and shrugged, giving Hugh a grizzled old-bear's smile from little brown eyes sunk in pockets of flesh.

"All this to-do," said he conversationally, "now you're all here, we can proceed."

"I need a swift word with Master Fentiman."

"Not possible, not possible. You'll have to wait. He'll not brook a stay at this juncture," rumbled the bear, not unkindly. He added cryptically, "I'm John Block. Her tutor. Your servant, sir."

Whose tutor? What juncture?

"Um, this is passing urgent."

"Then we'd better find if they're come in." John Block pushed his chink in the door wider, disclosing the room beyond. "Nay, too late, here come your people. You'll have to hold hard. Beard him afterwards."

Hugh saw a broad chamber with a descending stair from a gallery, much gleaming woodwork and as much shining plate as could be wedged on available surfaces. In the thundery half-light, the gleam looked sickly. It contrasted with the denuded state of his uncle's court cupboards. But then this Fentiman had backed the right horse, that of Parliament.

"This is the moment. We'll go in," said old Block. Behind him the ginger maid reappeared in a rustle of skirts and tried to peep over their taller shoulders.

"Here we go at last," she declared. "And 'tis as well, the air's black in there. Master don't need no thunder clouds, the way he loves waiting. Been waiting hours." She perked naughtily up at Hugh.

Here came a serving man with a great platter of things to eat. "Shift over, Nan."

"You can't take that lot in yet, till Master haves his say."

"Ain't he got going yet?" Then noticed Hugh, deferentially: "Trust you weren't hurt, sir? 'Tis a great stir th' upset's caused and no mistake."

Hugh asserted no, not hurt, and grimaced suitably ruefully, then bethought him sympathy was not what he wanted, but a pork pie, such as this helpful fellow in transit for the big room, bore aloft inches from his nose.

He seized a golden castlelet. His damp shoulders and tired muscles twinged. It was no moment to announce he had naught to do with the visitors, and was sworn enemy of Fentiman's in the conflict, as well.

"Where's Master Fentiman?" he asked, brushing crumbs off the mud on his sleeve. He wanted to find Fentiman more than play games guessing what might have all on pins waiting: he was anxious to find the Fentiman sleeve to touch, to draw him aside, tell him, "This is urgent: your good son, Tom..."

He followed the general tide forward into the big chamber. There was no mistaking Fentiman, impatient, fiddling with his cuff. Hugh felt his uncle had misjudged the comparison: reptile he was not, rather a large black galleon sailing about in stately fashion in front of the lesser ships of his household. His nose was high, his visage hewn from good quality rock. A swag of jowls had started to sag off the square jaw onto blindingly white neck linen. Hugh considered that had Fentiman not opted for worldly show (all that plate must mean something), he was such a one as to sail off and found a colony (Fentisylvania?) single-handedly.

In short, an impressive man with a presence, which supplied a small thundercloud brooding over his head in support of the real one still brooding outside.

Hugh was stranded on the wrong side of the room. Two opposing tidal waves were lapping in; the house servants, and the newcomers showing signs of thundershower and rescue in the rain.

What were they all awaiting? It was as if a Progress of old Queen Bess had come to visit, and matters hung between awful preparations and what mood she chanced to be in.

Here came that straight-faced young man, leading in the lady Hugh took for his mother by their noses and curious eyelashes, those of a flaxen pig in his case and in hers of a silver one. They displayed an air about them reinforced by the humble way in which Fentiman advanced to greet them, with much hatting, bowing and what-not. He was not a humble man, Hugh observed: this was for show. It did not suit him.

"An auspicious occasion," quoth he. "Allow me to bid ye a most hearty welcome."

All bowed. The lady looked down her nose at her host and then round the four walls as if she had seen silver plate before.

"Pity you do not look to the state of your banks and bridges."

Fentiman bottled. "We were merely anxious that the roads

23

be clear of King's men and deserters. We could not hazard you journeyed ere this. This climate of ours—" (here he permitted himself the actual relief of tutting) "Untimely."

The lady made a dismissive gesture. "Indeed. And despite that and the state of the realm, we stand here. I acknowledge the deathbed wish of my late husband as to this match he was so set on. For the sake of old friendship, so he said. This I gave my word upon. As one does in such circumstances."

"Dear lady, it is my great wish." Fentiman bowed fulsomely.

Ah, thought Hugh, matchmaking. The clue at last as to the occasion before him. Matchmaking: that nightmare.

"And where is Isabella, then, pray?"

This could continue for hours, thought Hugh. Shall I be driven to shout, "Fire!" to break up the proceedings?

The prospective bridegroom stood turning one gauntlet glove in the other, a boyish colt's way of standing belied by the self-aware face with no smile nor blink (nor expression, really). He stood there in his black with its silver lace, the only lapse from perfection the ripped sleeve. Hair of course to match the eyelashes, flaxen fair, and beneath this helmet shone two blue seas experiencing doldrums.

Hugh temporarily distanced from his mission and fortified by the pork pie, was intrigued. He hoped the young lady would come in like Helen of Troy and make the young hound sit up a bit. He looked round for signs of the prospective bride, for display to the bidders (he knew how these things went).

So, leaning back against the linenfold, he expected name and lineage were wooing coffers. Fentiman wanted the match. So had the dear departed. What about the young people? Wasn't it said, when lovers kissed, one heart would be warmer, one colder? But with arranged matches?

24

He would not think of his own.

In front of him, the pantomime of someone else's.

This Isabella, she would be the heiress, because of Tom. Tom might be about to alter all that, if there was a reconciliation. But as matters stood, she was a worthy property. Worth a bid.

"I have summoned Isabella," announced Fentiman, smiling purposefully. But the staircase remained innocent of his daughter. It was a watched mousehole with many cats. Everyone craned a neck upwards.

"Where is she?" ran a whisper. "What's amiss?"

Then, a sentimental aah, and witless smiles from silly women. "Here she comes…"

She was tall, young and under-rehearsed. Someone had miscalculated, for she was wearing an unfortunate shade of dung-coloured brown. Perhaps her father had ordered the cloth for this occasion, but her looks and complexion were struck stone dead by that shade.

This Isabella was her father's statement of his position in the world, thought Hugh. He waited to get Fentiman's attention. Isabella was a temporary sideshow in Hugh's attention, not the main stage. He awaited his opportunity, fretting. As for this maiden who was to be matched, he wondered if she cared for her brother, who might well be dying up the road?

Fentiman signalled his marriageable property to descend three more steps, then froze her by a large gesture of presenting her, and brandished a smile. His asset, evidently unused to being paraded, looked at the stair treads, ready to run away, shy as a faun.

Hugh felt sympathy, mildly. This Helen of Troy ought to wear gentle colours, even coral, even pink: Isabella was not favoured to launch ships. Why was her hair strained back, no tendrils?

The Parliamentary hens as yet wore their fine feathers. Why not she?

Fentiman should have let the travellers retire to gather themselves after their dampening at the ford. It was unfortunate his urge to demonstrate his daughter, his hospitality and his place in the world all at once, overrode common sense. Also, Hugh could have got to him sooner.

All eyes still looked the one way, as at the now banned theatre. The focus of interest, marooned on the staircase, stood still as an effigy. Malign providence let thunder roll a last time.

Poor creature, thought Hugh. I recognise this. I've been the sacrificial goat – lamb, in her case – unless I'm mistaken, that boy cares not a fig for her. Nor is this sister of Tom's smiling or venturing eyelashes upon the young man. There is a need of something of the sort, if only to fix the his attention and animate him in the presence of his pearl. Are not all heiresses pearls? The cross kitten maidservant, now she would have smirked, which might have stood a better chance of success; dimples, a pout, artifices.

What had this untried maiden to offer? A bosom, a complexion, and by the pallor upon it, a sharp headache.

Her father was actually boring to a close. In two minutes, Hugh could dart forward and beard him.

He was not alone in wishing matters to progress, for as the tableau showed signs of sticking, the bridegroom gestured to his servants to commence fetching in luggage. A big man and a smaller version, in larger and smaller liveries, still with muddied half-cloaks over, tugged off their boots to move as indicated towards the stairs. Each held a casket. Some of Fentiman's people began to circulate with flagons. The men with the luggage waited for Isabella descending. As her skirts cleared the last step they ascended. One had the wrong container, evidently, as the voice of the bridegroom rang out to stop him.

"No, no. Bring that back here."

Halting, the man's stockinged feet slid on the beeswax and he went down on one knee with a bang. The brass-banded box shot from his ham hands, the catch gave way on impact with the banister, and its contents, a waterfall of lace, shot out and carpeted the stairs.

The tide lapped Isabella. She had never had a better presented gift for dramatic effect. With it she received a shaft of feeling at last from the bridegroom's direction, presented with the lace.

Her dreadful day lightened, as at a charm. The equivalent of sunrise transformed her face. She looked up from the floorboards, arrowed by the glance's approval.

Greateleate was standing there focussing over her shoulder in reproof of the clumsy servant, bored, displeased. A stranger stood directly behind him, one of the newcomers in a flung cloak, muddied like the other travellers. She took in the wreck of a well-boned face that had been handsome, dishevelled fall of hair, and that he had been smiling because he had watched her when the lace fell: the wrong man.

Down a well-shaft her heart fell. A gauze of presentiment darkened.

She'd turned away. Hugh insinuated himself firmly forward like a man trying to get his ale served when there is a press in the tavern, succeeded, murmuring, "A word aside, if you please, sir," and had Fentiman into an alcove where a curtain in blue and green thread work would fall if he pulled the cord. He managed to brush his hand and pull as if by chance, the barrier descended and he began to speak.

"Forgive me this intrusion. I bear a flag of truce, if I may so put it. My business, sir, is this. Your son Tom lies hurt at my uncle Malahide's house. I entreat you to come with all speed, or, to speak plain, you may find no son living. I apologise that I needs must break in upon your occasion here…"

"Tom. What mean you, Tom?"

"Your son, T—"

"I own to no son," reverberated Fentiman under his breath. "And you, sir, have entered my house on a false pretence." He seemed as outraged by the latter discovery, his whisper gaining a head of steam like a kettle and rising in pitch.

Clearly, he had been fitting himself up to impress his visitors to the exclusion of all else, and found it difficult to adjust his mental sights on the stranger.

"I own to no son but he who will shortly wed my daughter. You are uninvited, sir: kindly get you gone."

The tone had sharpened. Was that pride which flashed in his eye? Hugh actually stepped back from him. So pride had been the issue, then, when Tom and parent parted? Perhaps it had, with declarations on either side neither could forget. But poor Tom lay a-dying.

What could he do now? He had no pistol to clap to the Fentiman temple, after all; nor would that work, he solitary in this nest of Parliamentarians. He tried again.

"Come with me, sir, before it is too late."

"I have important company, I am about making a match for my daughter, sir, and I will not have this matter compromised by your presence under my roof. I would not be seen entertaining Royalist desert-supporters. Must I have you thrown forth?"

Fentiman glared at Hugh; finding the enemy not merely at

his gate but calmly eyeball to eyeball with him was not a sight bringing him satisfaction.

"Open that door there and leave by it."

Hugh could not talk to him. Pride had armour plate. Perhaps boy and parent had never got on. Or simply crossed swords when the son became a King's man. Over matters where King and Parliament took up arms, hadn't sons, brothers, friends, divided?

But Hugh dug his heels in. Hadn't he seen breaches healed? He'd seen tears shed and embracings after a fright brought dear ones back to their senses. He'd not expected a rebuff. He could have stayed at his uncle's and warmed his bones. Still expostulating to himself, he found himself backed to the door indicated, and even as it was shut on him he could hear Fentiman's voice in the background raising a toast to the prospects of the match.

The door had yielded slowly, and in the passageway Hugh found the human doorstop again, John Block, too rheumaticky to quickstep aside from his eavesdropping. Hugh was too ruffled and dismayed, more than was usual with him, to say anything to the big man at all. He felt like a tomcat whose fur has been rubbed up the wrong way – wanted to run back to the roomful and make a scene, show Fentiman up before them all, shout How Could You, and Be Reasonable, and harsher things. But that wouldn't help Tom.

"I heard – is it true? Is it? Tom lives?"

Hugh grimaced. "He did when I left him. Now who knows? If the barber surgeon came – there was a bullet to come out."

"Tom, Tom living…" Of course, he only registered the hope, not the doubt. He seemed very affected.

"What's Tom to you?"

John Block shot him a look. "Whose tutor do you think I was

before I was Isabella's?"

"Ah."

"The timing, that Master Fentiman should be here! He's only come out of London to get up the match. He hath kept Isabella here in the country, out of the world, of course. Now that this Adam Greatleate hath inherited, we see Fentiman rushing up in order to prevent some other schemer wedding the Greatleate acres."

"You don't like the match? Doesn't your Isabella care for, er, acres?"

"I'll lose her," said Block, downcast. "What will I do?" He looked at Hugh, too sad to dissemble. "But she, oh, understand, we read, we are company, we converse, she's not one of your poor emptyheads with an embroidery frame and half wits... Oh yes, I knew I'd lose her some day, but not yet, you comprehend."

The pity of it was that the accomplishment the tutor had neglected (for which he could hardly be blamed) seemed sheer feminine wiles.

"The match may not go ahead. There's always that."

"She wasn't in looks today," ruminated Block.

"Perhaps that's good?" offered Hugh consolingly. "But now what's to be done about Tom? Might his father climb down?"

"No, and he can't, what's more. For what he's told us, and told the Greatleates—"

"That Tom was dead to him?"

"Worse. That Tom was dead to us all. Killed at Naseby."

"My hat! Has he."

John Block's little eyes sparked. "He can't have Tom a Lazarus, can he? Needs Isabella to appear his heiress, doesn't he, no shadow of doubt there. I tell you this, er, I missed your name?"

"Hugh Malahide."

"My Master is a man who rides high in the late times, prospers, but lacks land. Wants land. In particular, wants those Greatleate acres."

"That's it, is it? Tom can't expect his father at the bedside, then. I dislike returning to tell him that, if indeed he's in any shape to hear it. I'd best go, anyhow. Thank you."

Block however banged his fist into his palm. "Isabella."

"What?"

"She'll come. She will."

"But she's in there." Hugh indicated the big room he'd quit. Sounds of polite jollification issued forth.

"Can you skulk a bit? I'll get her out on a pretext. The visitors need to retire and preen up a bit."

This house was a labyrinth of doorways and passages, behind the big chamber. Hugh opened a broom cupboard before finding the place John Block meant for him to wait in, and then he was surprised by what he took for linenfold opening to disgorge Isabella, coming down a narrow servants' stair in a rush, her skirts filling the space. She was improved into a two-coloured rose, white and pink; the shock of the news about Tom had painted her cheek. But she spoke steadily. She was, he thought hopefully, not silly.

"Tom really lives, but sorely hurt?"

"I am here in hopes of fetching him a lifeline."

Isabella visibly gathered herself. "Then there's no time to lose. Father must have had a false report after Naseby. I can scarcely believe what you tell us! Father hath bid me retire, so I doubt he will send back for me. They'll be weary, they'll be unpacking, won't they... and Father said he wants me better-favoured for the morning."

Old Block seemed to have got his bulk wedged in the

31

corkscrew of the little stair, for Hugh heard his voice coming from above Isabella's shoulder. "Thundery days don't suit her," it said, as if he'd always warned her to avoid suchlike, as parents might warn children of elves in the churchyard, or of converse with strangers.

Which latter risk she was now faced with. Hugh felt he should have some familiar at his elbow, to swear good offices in the matter, like a wizard's black cat.

"Give me two moments," said she, and turning in her skirts as if twisting barley-sugar, was gone in a flash of ankles and petticoat.

When she came back he could see little of her but cloak and eyes. He hoped she'd shed the unlovely brown garment and trampled it before throwing on something warm.

Block saw them out into the concealment of darkness. Hugh fetched his horse. He put Isabella up with him in the shadows, took pains to seat her as impersonally as he could and not clutch her, though the folds of her cloak hardly permitted his offending her. He sensed her shy as a hind.

"Sit tight," he said. "We'll be there in no time, you'll see Tom, stay a little and then I'll convey you back. I'm sorry about the horse; my poor mare came in on her knees this afternoon and it seemed more urgent to get here than to cut a dash, hence the cart horse."

"Had you brought a chariot drawn by giraffes, in the circumstances, it would have done well enough," she said, which he liked. Was she an original? "It was providence, their upset in the stream. Everyone the worse for wear has retired to recover. Had not Father insisted, they'd have dodged all the greeting and show." And she sighed in a tide through the cloak. "I know I wanted to."

"They can't have felt at their best," he said, irony not quite concealed. "Let you off the hook to slip out, though. That old rogue Block, fortunate I chanced on him. Does he always, er, listen?"

"He needs to know things, he says."

"Tom a favourite of his, I gather."

"Yes. Our hearts failed when we heard Tom was dead at Naseby. He cried as well as me. How could Father have said it? How could he?"

"When did he hear young Greateleate inherited?"

"About then."

"I daresay…"

"Father won't see good in Tom. They had such outcries. The pictures shook! Father is ever right, and, Tom a worm, in his eyes. Tom used to laugh at Father, and that made it worse."

"Always does."

"Tom was always laughing. Must I lose him twice? Will he live? I cannot bear it a second time. Oh, forgive me. I am talking too much because I fear if now, 'tis hopeless."

He had hoped she could have gone on whispering, to cling to the first phase of three: some hope, fading hope, despair. Tom might well to be dead already. Naseby would have spared him for nothing.

"Naught to forgive. Your feelings do you credit."

Crossing the stream distracted them both, because she was anxious not to return with tell-tale dirty shoes, and he had to dismount without upsetting her, pull on the bridle, discover anew that his boots leaked. Then he couldn't remount without dirtying her, and so walked at the horse's head, which held them up a little, but not more than could be helped, in the circumstances.

At his uncle's door, where a small sun shone in the porch

33

from a bull's-eye lantern, he armed her down, tied up the horse. "Now you're courageous," he had to say, in case she wasn't. Now to face the fate of the wounded man.

"Yes, yes," she responded.

"Right then." He seized her arm and together they ran like a tornado down the passage towards the kitchen.

Isabella flinched firstly because the man she knew for the horse doctor was standing there over the apparent corpse of her brother. Fear slapped her. In the big kitchen, light from the fireplace outlined the group in front of it like cut-outs until her eyes adjusted from the outer dark, filled in the detail. The serving maids knelt, hands touchingly clasped in a quick prayer, their aprons tumbled, and with them the anxious sporting dog, red-rim-eyed as if next he too would weep; or howl.

She chiefly registered, however, the turn towards her by the statuesque old woman and the horse doctor. The ancient man who could not rise swivelled in his chair. They were grouped around the body of the man who could not notice.

"Bravo, young mistress Fentiman," offered the old man. "Alone? Your father not with you?"

"I'm come too late," she quavered.

"Nay, mistress, you're come timely," This was the warm country voice of the horse doctor, and Isabella gasped.

"Benezer, what are you doing to him?"

"Who else'd come? I got the bullet out, an' who else'd try it, see? Mistress, do you come forward an' take his hand, this just a faint. If he comes to, mebbe he'll know you. I got to have one more go."

Isabella sank to her knees, had Tom's hand already. "What do you mean, 'one more go'?" Ebenezer held a pair of pincers. She shuddered, knowing he used them on horses.

"I want the plug o'leather, or 'twill fester."

"From his buff coat," came Hugh's voice in her ear. "The shot will have carried that in first."

"Hold hard."

Isabella had one glimpse of the angry red mouth of the wound, hastily shut her eyes. She held Tom's limp hand to link with him. She scarcely could recognise him, so bloodied, drained and changed. He was merely a hurt man lying there, his spark and identity wiped away. Anyone's brother.

Someone touched her shoulder.

"'Tis done, he hath the piece," Hugh Malahide's quiet voice came like the tide on a beach in the distance. "You can look, now."

She opened her eyes on a secure white bandage over wadding which the man who cared for horses was securing. At first she only saw the bandage and the hands, then the room began to return, the murmur of voices. Then she couldn't get up, remained shuddering on her knees.

Even then, as they went to remove Tom's hand from hers, covered him with a blanket and laid him back on the makeshift couch, she registered that the pulse in his wrist as it passed through her fingers beat still. Only then did she take heart.

Ebenezer laid a nasty little object carefully down in the pewter bowl on the stool. It was impossible to see what it was, but Hugh swore to her it was the bit of leather sought for. He hoped privately that the shreds of Tom's shirt that would also have been in the path of the bullet were clinging to the disc of leather.

If it was all out, the hurt could start to mend. If not – but he thought the horse doctor had been skilful.

"He hath been spark unconscious," the old man was telling

her, "the better so. He's missed the excitement. Don't you turn faint, now! Luisa, is there a drop of brandy?"

The hot brandy and water went crashing down. She heard the man who had escorted her explain why she had come ("bravely," she heard, but queried if she imagined this, or was it the brandy), and of the events at Fentiman's.

"She escaped," he was saying.

When she recalled this evening, the mind's-eye pictures were as if down a tube. The clasp of her hand on that of her unconscious brother was the focus of alarm and fear. Voices came distantly, offstage, from the shadows.

In her ear, a rather closer voice made her jump.

"He's resting. Not failing."

Isabella gained a hold on herself.

"His pulse beats." As she attended upon this man, she saw him visibly write reassurance on the expression with which he was favouring her.

"There's life and hope," said Hugh, giving her the platitude he had used at many life-and-death-beds. "You had best come again. Tomorrow? I hesitate to keep you now, because of the circumstances by which you came in the first place."

"But, how can I leave him? Oh." And wrestled with childish dismay, emerged, with resolve. She turned to the horse doctor. "Benezer, keep this matter close, that I came here. Promise."

"I dare swear nobody's get this from me," assented he. "All I'll be saying, th'old mare gone lame again and that's why I came."

There was no more unified cause than a lost one, thought Hugh. The single kitchen here, multiplied nationwide, would have won the day for King Charles, had only kitchen maids, old men and out-of-work combatants each led regiments and had cash to pay the courageous.

Tom had fallen among protectors. Isabella swallowed and blinked and looked round at Hugh's uncle and the women, included Hugh.

Perils bit. Would she be discovered missing, or even worse, be revealed at the bedside of the Royalist brother? As if a curtain parted Isabella took a step into an alternative crisis to her alarm at the sight of the bridegroom.

"If my brother lives, 'tis thanks to you all," she said. Hugh stepped up with her cloak, tented her in it and she steadied herself up, yielded to his pushing hand and permitted him to steer her out of the kitchen, out into the waiting, concealing dark.

"I dare not speculate," was all she said as he piloted her back to Fentiman's.

"The bullet's out. And the bit of buff coat. And, yes, keep from speculating. You had best sleep a wink on and off tonight. You'll disappoint Master Block if you aren't in looks tomorrow."

"Life hasn't been a flat calm today, oh, what next…"

"Only that I miss my footing at this wretched ford and you have to save me from drowning," said he calmly, "if we survive that, tomorrow you must take the next chance to slip out to see how Tom does. Not easy, with that houseful."

"Father hates waiting, he's too eager to bargain my settlement, and then there's what they want of him in return for their acres. It is too plain he is after their land. I am not an equal exchange, I discern, for acres." Her voice had tailed away. He thought she nearly had said, not party to my fate.

Of course, her position in the world would be settled for her. Hugh, of all people, knew the way of these alliances, these matches.

This was hardly the moment for a lecture on the advantages

of netting a prosperous, landed, fat and victorious Parliamentarian for her husband.

Tom's broken and defeated return pointed a sad moral. She ought to be practical; if only as prudent. For all his own calamity of an arranged match, he knew that in this divided, ruined England, security, even spouses, were going to be scarce. And needed. In Isabella's case, to escape from Father.

He let himself say. "Keep your concerns for Tom quiet. Attend to your father. Smile at him. Er, smile at Master Greateleate. And let us hope, for a start, they've not missed you this evening."

"I've the key to my bedchamber door in my pocket. I locked it and left John Block on guard to declare my headache hadn't lifted. I do not fear they will have forced the door," she was suddenly vehement, with a first flash of woman's eyes, as he noticed as he dismounted her, "certainly not Adam Greateleate."

She minded, then, that the bridegroom had not aped affection.

He had pulled the horse up a little way from the house, amidst sheltering trees. A hunter's moon was caged on high by swaying branches, and the air had cleared. With it, at last, her head, as if the twin crises of her day spun off and allowed the imprint of the moment.

Inadvertently she found herself close to Hugh. Standing closer than she would have, due to a damp tree trunk on one side and the warm horse on the other, lit by the lantern of the large moon, for the second time that day she was pierced by his approval. Isabella again flinched from masculinity, breadth of shoulder, straight back, and that once he would have been handsome. She was under-rehearsed, in the sudden proximity to a man to whom she was neither pledged nor about to be sold for acres.

"I cannot think why you have been so kind."

He could. It dulled the edge of despair. For the little spell of diverting himself he'd put action for an injured confrere as a buffer for his personal last ditch.

Hugh Malahide, friend and neighbour. Hugh Malahide, beaten malignant. Hugh Malahide, putting a front up, postponing the truth, the still, quiet moment alone with himself.

"Go in," he said darkly, "go in. I'm no Samaritan, only the usual self-seeker with naught else to do."

She fled.

But he thought she hadn't been aware of him, that was what came of being older, more worn, and at that last utterance, more truthful, than the blue-eyed Adam Greateleates of this world, who made her fearful.

Chapter II

When there was no more to be done for the wounded man, he blankly dying or sleeping and they could not yet know which they left him with a watcher of the womenfolk. There was a pause. It was this point Hugh had been trying to stave off.

His involvement of the afternoon, though spurious, had proved a dockleaf to the sting. Now for the barbs, bitterness, dregs drunk, the void of hope.

Since his uncle didn't sleep and as presently nor could he, there was a second night watch that midnight, while the big moon blew in the clouds. It began then as if telling a confession, and for three days and nights, in fits and starts, Hugh told his uncle bits and disjointed pieces. He was putting off the small moment of facing himself and declaring what he now would do.

But he had made a beginning.

"I lost hope," he made himself say levelly, "whatever hope is, after Bristol… the last city, the port, the trade; whatever fell, Bristol was a symbol of survival. Wearing a touch thin, but—" He shot a look at his uncle. The old skeleton was being fed soup by Luisa, to spare his shaky old hand. Food and bread he could cope with well enough, but he said, glaring up at Luisa, "Liquid's untidy." Serenely spooning, she continued, pretending not to listen. The old man was glad of the moment with the soup to conceal from his nephew how upset he was for him.

Rupert had surrendered the city of Bristol a month back. The expressions of sorrow – indeed of despair – that Josiah felt as keenly as every King's man left standing, would not gainsay the event.

"You were ever the Prince's man," he responded. "That the Prince asked for terms was not to his discredit. He hath been sore pressed." His nephew's jaw tightened and a gunpowder gleam shot from his tired eye, sharp enough to have caused a lesser elderly to choke on his broth. Josiah did not choke; rather, he registered there was spirit still in Hugh. He was relieved.

"'Tis not the Prince I sundered from." Hugh started out of his chair as if a keg of gunpowder had felt the proximity of the slow-match. The singing bird in its wicker-bounded world let forth liquid alarm notes as the cage swung in contact with Hugh's skull, who steadied it as if it was his hat, tramped to the window, there looked out, the man at a masthead who sees no landfall. Behind him, the birdcage swung diminishingly and his uncle applied his camel's-lip to the soup.

"Who else but Rupert could have won this sorry conflict? Had the King no nephew, would we have outlasted the campaign that first season? The difference, in being bred to arms, and sitting in Whitehall or Oxford hearing what you want to hear, believing in the Right you bear... I laid down arms upon the tidings that the King revoked Rupert's Commission, I gagged on that... nor would my men go on." His men had the consolation ahead of homecomings, of open arms, the prospect of mending their old pattern of life. It was easier to talk about Rupert than explain he personally could not go home, and impossible to begin to say why.

He swung round, the bird, incautiously, trilled, felt the atmosphere, and saved it for later. Josiah, gathering up, avoiding a platitude, threw Luisa and the soup bowl to one side. She melted from the room to leave the words between the men.

41

Josiah glared to cover up what old age does when fronted by one's favourite brought low.

"I dare say I am the oldest set of wits in the hemisphere," he announced from his lair deep in the armchair, as if his mind wandered along the tracks of the witless and had left Hugh behind. "Do you know when I was foaled? People say 'Goes back to Good Queen Bess,' 'tis said of some poor fumbler: poor old fool. Ah, but I beat that, you know; I was foaled in the last year of Bloody Mary when we had a Spanish King. Can't be worse than that, you'd think... be amazed, how the Almighty's blown the weathercock over the years."

He's right, get some sort of perspective on it, Hugh urged himself, and overstrung, visualised a pageant passing: Dago King Philip and his cockleshell Armada; heretics crackling, Queen Bess ageing in a ginger wig, his uncle mewling in the cradle. He felt fevered, but, alas, sane.

And he came to sit beside that infant now his nine decades older, and was grateful to his uncle for still breathing. Hugh took the claw hand. "I know," he said, "you're a survivor, praise be. I am only the man who had to hang the white flag out. Time I woke up. It was all too real, I believed it was a nightmare. Nay, best face reality. This last while hath loomed too large with me."

He withdrew his hand from the old man's, clutched his own two strong ones together and condemned himself for self pity. In these days others, numberless others, were sinking in the same boat, in the same tide.

"'Tis a bit of a body blow to know we will not win, and yet we live, and are, probably, kicking," said Hugh.

That was a flash of the old Hugh, at least.

It was all comparative.

Up the hill, the young lady, now in her nightshift, was leaning on the windowsill watching the inconstant moon. The moonshine did not comfort Isabella. She been anticipating she would be struck by lightning at the arrival of the bridegroom, but despite the actual thunderstorm of that man's arrival, no elemental force had accompanied him. She was trapped as bait for those acres, for the inevitable fate.

No doubt she was her father's maiden asset: to guard her as such, she had lived closely kept. She had not been prepared for the world.

She had reacted to indifference with pain, but even then, maybe in reaction to the dreadful day, in a new sensation had received a flash of most un-puritanical femininity, keenly inopportune; it had been caused by proximity to a total stranger.

Hugh came downstairs on the third morning and gathered favourable reports on the injured Royalist. Luisa had gently been sponging him, a towel over her arm, basin cupped; Hugh offered to shave him on the morrow.

He felt an odd fellow-feeling for Tom, not for being weak and feeble, but for not being able to go home, either.

They were avoiding that topic.

"You're still eating more than he is," he told Josiah, who was facing the day dispatching bread and butter with the crusts off and drinking small ale. He would have offered to shave his uncle also, but felt this might be tactless, for tufts upon his face represented planned beard and whiskers and which bad judgement with his shaky hand, there was no telling.

"You'd best join me."

Hugh hacked at the loaf, discovered hunger, being human after all. "Good grief," said he, "I'd forgot good peaceful mornings. A health to us survivors."

That's better, thought the old man. The tankard half-hid his nephew so he beheld rather more pewter than the ageing face. He'd seen the young man, so handsome, with the well-placed cheekbones, that eye, become a wilder, stronger man. Adversity had brought Hugh into his restless masculine self. Experience in his ultramarine blue eyes looked back at Josiah, who saw the man of action sitting drinking a morning draught, action curtailed.

O, apostrophised the old man to himself, angry at life, caring, why had Hugh of them all, to lose. It had been the answer. He knew more than Hugh realised. Now, the wrong answer.

Perhaps it was unfair that he had never liked Athalia.

No, it wasn't unfair. She was too confoundedly pleased with herself.

He wanted to say to Hugh, be my steward, stay: but pride forbade, in case Hugh refused, and hurt him.

Survivors, thought Hugh, scraping back his chair. These three days had helped. Here he was, no longer as large with himself – a tiny fly on the clock face of the tick of years, reduced, but not, he hoped, not less himself.

It was the wretched self that ached, but this he put from him and looked out at the autumn morning, shawled with cobwebs. He remembered Tom, was ashamed about his preoccupations, while he still had limbs and strength. Then he saw Isabella coming, in her cloak. He went to meet her.

He had got involved with this sub-plot to his own, had fetched Tom's sister up twice from the willows at the stream where there was a slippery plank bridge for foot passengers. He had warned her his uncle's meadow was Royalist territory, even yet; "Mud is much the same, whose-ever," he'd said, making way that she might avoid the worst of the pathway.

"I share Tom's persuasion, never doubt." She sighed,

relieved to tell this truth out loud away from Parliamentarian father, bridegroom and future in-laws, all black as crows.

Yesterday she could not come, what with the visitors and what she had to do with the housekeeper. Old Block however had stepped out, making heavy weather of the plank bridge and needing an arm across. He had paused to blow a bit halfway up the meadow and to inform Hugh about the dinner with which Fentiman was feting his guests. Hugh had not liked to ask if Block had actually been present, or at the keyhole.

He'd rubbed his hands together when mentioning Tom's sister. "Bit of lace, her mother's pearls; for all there's Madam Greateleate looking down her nose, dressed as a silk and taffeta jackdaw, as if we all should dress like jackdaws nowadays…" He let the little eyes twinkle, indicating Isabella's better curves with his two hands, shrugging to excuse his partiality.

Hugh took hold of the cloak from Block as he stumped into the house, threw it on a peg in the hall. "I'm glad your young lady was in looks. Curious, this shift in what's fit and what is not, with the change of times come upon us. Goodbye to the colours. We're in for a black rainbow."

"This the door?" Block let Hugh show him the way. "Thank you, I am no greyhound when it comes to stairs. Phew. Yes, Isabella's looks are brightening now Tom's improving. I heard—" He acknowledged Hugh's eyebrow, unperturbed. "Overheard – the bridegroom getting the credit, there he is leading her about by the hand making speeches in her ear, and that bevy of silly old dames cooing and oiling their tongues and…" He had reached the landing at the top of the stairs, reared round at Hugh and performed a rheumaticky mountebank version of Adam Greateleate's smooth manner as he led Isabella to and from. It was not a pretty sight, and made Hugh laugh.

"At least the cold dog's warming up," he said.

"Yes." Block snorted finally. "But let's say Tom's put her in looks, not the likes of that one." He hoped so, evidently, as did Hugh, picturing Isabella and the bridegroom. He now opened the sick-chamber door and left Tom and the tutor to their reunion.

Well, this day two mornings later she'd managed to slip out. And early, to dodge the Greateleates, her father and the half-dozen guests before they quit lie-abed chambers. They had been up late, Hugh supposed, after the feast.

Not so Isabella. He brought her in to speak to his uncle. As she bent to enquire how he did, gracefully, Hugh speculated if the Greateleate boy appreciated these assets she brought him, if he cared. Was it only John Block, no suitor, who valued her?

Hugh's uncle tilted his head to look up at her, crossly because he was chained like a prisoner in his chair.

"Goodmorrow, lady," Josiah had said, "have you roped the bed-sheets, climbed down?"

"By heaven no, far too visible in broad day, no, I am bribing old goodwife Jenkins in the gate cottage as a first line of defence, to say I am most days a-visiting. She is both blind and deaf and simple. So there is no judge or jury would prove I was there or no."

"That old witch is likely twenty years my junior," complained Josiah, "will she remember the bribe, then? You don't want a good groat wasted."

"Nay, the coin goes into the palm of her son Sammy, and he'll get her a few comforts she can do with."

"How do you escape the house, then?" asked Hugh. "If not bedsheets? Have you a passage underground?"

"Master Block taps my door to give Coast Clear. It feels as if I am making off with the silver spoons. Block is my ally, each time I bring back your meadow on my shoes he cleans them for me. We conspire together."

Outside the invalid's door, Hugh stood aside for her to precede him. "Tom's stronger today," Hugh reassured her. But she ducked away from him, dark eyelashes hiding irises amethyst coloured. He'd bitten at her the first time he'd taken her back to Fentiman's, had given way to his own problems, It was clear that one look at him then had startled her, and he regretted his effect upon her. He had added to her difficulties. During these snatched visits he had been attentive, it hurt him a little that she was wary, stood back from him physically. Perhaps his nerves were still raw.

The door creaked as Hugh opened it. There was Tom in bed, propped up. He reached out to his sister. She knelt down to his level, held his hands.

"There you are, Bella."

"That bit of your complexion I can see under your foliage looks less like the bed linen today."

"The foliage, as you call it." He rubbed one hand over his stubble-field face. "Has its days numbered. Hugh here's going to shave me. Then you can admire me again."

Hugh wished she felt as easy with him. Excluded, with a pang of trespass, he turned to slip away.

"But stay," Tom called, preventing this manoeuvre, struggling to sit up higher, tawny whiskers and equine nose giving the impression he was about to whinney. A horse cast in his stall, thought Hugh. He hauled Tom up a bit on the pillow.

Under the whiskers, ah, a first, Tom managed a smile; he spoke to Isabella. "I couldn't sleep last night. This fellow came to talk when he found me in need of company in the night owl's small hours."

"He's mending," Hugh declared. "This is the first stage of plaguing the life out of us."

Isabella managed half a glance towards him, shy as a creature. He saw more eyelashes. At which the self-announced self-seeker felt coals of fire. Then she blew on his embers by raising her game. She blushed at him.

He turned aside, allowing them their comforts to one another. The room in which Tom was now garrisoned was hitherto the particular nest his uncle had drawn about himself decades ago, which he had deserted now he was beyond stairs, cat-napping in the rampart of cushions in the parlour. In Hugh's mind-picture this bedchamber had lived unchanged since last he set foot. It was still a colourful, untidy treasure chest. There was the little carving of the Lion of Venice, paw on book; there the pair of watercolours of that city taken from across the lagoon, hung unevenly, and behind the door a long-nosed mask hung up by fading ribbon. Trophies of long, long ago, when Josiah's father had taken ill in the Ambassador's train and died suddenly, occasioning Josiah's youthful single journey to the great overseas. There was the pink and gold tapestry, now lightly moth-eaten, where a unicorn peered into a fountain and dewdrops round as apples popped out around its dainty hooves upon the needle-worked grass.

Tom lay stranded as if spat out by Jonah's whale, in the clasp of the feather bed. First he had been feverish, then bloodlessly pale. Hugh listened to him telling Isabella, as elder brothers do, that she had grown since he left her as a twelve-year-old, in the other lifetime before Edgehill.

"What a room," he said, including Hugh again, "does the rest of the house match up?"

"Josiah is a hoarder, with all the implications in a long life

48

in one house," said Josiah's nephew, "few live to ninety, have an Italian wife, or once did. There's her books, her music, too, all kept."

Isabella had risen, looked around, standing under the tapestry. Hugh didn't doubt she still could catch a unicorn. He regarded first the gentle beast, then called up words his uncle had once spoken.

"I always hoped the maiden would come." Josiah had sighed. "She did; ah, but alas, briefly." She lay in the churchyard. Luisa had come as her duenna, went in her stead to run the house; went everywhere? On that, Hugh had speculated, but had kept this to himself.

Tom's voice recalled him. "I thought that I dreamed when I woke up in this chamber."

Isabella touched the little lion of Venice. "Treasures like to be admired. They weren't meant to be ignored."

"What's outside?" asked Tom. "What's the outlook? I can't see from here."

"There's a bowling green." Isabella smiled at her brother, heartened he was better. "Untended." She turned, the smile didn't falter as Hugh crossed its path, her first real smile towards him, with the eyelashes, as she continued to turn and wasted the smile on the room and its haphazard, faded trappings.

The abdication of his personal creation of chaos when stairs had defeated Josiah had evidently been easier than spring cleaning. There were jars of moulting cut quills, a precautionary mousetrap, empty, padded old Tudor suits cast flat like effigies. On the previous night, they had seemed to waver and stretch and breathe in the hallucinatory flare of the candle, as Tom cried out the injustice his father had done him.

In daylight they were inert again, and Tom seemed eased.

Isabella stroked a finger upon a quilted doublet. Dust rose.

"'Tis as with a suit of armour," reflected Hugh. "The dimension of the wearer's there."

Isabella blew dust off her finger. "Your uncle can't think this mode will return again?"

"Nearer, that these represent his young man's self, he can't throw himself out... those doublets, so real, as if," he remembered the previous night, "as if the quilting might breathe and shed the dust, and it be fifteen eighty-nine again."

"And she be there, from Italy."

"Ah," he said, "she's waiting."

Did he only want to talk to forget himself? No, his interest in Isabella had deepened. How was she feeling? Would she desert Tom and take the wide Greateleate acres? Could she own her brother, if she did? Tom had risen from the dead unbeknown to the bridegroom, who expected to take Isabella as Fentiman's heiress, his sole child. Fentiman could clearly not disabuse a son-in-law with acres.

Tom, who had always been laughing, had not been laughing last night.

At this point, Hugh had forgotten himself and his own woes; he pushed back the sweep of hair from his brow and smiled at Isabella because she had been brave and was here holding the hand of her disinherited brother. It was timely that she returned the smile back at Hugh, for all that she fronted him where the light from the window was not kind, showing the scattering of pockmarks down one cheek and that his face had aged before his hair, barely silvered, like the guard hairs of a tabby cat. The lines round his eyes bit deeper with that smile. She felt the attraction of character, saw the dark blue eyes.

She was unused to masculinity. As if smiling back had been

too personal an act, she turned her head away. If at that moment he had offered to teach her the alphabet she would have hung on his words, aware of an un-Puritanical, pleasurable inner arrow.

He was relating something acceptable, as it happened.

"We had to sweep a crow from up the chimney before we could light Tom his fire and fetch him up here, black and dusty, petrified, like a clergyman awaiting burial."

There, attending to Hugh, and turning as he led her around the room and the stranded Tom, Isabella heard more of the history of his Italian aunt and of Luisa.

"These anti-papisticals will not have it that Luisa might be as good a Protestant as any of us. Oh, the universal truths noone believes, that old Queen Bess died a maiden, that the King of Spain be a Christian, and so forth."

Tom entered the fray. "Faith can't be proved, yea or nay."

"That's what I hold against the Godlys, forcing their views, whatsoever, on the rest of us." Hugh shrugged, "Saving your views, lady."

Tom grimaced against his cushions. "I wouldn't care to join a Heaven full of Cromwell's crew. Now they look to have won the day, what they intend to force on us here below is quite bad enough."

The Royalists and the Royalist's sister sank in gloom together. The sun, not temporarily, had gone in from their day. Offstage, in the indigo cast of twilight, King Charles would call a Council of War, while Prince Rupert at Belvoir Castle, furious at the slanders done him, would shortly have the bitter ashes of satisfaction that his detested adversary, Digby, the courtier now become Lieutenant-General, would lose the Northern Horse. Night, of King Charles and King's men, darkened on the path to a Puritan horizon.

"Have you tidings?" asked Tom.

"I've put nose to a broadsheet. The Prince hath yet to see the King."

"Will you return? If there's a mending between them?"

Hugh essayed dispassionate reasoning. "For Rupert's loyalty, he hath got pains. For mine, I'd return were there more to do than, than to be ground down one by one like loiterers cut off by the tide. My men have high-tailed for home. I could return to Oxford—"

"Too late." Tom shrugged as much as strapping and soreness allowed. "Too damned late. What'd we be, but dregs of beaten regiments? That's all it would be, I vouch for it."

"Aye, they've coined a word for that: Reformadoes."

The bedroom door opened and the sporting dog sidled up and placed his browny-pink nose on the bedclothes.

Even the animal looked mournful. Tom launched another shaft at the fellow defeated soldier. Had Hugh been that dog he would have taken refuge in the same expression, and probably hidden under the bed as well.

He attempted no expression when he heard Tom asking, "You could go home? You are but a-visitor here; that's so, isn't it?"

Hugh thought of the King's reply to his small son when they were out on the roads campaigning. The Duke of York had asked, "Can we go home now?"

And his father had answered, "We have no home."

He replied, "Let's say I don't choose to."

"What, are we fellow creatures?" Tom was brightening, tired of being abandoned on his own.

"As yourself," Hugh told him, "I lack the welcome."

"No wife?"

Rupert, the cause of the King, his leadership, the phoenix of command as a soldier: all had crashed. Yet these he could admit to, they were universal. Tom had these. He couldn't go home. So Hugh made himself reply to Tom. Isabella saw the lines clench on his face.

"She is a good little woman," said Hugh humanly crossly. It was his turn to look away whilst gazing as if with interest at the autumn leaves dancing out there upon the bowling green.

Isabella made mental adjustments unbecoming to a gently reared maiden.

But he didn't see these, instead Athalia's tight face with its conviction that her dowry had purchased him body, soul, beliefs, and most unwelcomely, as her poodle. His refusal to be patronised, spoken for, or worse, to wag for a titbit, had cost him dear.

('What would you be without me? A nothing.')

He had felt his obligation to a bankrupt, loved parent was over-riding, on that betrothal day years ago. Athalia had demanded that her house and her line, of which she was the last, should be decorated by the best looking man of his generation. That his looks had not lasted had been one of her complaints.

Hugh had left for the conflict as might a man galloping a willing horse over a burning bridge to freedom.

King Charles could do nothing for him now. He would have to find his own path. But how different the coat tails of defeat to the peacock train of victory.

I'll not go back, he heard his inward voice. That's the only certainty I do know. When am I going to have the thunderbolt I need, of inspiration?

Then a lesser shaft penetrated. He had just experienced unbuttoned relief at mentioning the truth. Perhaps he, defeated

King's man, had faced his new beginning.

The attendant reverie stamped a hold on his features.

Tom reared up in bed, recalling him, "I'll make Father suffer for what he's done to me. To have him deny me, me – sheer vindictiveness, that's what, and two can play that game…" His voice was strained, high pitched, and Isabella flinched. And Hugh Malahide forgot his wife in the sudden glimpse of trouble brewing in the flash of Tom's red-rimmed eye. With his faintly equine cast of countenance he looked like a bolting horse.

Uncontrollable.

Only then did Hugh think they might be harbouring a cuckoo. He fumbled for a commonplace to smooth the moment. "Put it aside. Get your health up a bit, gather up."

"How can I, with Isabella about to wed my inheritance to some mountebank Father hath imported? My prospects go with Isabella to him. Even the pearls round your neck, Bella, they're mine."

"I wish to take naught from you, Tom."

"'Tisn't your choice, is it? Marry and what you get from Father goes to your fat husband. To cheer him into smacking your cherry lips."

"Don't." And she visibly paled, losing what cherry she had.

"What do you expect? My thanks? I wish I'd got myself into Basing House and shut up safe in there, not dragged in here, I swear it."

Basing House was a last bastion, probably anywhere, a refuge likely to prove temporary, with the New Model Army sitting outside it this minute, as Hugh knew.

"Why didn't I? Because I looked to my blood and kin to own me."

Hugh intervened in a soldier's tone, "Call Isabella family

enough for this day. She's owned you despite it all. Once you're a touch stronger we'll set up some way to heal the breach."

Tom had slumped back on his pillows, white.

"Sorry." He shut his eyes. "Sorry, Bella."

And they were sorry for him.

Isabella was late leaving. Then there was a delay between going downstairs and quitting the house, for even as Hugh followed her out onto the landing, they heard unexpected cries of excitement in the hallway below.

"Whatever's afoot?" he said aloud.

It looked like a boiling-down of Christmas, Fair Day and a tug-o'-war below them. A crush of happy people.

The sporting dog burst between Hugh and Isabella, nearly upsetting them in his haste. He understood more quickly than they. The melee resolved itself into a stout soldier in a buff coat, clutching aloft and holding round the knees, his wife Jane, her cap over one eye; at his boots clung the barely walking child, at his other side was Jane's sister, the other of their maids, hugging him, her cheeks bedewed rosy apples.

Behind this human maypole, the statuesque Luisa pushed Hugh's uncle in his chair, and they were exchanging united glances.

"Safe an' sound, see!" cried the newcomer. "Oh Janey!"

And, "Oh Brownie, Brownie!" as his dog jumped up at him. "At last!"

His three successive cries wrung the heart of his wife, his dog, and everyone present. It was clear a wallow in emotion would be essential for half the morning, and Hugh thought they'd leave some over so later even he might join in. His heart ached.

The morning seemed very calm and still after that, the downs above the valley blue in the autumn haze. Already the warmth of the day reflected back from the brick and flint housefront and took a good aspect of southerly sun. Josiah would look up to the chalk ridge in the distance of a morning, as if at the line of a sleeping beast. Whereas the Fentiman house sat in the shadow cast by the downs, cold to match its Puritan sympathies.

Between these two houses of opposing parishes, the symbolic Rubicon of the little stream divided the sunny run-down house and its water meadows, its farmland, from the single boggy field which was all Fentiman could claim.

His wealth lay in London coffers. They were not the sort of riches he could throw wide the casement to admire of a morning. The lack of this had lately got to Fentiman, because all he could proclaim at his country retreat was his rather grand gates and a cottage by.

At which Josiah had poked ridicule, for decades. Perhaps it was for the best that St Joseph's on the one hand and All Saints on the other made sure the enemies sat in separate churches of a Sunday.

Isabella, daring to enter the Royalist house sheltering Tom, was creeping out as if meeting a lover, even as an actual bridegroom was ingratiating himself with her father. She was about to be traded for those acres he was angling for. The fool's paradise that silly maidens conjure up of their lover had sunk in the gathering gloom upon Tom and his prospects. All that was needed now was for her to be discovered visiting the disinherited Tom by their father. She bit her lip, but here she stood, bridges burning.

The stranger noticed.

"You're between the two fires, aren't you. Three, if including Master Greateleate. How, er, goes that matter?"

"It would stick entirely, if his liking were the test." Why had

56

Tom said – Cherry lips? Isabella in a flash threw toys on the floor, gave Hugh eyelashes, womanhood. She had been bought for money, sold for acres. An heiress was a commodity. A rise of spirit disdained the insults of destiny. Yet, she was her father's child; worse, she was his property. But what locksmith would free her? "Tom was right. Were it not for the great settlement, which is too truly Tom's by right, Adam wouldn't look at me. This grows harder still, day by day. I watch Adam winding himself up to act the part..." Too late, she had brandished aloud what she should neither say nor recognise. She, in the shape of her dowry, was mere bait for acres. She bit her lip, insulted, disadvantaged, alone, with no champion to carry her favours.

The worldly man was amused at the bridegroom needing better lines.

"Enjoy the playacting: our theatres are closed down, he's your best entertainment."

"He still needs the book," Isabella, exonerated by his light tone, rallied, "but there; Father's wealthy, there are inducements. So he acts the suitor. Block hath unearthed that they haven't fared scot free in the conflict. Maurice burnt a house for them. But the land, the wide land... Father – Father..."

"Father hath let the idea of Greateleate acres go to his head."

"Maybe, and I, I, represent the only bait he's got." The maiden who had hoped for moonshine, had been staked out to catch the land her father was after, with arranged dowry.

Scapegoat, considered Hugh. Or caught in their mousetrap.

Isabella, who had no wiles, told the truth. "It could have been well. If Adam but took to me. He's bored. If he has to have me why can't he pretend?"

Hugh refrained from explaining most pretences ceased at the altar, rather than in this case, earlier. "I've only glimpsed the gentleman. From that, I hazard he doesn't act the part anything like well enough. Besides which, you'd know."

Athalia had not pretended, once names got flung over pulpit.

"I am ashamed."

"Are you? Whyever? You're the best of them."

"Oh, no."

"Now, why?"

"Because," and forgetting the embroilments and everything, she faced up to what hurt. "I couldn't draw him. Pearls or no."

"But," countered Hugh, feeling senior, at a lofty altitude, "but, he's not worth, er, pearls, is he?"

"Yes – no, but don't you see, it would have helped."

He did see, descending in a rush from his lofty height. He'd been tied, like this, to a bored stranger. He knew John Block's sentiments about her, and that she was a loyal sister. He regarded her.

"You could say nay?"

"To Father?"

"Mmm. Greateleate could say nay?"

"So I kept hoping, but those pearls are real, not a figure of speech. Two days hence Father's birthday comes. John Block hath heard a word—"

"Overheard."

"The birthday fete will also set off the signing of the marriage contract, round off Father's celebrations."

Before Hugh could formulate a reply to this catalogue of inescapables, movement on the further hillside caught his eye, thus saving him. He had focussed upon two horsemen, small as toys, emerging from the trees that masked Fentiman's, at walking pace.

Isabella saw, too. Autumn sun became winter frost. "I'm

about to be caught. 'Tis Adam and my father."

"They aren't heading this way." It was Royalist mud on this side of the stream. He hauled Isabella behind a bush which still bore leaves and looked out.

The two little figures were not for the ford, either.

"Worse. See, they're going to meet me, at Goody Jenkins's cottage."

"The devil they are. That's untimely."

"To think it has answered so well, Madam Greateleate approves of good works – 'your duty, girl' – yesterday she praised visiting the poor – Oh, this is my Naseby…"

"We are yet nearer the cottage than they are." Hugh began to bustle her down the hillside, for once pleased she was cloaked in his unfavourite dull brown, so her presence wouldn't shout itself to the riders as an eye-catcher. "Can you run?"

He had her to the stream where they were masked by the headdresses of willows, dragged her along the bank. Thank Heaven the path had dried out since the storm so her skirt tails wouldn't draggle.

Now he and Isabella had pounded out opposite the collapsing thatch of old Goody Jenkins's hovel within one dash, but for the stream. Why wasn't there another plank bridge?

Behind the opposing willow fronds a stout blacksuited figure emerged from the low door of the cottage, wearing a severe black hat. It was John Block, with a basket on his arm.

"He went in my stead."

"He is not disguised at all to resemble you, mistress." They watched, she panting, whilst the old man stepped out with his rolling gait slowly up the path away from them. It was no use calling out.

What to do? There was not so much as a stepping stone.

Fifteen feet of shallow-looking running water kept Isabella as far from widow Jenkins's door as from the Americas.

Hugh had known more than wet feet, in the army. "Forgive me, lady," said he. In the act of speaking he put Isabella up as if seating her sidesaddle on a horizontal willow bough, vaulted it with one hand upon it and dropped neatly into the water. It was as cold as charity.

He laid hands on Isabella, finding her warmer, though startled. She clasped him in a reflex action, he caught up her skirts and cloak and took steady steps to pop her upon the Parliamentarian bank. And he himself, most symbolically, remained sinking fast in the tide.

"Run!" he urged, "run!"

There was barely time to extricate himself and the weight of water in his boots, in order to conceal himself back in the nest of willows. He watched Isabella pelting like a deer up the slope, hitching her skirts up, amazing John Block (he turning, mouth a round O). She put her arm in his, and they were idly strolling up the path fifty yards from the cottage when the riders rounded the corner and beheld them.

Isabella was not pink from the autumn sunshine. Adam Greateleate thought the sight of himself had occasioned a blush.

"Isabella and John Block were dancing."

Chapter III

Hugh Malahide sat in the kitchen with his feet on the fender, listening to the tale of the happy homecomer. It was a good story and a long one, lasting without more than half a dozen repetitions well into the next day's session, by which time Hugh was half-listening for footsteps of visitors for Tom.

But noone could get away today, it seemed, and so Hugh listened to the long tale as Harry, big and brawny, held the floor. He was an out-of work sergeant of pike, due to the downturn in King Charles's fortunes of war. As he had run out of knees to sit wife, sister-in-law and dog upon, all were squeezed together in the high-backed settle like a nest of owls. His dear ones. He hugged them and gesticulated and talked and talked and talked. He was a realist, too.

"And they Scotsmen," he was saying, "no such creatures, say I, for all we saw a hair or hide of 'em. Coming shortly! My eye. In th' finish, I tell'ee, all we got was Leaving shortly. An' that's the truth. Naught left for we, I says to my mate Amos, an' King Charles hisself couldn't ask more from we. So I'm for home, says Amos, and so said I. Couldn't wait, to, to—"

And there he was, grasping his family and raising his tankard, and beaming. They all beamed back. He was infectious.

Neither Isabella's lightfoot patter nor the heavy tread of John Block crossed the threshold. Hugh's pricked ears continued to distract him even later when he was counting up the rents his uncle had come in at Michaelmas, so he had to start clinking up the little pile again.

"Not everyone's paid up, have they? Want me to see about it?"

"Would you?"

Perhaps I won't have to ask him to stay, thought the old man. Perhaps he'll want to.

"Least I can do," said Hugh absent-mindedly. He was good at seeing cogs in the machine turned as they ought. What Athalia had gained, was by Hugh refusing to sit indoors and be a lapdog. He'd set himself about learning and listening, about her lands, discovering; then informed about market prices, the best corn, which of the tenants swindled the bailiff. Athalia had gained the smoothest running acres in the county because Hugh tried to pull his chestnuts out of the fire that way. When he'd left, he'd been able to take a clear conscience that Athalia had a far better run estate than she would have had without him. It papered over some of the cracks, though not all. Perhaps the discipline involved, of living some sort of life whilst empty of heart, had prepared him for becoming a good army officer.

"Hayman is no rogue," his uncle was excusing, "but he hath had two boys killed and the ginger-headed one hath come home on a peg-leg."

"He ought to have come up and seen you about it. I'll look down and see what's to do."

All the time, Hugh was wondering what had kept old Block, and Isabella. Why hadn't she come? Had Father glimpsed the pantomime in the willows? Had he got wind his daughter was deceiving him about Tom? Or had those pearls garlanded her to advantage with Greateleate?

He hoped Fentiman's heavy personality had not made mincemeat of Isabella. It wasn't fair, really, to have involved her.

But Tom had been in such straits.

But… as he made himself write the list of his uncle's tenants, his mind ran on the two tracks still.

It was a long day. To divert himself he went upstairs and shaved Tom. The equine cast of countenance saw daylight again, pale as a blaze. Then they tried cardplay for an hour, passing the dregs of their army pay to and fro. The Tudor effigies must have roused themselves and rustled their strewings of lavender when Tom at last laughed, having won the hand. The candle end guttered its yellow light to show the Tom who had always been laughing, long ago.

Perhaps he'd laughed too soon, for by morning Tom was sitting up in bed fretting, tossing his mane, and in Hugh's imagination, laying his ears flat back as if about to show temperament. The maidservants, one each side like matched ornaments, threw a clean nightshirt over his mending, strapped torso and retired hastily.

"Father's birthday. Hope it rains," fulminated Tom. He pulled himself shakily up on the bedpost. "Still heaving," he complained.

The childish wish for it to rain on the unjust might have been humorous had it not been clear Tom wasn't joking.

Hugh, not being able to make it rain, abandoned the bedchamber and set out upon his uncle's business. He saw three tenants: one shifty, one unlucky, with sickness in his beasts, and one who paid up. That was a start. Hugh, wanting to spare his mare Bonny who had come home so thin, put his boot toe to the white chalk ribbon where the path cut the turf above the valley.

In the perspective below stood the little thatched cottage of Goodwife Jenkins and the bribeable Sammy, which guarded the too-grand gates to Fentiman. A small figure, presumably the very

Sammy, was swinging the gate even now, then shutting it behind two riders leaving. Hugh saw a set of grey hindquarters and, merging more with the background, a bay. The horses half turned to follow the track and he got the profile of the pair of horsemen, cloak by cloak, hat by brimmed hat.

They had an air of kinship already. Hugh thought Fentiman and Adam Greateleate were going to suit each other.

Well, they were for a little trot out, were they? Perhaps the birthday preparations were in train, and proved tiresome. They were going off to avoid the hubbub. Quite a celebration, crowning the birthday by signing the marriage settlement. Isabella was the surety for acres.

The riders dwindled. Temptation crept upon Hugh. He gave in to it. He wanted to know how Isabella was feeling. He'd failed to enjoy the picture he'd conjured up of Isabella exchanging the usual tokens, gloves, say, in taking Greateleate in authority over her.

Even in place of Fentiman her father, Adam didn't seem quite the nonpareil he'd want were she his daughter. Could she cope with what came with these particular acres? Yet the whole package, Adam and all, would spell security after the stormwrack of the conflict, which had so roughly thrown Tom and himself on an uncharted shore.

King Charles's ship had foundered, with its motley crew.

Not quite pleased by his mental comparison, Hugh shook his shoulders and strode down the slope to march bold as brass to the oversized gatepost, hailed Sammy out and administered what Sammy liked best, along with a question.

"Thankee, sir," smiled Sammy, butter-wouldn't-melt; "Nay, they'll be gone a coupla hours, they've gone to fetch Master Hazeldene to the feast." He clinked Hugh's coin, swung the gate, and Hugh went a second time to storm Fentiman's.

It didn't look much more cheerful in broad day. No thunder rolled this time, no downpour, for all poor Tom wished it to cloud his father's festivity.

Hugh skirted the courtyard of his first entry, himself concealed by the trees gibbeting the gateway. He trod carefully on, turned a corner, hearing clatter and voices from the left of the building. Ah – baking smells. The kitchen. They'll be manning the spits and ovens. He could do with another pork pie.

The casements were most helpfully steamed up and he wandered by, ready to be glib if challenged. He kept his footmarks off the gravel: my silent cats'-paws, he said to himself.

Mullions were set in the flint on the long front of the building. It was a very unyielding looking house, all hard edges like the faced flint itself. He found an alcove where a lead pipe, dated 1633, fell from guttering high above, and there, shielded, he could peer in at the end window. Within, he was rewarded by a most unexpected sight, one which quite took his mind from the complications of trespass.

In a book-lined room, Isabella and John Block were dancing. Between a pair of globes at one end of the floorboards and two torsos sagging under the weight of a substantial chimney breast at the other, they were treading a measure for all the world as if here the performing bear and its slip of a keeper.

Hugh was fascinated. Block was earnest, empurpled, and by his bottled expression, humming to give the semblance of music. Hugh beheld Isabella turning, stepping, following old Block; he saw her neat ankles when the advantage of movement belled up her skirts, the little waist, the rising breast. Only when she revolved and showed her averted face did he comprehend how miserable she was.

Block knew, all right. He had stopped clumping about and humming, and was tenderly patting her shoulder. She told him she was sorry (Hugh could read her mouthing the word), and they were at it again, John Block now beating the air with one hand to give the rhythm. All of which very rapidly took his toll on his breath. Hugh became anxious for him, at his age – indeed so anxious for the old man that he tapped on the window and gave him a start to add to the heavy breathing.

The window opened, nearly putting Hugh's eye out, and a heated Block was revealed framed in the tall rectangle. "Phew," he said, "thought you were me out there, for a minute, watching." The little currant eyes assessed Hugh. "You'd best come in. 'Tis safe, I've turned the key so we could practice undisturbed. Fentiman's out, anyhow."

He extended a hand and hauled Hugh up, who took a step over onto the window seat, and down with a crash.

"Yes, we're having a little rehearsal for tonight," John Block, quite unselfconscious, indicated the cleared floor space and Isabella, she overcome at being discovered being put through her paces.

What had Tom said?

"Oh, Father keeps Bella mewed up with old Block and the housekeeper. Out of the way, out of the world. There she's stayed, what with the conflict. Not even little pleasures. Father thinks London is no place for maidens. Doesn't say much for the God-fearing nature of Parliament's men up there, does it? Father thinks the world of a dull life – for others. I should know. Sin's in the pleasures, he'd have us know. So Bella wasn't to have them."

Not even little pleasures, it would seem. What had he thought of Isabella that first time? She lacked wiles. There was something warmly endearing in old Block attempting to supply last-minute accomplishments.

He nodded at Block, turned, more gently, to the under-rehearsed maiden, asking, "I hope you're teaching him thoroughly?"

She couldn't reply.

Block set about rallying her, taking her hand, wanted to start anew. "Could you hum this time?" he asked Hugh. "Nay, better you save my strength, would you take a turn with her? I have not the breath for more."

Hugh stepped forward, therefore, counting the measure. Indeed, he was guiding her when she turned away from him and hid her face.

"You have but trampled me the twice," he said, hating that she was trying not to cry. Her back hair had escaped, presenting dark brown silk, encompassed by the arm of Block. He attempted to rally her but failed, pushed her onto a stool and patted at her. Unsuccessful, he turned to Hugh.

"She's been like this all morning. Can't get a word out of her. You'd best try."

The supreme sacrifice, he indicated Hugh in his stead, and himself trod disconsolately to the door, produced a key, unlocked it, brandished the key and a turned-down mouth in their direction. "I'll be back. Not listening."

He had actually locked them in.

"Bad day. Tell me?"

Isabella was trapped with the one person she could no-ways tell.

"Is it Tom?"

Not Tom. Of course not. He had not thought it would be. She was shaking the flow of tendrils, indicating not Tom.

What might she not be able to confide in old Block? "I am not family," he suggested, "nor old tutor, and I won't talk."

"Yesterday," began Isabella, after three false starts, and a bottleneck, "yesterday Father was full of my duty to be a credit to him. I was wearing the pearls. He made one of his speeches, that he would shortly be entrusting me to Adam, and so forth, Adam had been his choice…"

All about Fentiman, then; no mention of her happiness.

"You had been a success," he suggested, silver-tongued.

"Did better, at least. I must have. Everyone remarks Adam's good looks and my fortune to get the match – I kept thinking whatever could I do to bridge the barrier between us, Oh."

Hugh dreaded to think.

"And?"

"Yes. I believe his mother told him to take me behind the curtain in the big room, to kiss me…"

"He took his time," he offered, "only slow in reaching the point, surely."

"No, no. 'Tisn't that." Why had she started? Trapped, she turned away and told the bookbindings behind her on the shelf. "What it is, is that I couldn't bear him. Oh." She put up a hand as if the books in a row were no protection. "He hath a slippery, cold tongue."

Hugh felt exactly like old Block. He was at a loss for whatever he could say to this unprepared maiden, was jolted quite out of himself. He held up her hand against his face. "That bad," he said.

Touch visited a new sensation upon Isabella, followed by eye contact, which cannot feel, but seems to. She met the blue of his eyes, in shadow, deep as night, while he kept her hand against the rougher leather of his face, under the splay of lines created by

69

the expression of strength and feeling.

Greateleate faded. She focussed on Hugh.

Don't be sorry for me. I'll not stoop to playing you for that.

He read her clearing eyes. "I have one idea," he began.

Perhaps he had been brewing it; it pounced.

He released her hand. Why hadn't it come into the open of his thoughts? Because it was none of his business. Yet... "Tell me truly. Do you, could you, want this match? Want him?"

He put it to Isabella in a low tone, sternly.

"I could not," she told him quite steadily. He believed her.

"Then, I have a battle plan. Remember this, when there's heavy fire, unless you're directly employed in putting match to touchhole, you keep your helmet on and your head down." He was smiling at her.

"You are not actually going to bombard Father."

"No, I am metaphorical." Hugh gestured, now alive from his fingertips to his down-at-heel boots. "I concluded but a moment ago 'tis high time your father had a birthday offering. Any bombardment resulting will be purely self-inflicted."

"Whatever could you do?"

"Ah," said he, "if you'll trust me I'd rather not tell you. If you don't know you won't have to feign innocence. I shall tell Block and he shall have a veto. Will that do for now? If he says me nay, so be it. But I believe he will form reinforcements."

Intrigue lightened Isabella's eyes. It lifted Hugh to see her brighten. Upon that, he advanced, offered a formal hand, bowed, not playacting: "Come, first we will finish our measure. Dance with me."

He suddenly, keenly, wanted them to tread their measure. Exhilarated, he had Isabella in a whirl. Even as they were caught up in these dance formalities, her unbiddable tresses escaped untidily and fell upon her lace collar. He did not repress his flash of pleasure.

Block, with maladroit timing, was grating the key in the lock, entered, registering his dear girl had returned to life. The currant eyes approved Hugh's efforts, so far as he was aware of them. He straightened from re-inserting the key on their fastness. Temporary cunning passed over his features, and his whisper relieved the pressure of new information. "Warfare's broken out in the kitchen. Who d'you think's come back from the army? Black-eyed Simon, that's who, and he don't think Nan's been faithful. She's thrown a tray full of pastries at him. They're all taking sides. Dear, oh dear."

"At least he's caused a diversion," Hugh recalled Nan, the ginger kitten. Poor kitten, spitting. "Will the welcome outlast five minutes?"

"They won't waste an argument now they've taken up battle stations."

"I must ask a word with you, Master Block, before I get me gone."

"Oh?"

"I've concocted an idea concerning this match and your young lady. You are to have the yea or nay to it."

He looked at Isabella, as did Block. She nodded at her tutor.

"Mmmph, we could do with a straw to clutch." Ruminated he. "Isabella, will you away?"

"Nay, I've had two hours of Madam Greateleate today already. If I brave the parlour it will be yet more sniffs and recoils. I was sore tempted this morning to say quietly that Prince Rupert be no more a warlock than Father."

"That's a corner to defend," Hugh said as he watched Block advancing yet again on his keyhole brandishing his weapon, and then beckoning to them.

"You could get a job at the Tower of London with that thing," Hugh indicated Block precede him, "Adieu, lady, whilst we sort out our birthday offering." He was aware his eyes were dancing.

Had Isabella been a realist she might have called him the interloper her father would have done. But she was held by the interest in the blue eyes, and in the shadows by the door there were less lines on his face.

The little room, Block's own retreat, struck Hugh as the one snug corner in the unwelcoming house. There were books that looked as someone read them, a table with its woven cloth blotted here and there with ink spots, crowded with pens, wax sticks, crumpled paper. The fireplace was laid ready. He pictured Isabella and Block cozily by the fire, books to hand, fingers in the ginger jar.

Hugh spoke straight, "Do you like this match? I have a feeling too much is done by deceit – do you? Have you thought, that Tom could detonate the whole pantomime of Isabella as the sole heiress by declaring himself?"

"There'll be the devil to pay." Block turned away, meditated, but emotion bested reason. "Yes, yes! She shouldn't suffer the match, nor would I have her to do it."

"Then shall we have Tom declare himself?"

"Why not?" Block spread his hands. "Why not! It plays the boy false; it matters not he's a King's man, only that he is alive and never buried. He's the firstborn."

"I have a horror of arranged marriages. I keep wanting to shout at Isabella 'Don't do it – I did – it is fatal."

"Ah. Pity."

"I've been thinking she should wed, for security, these are troubled times. Get her away from Father... yet..." Hugh thought that Tom's old tutor was the only human relationship she had, shut away as she was. What good was that to her? Tom, and all the young men, had been away fighting, except, of course, save-his-skin Adam Greateleate and his like. This repressed household, composed of silly bent-backed old women, daft boys, and that cross kitten maid, hadn't much to give Isabella.

Nor Greateleate, though, no, no; Hugh had been touched beyond admitting it by the tale of the distasteful, slippery kiss.

"I have been wondering of late," Block was saying, "if I might simply shoot Master Greateleate."

"That's the spirit," commended Hugh. "That makes two of us."

"I was going to say one of you Royalists crept in and did it."

"Ah..." From their smile of complicity, Hugh's eye fell upon the tabletop and by chance upon the least scrumpled of the scraps of paper. A demented spider had writ thereon,

"Epithalamy," it said, "on Isabella fair."

Hugh then read aloud, "Good cheer when Isabella nears.

A rose she is, and blushes wears." He gave Block a straight look. "This is dreadful, Master Block. How could you."

Poor Block had the grace to look shamefaced. "Don't look. I know, I know. I cannot write the thing. What did Master Fentiman demand of me but a wedding song for her! I have sweat blood over the thing. I detest the very task where she does not want it. Also I am a very poor poet."

Hugh rashly had read further. "Come night on Isabella fair. Let dawn be late and tread with care..." he read.

"Don't laugh."

Hugh shook his head and threw the paper after the others,

73

crumpling it into a hedgehog.

"I'm thoroughly down about it." Block methodically made several hedgehogs and threw them one after the other into the grate, saving the last one on the table top, next to a thumbed copy of 'Midsummer Night's Dream.'

They looked at one another.

"So, do I haste me back to Tom to see about the letter we need writ?"

"Master Malahide, I wish you would."

"Hugh?"

"Thank you." The old bear's little eyes smiled. "I answer to John or to Block."

"Take good care Isabella slips out when Tom's letter is brought in for Master Greateleate. She isn't implicated: Tom's living, she can be surprised and happy, but she didn't know."

"Right."

"See she's out of the line of fire, all the same. We are about the laying of a mine. I was at Lichfield in forty-three when the Prince sprang that first mine and burst the wall: I remember waiting for the explosion and then the moment it went up." Hugh was soft-footing it after Block past the sounds of voices raised still in the kitchen with the crash of pans. "Tell me, Block, of what persuasion are you in all this conflict in the Kingdom?"

"Survivor," replied Block.

Tom needed a secretary, but no second bidding.

"Say they'll be delighted to hear I am about to rejoin the family, once my small hurt is mended. Go on, write." He watched the loops and flourishes as Hugh twitched the brown-barred feather. "What I wanted was to get down there. But this business with Isabella seems to be ready quicker than me. Better this letter goes off directly than I wait until next week and too late,

Greateleate gets my rights as well as my sister."

"I've put: 'the bosom of my Father's family will very soon be rejoiced by its son and heir in person...'"

"Yes, good – go on."

"'To second the rejoicing they had felt on hearing I survived Naseby field.' Shall I put 'as told them hitherto?'"

"Write that, put it in."

Hugh thrust the paper for Tom to read over, "Want to add that you'd heard you are gaining a brother?"

"Why not? – put 'younger brother', too. Isabella's a woman, second-born, no Puritan dog of a husband shall put himself before me, a proud King's man. You said she don't like him?"

"Not a lot," confirmed Hugh ironically. "And why should she, indeed?"

Slippery customer, he said to himself. Poor Isabella; that kiss had not enticed her.

"Come on then, I'll sign the thing and we'll send it off."

Hugh fiddled, dipped the quill and passed Tom the paper to tell the Greateleate interest the Prodigal was arriving shortly. Unlike the Scots recruits.

Tom signed his name and a batch of blots.

He grimaced, sour that he was not ready yet to stride in and cause a sensation, with gasps, at the birthday-cum-betrothal. "That letter'll tell him I won't be cast aside. By all that's holy, I won't have Father marry off my prospects! Pity this brewed up so soon, I was all for being the skeleton at father's feast. But, once I jangle my bones in good health, won't I show him."

"You've penned your name to cool the Greateleate ardour. They'll visualise the marriage portion shrinking. Isabella isn't the single unimpeded asset they've thought her, is she. They've been—"

"Been gulled," Tom asserted. "Father's told them a tale. We've only put it straight."

Hugh removed the sheet of paper from the invalid, set to work with taper and sealing-wax. The cherry of wax bridged the two paper edges and yielded to Hugh's pressure of the Fentiman seal. Tom had kept it safe in a pouch tied round his waist, apparently.

Hugh tossed the ring back to him, threw aside the wax sticks and made for the door, but a raw tone from the bed halted him.

"Why are you helping me?" A sardonic red eye rolled at Hugh from the figure heaving on the bedpost to sit himself up. "Why?"

"Because you live, and I don't care for your father." Hugh conjured up the unattractive memory of Fentiman showing him the door. "Also you fight – fought – on the side I hold to. We stand here shabby as two tinkers together. I find this engenders fellow feeling."

He nodded to Tom and clattered downstairs to dispatch the redundant sergeant of pike with the letter, to go into the hand of young Greateleate in person.

There was neat time before the celebrations got under way to pull the noose on Isabella. He wondered if a mere declaration of disinheritance was all Fentiman had perpetrated upon Tom; that would have no legal status, would it? Not while Tom lived.

Next to give his old uncle a paraphrase of the letter. He stepped into the parlour. Josiah was peering expectantly up at him like a moulting owl from his supporting cushions. The deepening autumn evening made the fire brighter than the setting sun.

"Well writ." Josiah chuckled evilly. "I like a thunderbolt."

Hugh sat down by the big chair. Josiah was stranded

downstairs, Tom up, so communications between the invalid and the old man would have been as fractured as those of Pyramus and Thisbe without Hugh or Luisa playing go-between.

"We've writ a bolt from the blue. He's not going to like being found out. But we didn't implicate this house nor you any further. Tom's woes don't extend to making you suffer for harbouring him."

"What did you say?"

"A line to the effect he's in unspecified lodgings in Stonebury to complete his recovery."

Josiah, typically, bridled a bit. "Not ashamed to own him." He growled; but Hugh didn't intend Greateleate down here to sniff at Tom, nor Fentiman, for that matter, under his hat of self-righteousness.

Josiah was fidgeting. "Hugh, ought to tell you something, different tack, but…"

"Oh? What's that?"

Josiah bridled no more. That he needed to lean on Hugh, younger and stronger, cost him pride, unpadlocking the difficulty he wished to present as unimportant.

"D'you know, Hugh, that father of Tom's a thorn in my side, always has been, never got on. Of late, he's ridden high on the back of the damned Parliamentarians, up and up. Been trying to buy me up, that's the truth of it."

There. He'd come out with it. He watched the effect on his nephew.

"Oh, has he? Can he? How – how are your resources placed?" Hugh had sprung to his feet. "By the good Lord, you should have told me! I'd not have had Tom add a pennyweight to your trials. And if Fentiman's lined you up as booty—" It wasn't going to be old Block who shot someone, Hugh was so riled up. With an effort, he bottled himself and attended to Josiah.

"We are not yet a-sinking, not yet." Josiah was leaning forward pretending to poke the fire. Sparks rose, but nothing to those rising in Hugh.

"I will see about all the rents. I will have them in. I'd do – anything," he promised, darkly. He'd been blind. How could the old man see to things, and with the King's affairs in tatters, every Royalist trod a quagmire.

"I understand he prefers my southerly aspect to his," Josiah was speaking like a man mentioning the weather.

"My God, he hath his sights on the HOUSE!"

"Of course, I have denied him, denied him now some few times…"

"God's teeth!"

"Nay, Hugh," said the old man, "I do fully intend to deny him still. Would that King's men owned the advantage. Then I'd have given Fentiman the answer he merits. I still will, mind, there's still breath in me."

"But we have got into this business over Tom. Why didn't you tell me? We have added to the animosities with his father, which you cannot afford."

"Would I have thrown Tom out, to hide his head in a ditch, the state in which we found him? Nay, it was my choice to take him in. After all, what else to the good have I been able to do in the Conflict?" He cackled and threw the poker down. "I'm like you, eh, nephew: rather go down fighting than show the white flag."

"That's our choice."

"'Tis what I choose," said Josiah crossly. "Luisa hath the habit of getting me to take an interest. Lately, she hasn't had to remind me."

"I join with you in that," Hugh told him truthfully.

Thank the Lord, thought Josiah, I've come out with it and told him.

Chapter IV

The letter was out of sight, but the equivalent of a mine in the entrails of a castle exploded, up into the blue.

After an evening's silence and a night in which to speculate, Hugh betook himself outdoors. And while the mist still pressed onto the grass there came the roll and rattle of a departing coach, the scuff and splash and struggle of managing the ford, then the departure of stiff-necked indignation for anyone to see who happened to be handily sited behind a bramble thicket upon his uncle's hillside.

Hugh rose like Neptune from these thorny waves and returned rather cheerfully to the house, and described what he had seen. The heavy vehicle with its strapped baggage had crawled up where the chalk path rose, the autumn chiffon of mist swallowing the Greateleate train. "A strategic withdrawal," he reported to the heir to the Fentimans. "I must say they wasted no time."

"I hope it came to fisticuffs," cried Tom. "Oh, to have got there myself."

"The main thing is that they read, how did we put it, 'the bosom of Father's family will very shortly be rejoiced by the son and heir in person.'"

"Survived the field of Naseby."

"As told Father hitherto."

Tom wrapped in an old dressing gown transferred his grip from the bedpost and wavered to the windowseat, hugging the wrapper around him. "Father needs taking down a peg. I was ever at odds with him. He didn't discuss, ever spoke as if he was old Moses with the tablets of stone, over the most fool things. I once watched him eat a bad egg simply because he'd proclaimed nothing whatsoever the matter with it."

"Moses would be a sore trial to live with," Hugh said abstractedly, looking out of the window. There was a disc behind the cloud now, like the moon, reminding him how he and the King's army once saw three suns, by some freak of the light, and noone could tell what portent it might be. He was relieved there was but the one sun this morning: all he hoped, with hindsight, was that he might never see three suns again.

Tom's voice recalled him.

"I suppose that's cleared it for Bella, until Father next matches her."

Next? Hugh had never thought as far as that. Wrongly, he had considered the match an isolated business, once won, won for good. So had the battle on Naseby field been: the battle of all, for all.

Why did he have to remember? He remembered the defeat of Naseby every morning.

He made himself concentrate on Tom.

"At least from now on 'tis known you live and breathe. And while you do, prospective in-laws will say 'in the long run that boy and his father will reconcile.' They'll know Isabella's not the heiress. In due course, you will hold the two houses, town and country, the gain in fortune during this conflict…"

"And the pearls," added Tom sourly.

"She won't be decked in aforementioned pearls, roofs, coffers, quite as absolutely."

"He won't be reconciled, he won't," asserted Tom. "I'll show him I won't be bested…"

"Basing House is fallen."

For the second time, Hugh registered the tone as Tom spoke, and for the second time wondered why that kind of wound mended less well than the hack of swords. "Let the dust settle," he told him. John Block would have been listening and there would be an account shortly. Then he contemplated Isabella's future, and King Charles's. Equally uncongenial.

The next-comer was Ebenezer the horse doctor. He had a broadsheet from the wider world. He pointed at the crabbed text. "Basing House is fallen. Don't they Puritans crow."

They would. This had been as absolute a bastion as the loyalty of its owner. The hearers felt a chill, for all it was an expected death. Tom would only have staved off personal defeat, had he got there to hide his head. But it came as a shock. Now the sergeant of pike could expect no recall; Hugh's men had been right to leave when they saw King Charles's ship holed and sinking, and Hugh himself suffered an unwelcome mental picture of himself clinging to the bowsprit as his vessel sank in the gloomy Parliamentarian tides.

The long faces around him recalled him. And because he tried to cheer everybody nonetheless and rally his uncle's family of waifs, strays and supporters, in the end they felt better but he felt worse. By the time Ebenezer had drained the tankard Hugh issued, Hugh had re-lived most of his army career and discovered it Dead Sea fruit.

Tasting these ashes, he swung the door.

"Forgot to tell 'ee," the horse doctor paused, stuffing the broadsheet back up his sleeve ready for his next port of call. "Sammy says, back at Fentiman's, what a to-do! Seems ol' Fentiman don't take kindly to losing the match he'd got up. He's off after them."

"He's not! Followed the Greateleates? Really?"

"So Sammy do say. He got the gate open not an hour since an' off goes Master Fentiman looking black, an' th' two serving men with him. 'Tis fact."

"Well! Has he so."

"Never liked no for an answer, it has to be said, a fearsome proud man."

It would seem his character had over-ridden evidence that the Greateleates would actually deny his desire for their rolling acres.

Hugh stood in the porch watching Ebenezer diminish. The bad news had gathered. This went deeper than the little local drama of Fentiman and Tom. After cheering up the various despairs of the household all morning, he couldn't return indoors, be mewed up. Throwing the cloak around his shoulders, he shook himself like an unbridled horse in the meadow, tossing cloak, mane and temperament together, and rushed out into the sun.

Half an hour striding against the breeze blew off the low mood by simple energy. Hugh eventually came up against a barn on the hillside neglected by one of his uncle's less organised tenants, its thatch sagging off in a greyish heap, shielding a broken-axled cart and some sheep hurdles. The sheep were white dots on the hillside above. Hugh took a moment's respite from the wind, a reverie, merely existing without thoughts at all.

Movement caught his eye. Halfway up the slope a fellow human being approached, in a blowing cloak. He knew her; dreaminess popped, was gone.

Hugh found himself a fox surprised and implicated near the henhouse. An instinct had been lurking. Reason, repression, denial, burst like bubbles.

He lived, a feeling creature. Had his life force conjured her up? He had been wishing, was wishing, that now he had seen the

Greateleates off, now Fentiman had gone chasing after them, that Isabella must come – not to Tom – come to me.

It was Isabella's doing, next, because his garment made a contrast against the grey avalanche of thatch and she realised he was there. Her cloak blew like the sails of a galleon and she tacked to steer towards him in the breeze. Her hair fell in pennants on her shoulders. He saw she did not flee him.

Two voices spoke to him within.

Come – She does not know I wait for her.

Then: she must not know.

But he did not want to wait.

Speak, fool.

He made a great effort not to frighten her. He must never frighten her. He would do better than that reptilian kiss. It was beyond Hugh to delude himself to deny that his concern, he harshly saw, was not to fright her. Not to forbid himself. He sighed, but quietly.

She stood two yards from him, breathing, desirable, ready, and he was stimulated.

"Come out of the blast," he said, outwardly normal, "this is sheltered. Was yesterday awful? Were you brave?"

"Like Tom at Naseby, I survived somehow. I wasn't brave; no, I hid my head during most of the firing."

"That's prudent, which is probably more to the point. I think you achieved a lifting of siege, too, at the finish."

"Yes. And Tom's delivered his notice of survival."

She was noticeably breathing in and out after climbing the hill; he indicated the bank of thatch, but she wouldn't sit, so he did. He looked up at Isabella, and she was aware of his ultramarine eyes.

"I've seen my poor horses try to eat thatch, alas, such straits we've suffered. My mare is at last with her nose in the manger. I'll be glad to see her less of a gridiron, she's done her best for me." Cloak spread, hands on knees, wanting her innocence, he turned his eyes deliberately away to the long-coiled dragon's length of the downs. "Look at those trees," said he, indicating the foolhardy landmark on the top, blown askew by the winds of many winters. The tallest tree was seconded by slightly less foolhardy trees below. "They've a name. Do you know it?"

"What was it? – The King and The—"

"They are The King and The Maidens. I do hope there is no move afoot to change the name to Old Noll and the New Model Army."

At these smoothing words, Isabella came closer, subsided on the cloak upon the thatch. She was as near to him as if upon a blanket over the marital mattress.

"Benezer stopped first at our door," she told him, "Tom must be downhearted at the tidings of Basing House – I had to blow out onto the hillside to shake out of it…"

He looked at her, and she realised, "You too."

"Me too," he shrugged, deprecatingly.

"What they have been through. Poor Master Inigo, at his age."

The celebrated man had been carried out wrapped in a blanket. All the masques and the fete celebrations he designed were long gone.

"'Tis hard so famed a man is forced to leave like Cleopatra. Ah, I heard Lord Winchester hath scratched 'Love Loyalty' with a diamond upon his window pane."

"Love loyalty… Oh, Tom was heading there, but for the bullet hole."

"The last refuge," Hugh declared, "but hopeless; such,

refuges do tend to be." He shifted to look at Tom's sister and the bedstraws creaked.

Isabella breathed sharply in, and he inevitably, was pleased by her bosom rising. She turned away, at least half aware of this, "Tom was saved by finding your uncle's door."

Tom was getting more than his due as a topic. The dilemmas of Tom were neutral ground, not personal between the two people feeling their way to what next.

Hugh loosed a trial shaft. "In all these troubled times, should you not want the 'blessed knot'?"

Isabella realised the question to be loaded, but skirted surmising why; "Oh, what is it said of marrying for love? 'poor greenheads' or somesuch. No; if love will come, it does not come to call." She nerved herself, "Adam Greateleate did not call upon me."

"I thought not," he said.

"In your case?" (Did I hear myself say that? I should not have said it.)

So, she'd remembered I have a wife. Of course she did.

Athalia, buttoned over-neat, hair in a small mouse-shaped knot at the back of her head, the mouse smaller over the decade but the expression of complacency, deeper. He discouraged his mind's eye.

What could he say? "I cannot preach arranged marriages. So was mine. I married for money my father had sore need of. Athalia hath not suffered my extravagance," he indicated his jaded clothes ironically. "I'd only excuse myself that there are exceptions to the rule 'that which the wife hath is the husband's' – I have not been a charge upon her coffers. Nor have you taken Tom's heritage off to Greateleate's, either."

He made himself sit easily, straight backed. "She holds the

Parliament persuasion. There's no loss for her in the conflict. We took opposing sides early on. I sundered from her house." He could have added, willingly.

"And her love for you?" Her eyes fell to the bedstraws.

"I was an unsatisfactory lapdog." Then, honesty ruling his sensitivities. "And once handsome."

That brought Isabella's eyes up, dismayed, and her blush.

"Oh, lapdogs need looks," he said, but smiling. "She found I grew the less. May I say I don't regret it. I'd be my own man, so when the country came to arms I left on the excuse. I replaced the voice of the shrew by the siren song of a lost cause."

Perhaps it was a crass ill judgement mentioning Athalia. Should he never have said? He so seldom said. But matters were urgent enough without subterfuge. Hugh suffered a memory of his wife relentlessly pounding a small defenceless keyboard instrument.

The past was interrupted by Isabella's amethyst gaze. On the tide of lovely interest, Athalia ebbed and he asked, "Do you forgive the telling of my tale, lady?"

"I have no choice," she answered, failing to be enigmatic. The man who had been handsome received the faint feeling that Isabella lacked a woman to advise her to avoid him.

The moment was not to be jolted. "Someone took a pastry-cutter to you in the cradle, there are crescents in either cheek when you smile. I rejoice they weren't writ into that marriage contract, I see you have them still."

"I had them withdrawn, but left the bad temper in, and the scoldings." And the crescents smiled, as did the amethyst eyes.

"No wonder Greateleate fled thee. Why am I sitting here with impunity?"

"I might be saving tempests to catch you unawares."

"I am used to warfare, remember. Will the white flag be allowed?"

"Mine or thine own?"

"You're a Turk, with those crescents. I shall haul down, I fear it."

"Oh no, I detect you for a talker, you'd treat, not surrender."

She was new and sweet. He played with a kitten. His heart ached; and lower down.

Why did a chill breeze have to blow? The sun was fading fast. "What was your father's parting shot? Will he be long away, or is he for dragging Adam back the whole way bound and gagged? Did he indicate?"

"Father declared the agreement should stand because Adam's father gave his word. He is dead, so cannot gainsay. Equally, Father's case is weakened because a dead man cannot answer the charge he was told Tom was dead and by that, I became the heiress. Me."

"Tom breathes. 'Tisn't your fortune, but his. They'll hardly be importuned."

It had been a thunderous moment when Tom's letter got to Adam. "You should have seen their faces. Father won't be welcome on their doorstep. It is too like insisting a favour when putting a foot in the door."

"Literally. Will we have him back directly?"

"We have a couple of day's respite, 'tis a day's trot and a stay over on the way."

Hugh's connecting glance of amusement was that she had used, "We." Maybe he was anticipating the couple of days.

Isabella, too aware, glanced back at the man sitting by her. It did not help. The sunset lit the lines on the handsome face a touch unkindly. Why did physical attraction beset her? There it was; yet he had not touched, spoken – she was fool and worse – for why would he look at her? It was immodest vanity that he had a thought in his head about her.

She was neither ashamed nor bashful. Isabella rose and bolted in case he realised this. Of course Hugh followed her down the path, came up with her easily, the cloak over his arm, they were down the dampening grass, they were at the plank bridge. As she didn't want him to go she didn't want him to know that either; she stood with one hand on the rail, not dismayed about his wife, not for being older, but shockingly aware of him.

As for Hugh, he had noticed 'Midsummer Night's Dream' on Block's table that they had been thumbing. He inserted a planned felicity.

"… the business with Greateleate and your father hath ever reminded me of that opening scene of 'Dream', where Lysander makes his complaint that Demetrius should marry, not Hermia but her father, that was so partial to him…"

She should not have laughed, but absolutely did.

He saw the crescents, and her eyes. He wanted her to come tomorrow; he could still speak, and asked her, voice as soft as to an un-backed filly.

"Block, too," he offered, "I don't mind sharing him with you."

"Tomorrow," she assented.

The cynic in Hugh Malahide should have reminded him he now added a second lost cause to the first, Royalist one. Three, if he counted Athalia. But anticipation and hope, long absent from him, and possibly reason the same, came so welcome.

Hugh returned to sounds of sweeping and banging. In any other household than his uncle's with its look of having been ransacked and left to rearrange itself, he would have taken for spring cleaning.

Investigating, he discovered Josiah's lair was empty, but next door in the hitherto shrouded big room, a good deal had taken place in his absence.

"That you, nephew?" Josiah's disembodied voice rose from the depths of an armchair. "We decided we couldn't save Basing House. Moping would not help, we busied ourselves."

"So I behold. Luisa, good heavens, are you safe up there?"

Luisa, impassive, was detaching dust sheets put up along the gallery, dropping them like banners surrendering, to the floorboards. She had mounted a pair of steps to its extreme limit, even teetering was retaining calm and dignity. In the two hours Hugh had been absent he had missed a tornado. Logs in the fireplace lit and crackled, candle sconces still bore indigo tarnish. The candles made waxy loops and bows in the draught Luisa was releasing. Hugh stepped forward through the pools of dark and light and discovered that the back of a second armchair concealed Tom – Tom downstairs for the first time, and with his clothes on, so he merely looked pale, rather than the bed-bound wreck.

His uncle's head poked up like a tortoise putting its head out, with an expression of pleasure on seeing his nephew. "Couldn't sit in the little hole all winter now you're here," he explained, "the place more like home, eh?"

"More than I deserve," Hugh said, gravely. Luisa wobbled and he crossed hastily to steady the steps, coughing as the last dust sheet fell. The nearer chairs blenched.

"Good thing we hadn't dusted first," remarked Luisa. Hugh handed her down like a duchess. It was unlikely she would be dusting after, either.

Harry, Brownie at his heels, came in with his arms full of logs, took away the brooms and the sheeting. Luisa fetched a tray and glasses. The chink of a toast, the glint of tawny in the glass, took place in the chief room of the house, in use again.

Bravado rose with the raised glasses. Nobody said, 'Basing House is fallen,' no one referred to the day's ill tidings. Josiah, Hugh, the sergeant of pike, ate that night off a roasted capon, tasty with ginger and prunes. There was a suspensory triumph of jelly in which whole plums floated, like fish. They were affirming that inwardly Old Noll didn't defeat them.

"You are mending apace." Hugh heaved Tom out of the chair to get him to bed.

"What for," asked Tom sourly, spoiling the atmosphere. "What have I ahead of me? I could do with a toast to my homecoming, an event I conspicuously lack."

Had they been that tactless? But Hugh, that night, didn't attend to the woes of Tom. He put him aside, took better thoughts to bed. The slant of candlelight on the mantelpiece in the big room, the carved figures on either side, the goose girl, the beekeeper, the shepherd with his crook, were favourites from his visits of old; but even the kindness of Josiah eddied before his mind's eye of Isabella, temptation ready, new and sweet.

Would she want him? He had no newt's slithery tongue. Stretched out against his feather pillows in the moonlight, anticipating possibilities kept him wakeful.

He could have throttled John Block next day for coming with her, for all he'd invited him. Of course until Fentiman returned, Block, too, seized the chance to visit Tom. For the first time Hugh had to force himself to be delighted at Tom's improvement, listen to their prattle. Now the crisis was over, for Tom, their Lazarus, was mending.

Excluded from the 'did-you-remember' tales, Hugh lifted his head and met his own reflection unexpectedly in the glass of the mirror across the room. It was a nasty shock. He saw the ageing face.

When they had left he went out and relieved his feelings by splitting logs for two hours. Swinging the axe and feeling his muscles play deadened thoughts. Then he had no more logs to split. Leaning on the axe handle, he watched Luisa carrying apples in her held-up apron crossing the yard, and in her steady eyes read a message he could not interpret, for all she invited him to come indoors in plain English. He sighed, shouldering the axe. Luisa, too, must have been attractive in her youth.

Tom had too much to drink that night, and then as if he had reacted to the portent, Fentiman returned.

Unaccompanied: it had been an unsuccessful journey to recall the Greateleate match.

Isabella of course was kept within doors, and for a week Hugh fought off the urge to join Tom in drowning his frustrations. Instead he set about his uncle's tenants. His successes gave him a tale to tell of an evening and kept up everyone's spirits, except his.

He saw to it that Tom sent a message to his father asserting he was lodged in the market town, so Fentiman would think him there and not close by at Josiah's. They did not want him a-visiting.

"Done that," assented Ebenezer after delivering the letter.

"Good fellow. Don't you show me your new broadsheet. Keep it up your sleeve, I'm low-spirited enough."

"Don't ee want a look? King's still at Newark."

"I do not," said Hugh firmly. "Tell me any news from Fentiman's though."

"Dull as ditchwater there. Old Fentiman's been back since last Wednesday, not a thing since. I'll be up there again end o' this week, tell 'ee then."

Hugh now a cat on hot bricks to see her, suffered: what if Fentiman settled down for Christmas? Stayed for ever?

Tom had grown mettlesome and restive. Hugh had begun to match him.

"I'm the scratchy one," complained Tom. "What ails thee? I'm the one with no home."

"Ah, be damned. I'll get me out and chop down a tree and split it into spills, I think."

Tom took another swill from his tankard. "Dull the future."

It was the past Hugh would dull. But one cannot.

"So would the King."

Not for my reasons, Hugh thought. My wife in the past behind me. Oh, that turned shoulder. Athalia, indifferent, in the marital bed.

He couldn't tell Tom why he was on edge, and put the inward look in Tom's eye down to convalescence, the hot brown gaze busy thinking, thinking.

Hugh returned to fretting for Isabella. He thought he was a bad actor when he caught Tom eyeing him strangely.

Chapter V

"I care not for that Sammy." Ebenezer shook his head.

"He have a look in his eye reminds me of that beggar, market day, legged it quicker than greased lightning when the tavern caught fire, leaving his several sticks behind... Sammy says, Master Fentiman, your father, sir, be gone off at first light back to London, seemingly."

"There's news," said Tom, eyes glistening. He reached forward, clinked his tankard with that of Ebenezer.

The horse doctor inspected his patient. "Thou'rt a credit to me. Look at ee. Good as new."

"Bad as new," corrected Tom, with the equine toss of the head.

"I must be off." The horse doctor acknowledged him, departed, and the day ran forward for an hour or two until Hugh looked for Tom, enquired for him. He wasn't in the house.

"Where's Tom?"

Luisa shook her head, Josiah had no notion.

Hugh shrugged. "I had news for him, I've seen the ginger boy with the peg-leg, he'd heard Fentiman's summoned by his London friends, seemingly. I thought Tom'd want to know." He felt a presentiment, ahead of any reason. Reason could only tell him that now, straightways, if Fentiman was away, surely, he could resume with Isabella. But as he stood there in his cloak, questions within him whipped up like a cavalry charge.

"Why, here comes Block," realised Hugh, and before John

could lumber down from his horse, he had run out and held the horse's head.

"We've mislaid Tom—" he began whilst old Block caught his heavy breathing.

"I know, I know, I blame myself – look, Hugh, he's been up to us, he's cleared the valuables and run off, he's taken, taken the PEARLS…"

"The devil he has! He'd heard his father's left!"

"Aye, aye, he'd heard the coast was clear. He's affrighted Isabella. I didn't see him but she did, he shouted at her that it was justice, the treasures are all his, and made off like a whirlwind."

"What else did he take?"

"Isabella will know what there was in the strong box."

"A good cargo?"

"'Tis the pearls, in chief. Weight precludes the plate, and what coin there was, Fentiman took back to London with him. But the pearls! Fentiman will be furious, furious."

"There hardly will be a reconciliation now, will there."

"Fentiman'll say Tom's a common thief."

Hugh regarded his boot toes. Against the courtyard wall an espalier pear had dropped rock-hard fruit and the windfall apples lay squashed and brown. Autumnal decay seemed part of the bad news, the musty over-ripe aroma a breath of hopelessness. Tom a common thief. But – provoked…

"Isabella let him in," Block growled. "She's implicated, d'you see. The housekeeper, one of the boys, Nan, all saw her. They think she knew. She didn't. He hurt her arm when she tried to stop him."

Hugh's sympathy for Tom evaporated. "I'll come up." He grimaced, and jumping the trails of spat-upon brambles straggling the path, ran to throw the saddle across his mare and haste to Fentiman's.

Thinking, where does one dispose of pearls? Where would Tom have gone?

Could he be overtaken? And, why did Tom's revenge on his father come so quick while they were so unprepared?

The stable stall was empty.

Hugh realised Tom had not walked to Fentiman's.

Taken poor Bonny!

And she only just putting flesh back on her ribs. Hugh was fond of his moth-eaten old bay, felt a pang of indignation. Bonny's been shot at, half starved, got saddle galls in my service. Now to be stolen is adding insult. He thumped his clenched fist on the partition.

A figure darkened the doorway: John Block's broad beam, come to see what kept him.

"To your list of pearls and what not, you can add, my good old mare, and saddle, bridle, saddlebags. I tell you, Block, I didn't think a second time I'd ride the cart horse to Fentiman's, but I'm about to do it."

"Didn't I ride down on ours?" asked John Block.

Entering Fentiman's had the curious resemblance of entering an enemy house during the campaigns. At the head of his men Hugh had fronted frightened or sullen households, and had restrained looters; that he had been scrupulous over this had been his reputation. On one occasion, the lady of the household, left to man it, had first nearly shot him dead, and then offered him private surrender, later.

Now, marching into Fentiman's with only old Block in support, he found the usual lineup, only that he wasn't a combatant but the too-late apologist for his house guest.

The bent-backed old housekeeper, Nan gawping, and the remnants of the staff not departed with Fentiman to London, did not give battle. They were watching a mummers' play, with all its diversion in dull lives, openmouthed.

Forced formally to greet Isabella in front of them, he made a bow as if he had never set eyes on her before, got her aside into Block's little refuge. Unfortunately Block followed. Hugh had no intimacy.

"Your arm? What did he do to hurt you?"

"'Tis but wrenched," she whispered, upset at seeing him again, for Hugh, recalled to his military commander's habit, was stern without realising it.

"He's bruised her, whatever she says." Block patted at her other arm. Not only had Tom had hurt her, so had the demands she give up the shining cargo her brother knew to be upstairs, hissing of justice and his right. 'They belong to me, me, not to your husband whenever Father next gets up a match – you wouldn't deny me my inheritance, would you? Father has …"

Tom had turned her arm until she had shown him the key to open the strong box, so Hugh had to enter Fentiman's bedchamber where the thrown-down box glared at him, empty on the floorboards.

Fentiman's quarters were no more welcoming than the rest of his house, with massive furniture like tombs.

"How did that hanging get torn?" he asked.

"I tried to turn the door key and lock him in. I think he hurt his scar pulling me, but he got the key out of my hand before I could do it. He ran away."

Block bent rheumatically to pick the box up, distracting Isabella from wishing she were alone with Hugh. Dramatics made it hard to narrate Tom's revenge.

"Do you know the contents of the box? Is there an inventory?" Hugh was asking, the blue eyes far and near. What she needed had been chased off by events. She tried to tell him, to pen a list. Intimacy fled. Isabella bent her endeavours upon a curling sheet of paper and a quill whilst Hugh unknowingly strode up and down and made it worse, because she found she was counting his footfall rather than giving her mind to shining, vanished pearls.

Tom had hammered at her, loomed over her, hurting and pushing: a stranger.

The other stranger walked up and down, turning in a swirl of the old cloak, surefootedly graceful.

Then new steps beat the stairs, and the door crashed wide. It was the big man from Hugh's, who had been a pikeman. She dropped the pen and Hugh swung round.

"Harry, what's this?"

"Sir, sir, the rent money, he's taken the rent money!"

"Dear God in Heaven – no!"

"He have. You'd been gone not ten minutes when Luisa, she said she'd had a bad thought, went to check, come back white. 'S'gone."

"Does my uncle know yet?"

"Not yet, sir."

"Thank Heaven for that. O damn Tom, damn him." He'd never thought of that! Not to rob Josiah who'd taken him in. Betray them.

He found himself with his hands to his head as he paced the room, was confronting the shrinking Isabella, had thrown down the paper she, trembling, held, then cried out. "These are baubles! But my uncle! It is the bread from his mouth."

He continued, and she heard him.

99

"Tom's given your father the power over Josiah by this day's work, for Fentiman's been trying to buy him out, he old and frail as he is – oh, the cursed unfairness of it now that his rents are got in at last—"

Hugh sobered down from his outcry. He whirled round, adding aloud to himself: "And who told Tom of my success in getting the moneys in? My God, I did."

Harry stood there with his head bent. John Block sat down as if winded all of a sudden, on the window seat. Isabella felt of the people watching Hugh Malahide, only she could feel pain. The others were dulled by the blow while she bled and died and threw pearls aside.

It will kill the good old man.

Tom's sister she. He had cast her from him, cut her off with the deed.

Tom had taken Hugh Malahide from her. He had taken livelihood away from the house whose hospitality her brother had betrayed. Shame engulfed Isabella.

Hugh swung round charged with emotion, was in the doorway to depart. The blue of his eyes were arrows firing twin shots. The power and strength of personality and though she could not know it, his deliberately then throwing aside the choice of wanting her, overrode crisis.

The door crashed and he was gone.

He rode a cavalry charge of events, for all he actually sat astride his cart horse. Halfway up the slope to Josiah's home he discovered the coins of the last rent he had got that morning were still in his pocket, which added a crumb of comfort to the complications of fury and despair. They weren't literally penniless, not quite. The luck of it, that he'd not had the time to put that money in with the other! He would have felt better, had he not known how little it was.

He rushed forward to meet Luisa, devastated to see handsome, undemonstrative Luisa was crying. She looked up at him still in control of her features, but her large dark eyes shed giveaways.

"Oh, Luisa, don't," he said, "those are your pearls."

"I never thought he could do such a thing." She shook her head, scattering the tears. "What are we to do?"

"Not weaken," Hugh said. "Where's Josiah?"

"In the big room. He's had a little turn."

He ran there in his clumsy boots, noisily, and knelt by the big chair. Josiah had his elbows on his knees and his head on his hands. Hugh attempted to embrace him and was vastly reassured when the old man shrugged his shoulders to throw him off.

"I'm not dying," he said through his coat sleeve. "Let me come to a minute. Been a shock. I came over shaky. Better now."

"Get you a drink?"

"Luisa tried that one."

"Yea or nay?"

"Maybe."

They set about comforts of a practical nature. Of course, the move into the big chamber had facilitated Tom's plans, for the rents had lain in drawers in the old lair, Josiah guarding it – and there, unguarded, it had remained.

Tom must have forced the drawer while the women were at their washing and Hugh himself had been out getting the last overdue payment.

Which he fished out as a gesture, poured the contents of the leather pouch, chinking, into his uncle's lap. "There, see, we aren't worth what we were, but we're not quite for the hiring fair, either."

His uncle began quivering out of his broken scarecrow posture. "He'll be ashamed, the boy. Pity."

Pity was not the emotion Hugh felt at that moment, not at all; he had calmed down somewhat, but had a raw, red ache. He found it in him to admire the old man for saying what he did, nonetheless.

"Luisa told you, then."

"I asked. I felt something amiss."

Luisa had come in behind Hugh. "Seeing that you knew something, best not lie about it," said she, bending over to touch his shrivelled hand. Hugh recognised love and trust, even as an ache registered it as something he did not have.

Transfixed behind the slammed door at Fentiman's, Isabella bowed her head. Tears would not help. What had been a catastrophe when Tom wrenched the pearls away was only material loss; her father could do no more than he already had, repudiate Tom. But the Samaritans up the hill and their poor little heap of rents... Tom, Tom, how could you?

She began to copy Hugh's march up and down, sweeping her father's polished floorboards with her skirt. In his house, there was no dust for her broom, but she would not have noticed if there had been.

She should not have let Tom in. She should not have been intriguing with his Royalist benefactors. She was associated by more than blood link with his shame, his stealing.

Her father's heavy presence of the last fortnight, the lectures and Bible verses nightly before the bedtime candle, oppressed the house still. He would blame her, once he knew. But she had no alternative but to bear that.

She couldn't endure knowing old Josiah had welcomed her, she'd had kindness from them, and they'd saved Tom. The night of the bullet smote Isabella's recollection as if again she held her brother's limp hand, heard the dark voice of Hugh Malahide, and then his anger across this very room only minutes previously. She quailed. She knew right and she knew wrong, and that her family had done wrong to his. The make-believe of a hopeful outcome sank like wreckage, spiked by the twin guns of her brother's action and Hugh Malahide's stern face.

Up the valley, the household at low ebb began getting the fire to burn, warming the old gentleman in his rampart of cushions, folding the shutters. Harry's small son cried in his cradle by his parents' box bed; Brownie, beyond howling, slunk into the kitchen and hid behind the heaps of un-ironed washing.

Luisa offered soup that nobody wanted.

Hugh and Josiah sat in silence, pent up.

Thus, inwardly, Hugh: "So I couldn't hide away from the world even here. It comes to find me. No haven, even here, to shut out bad tidings in those broadsheets Ebenezer brings, or keeps out Tom, the thief. And – what a damn fool paradise that I would toy with Isabella." Dissolved, with the autumn mist.

The door opened, the maidservant Jane's worried face filled the chink, all eyes, then she pushed the door wider, withdrew eyes and her puff of white cap. Hugh heard her footsteps running away. There was a moment's blankness and the draught blew, then, unless he hallucinated, Isabella stood there, Isabella with her cloak damp to her knees, grave face raised. Curiously, she had never looked younger, facing up to him (for he shot to his feet) – and yet, he comprehended her straight back was expressive of more than carriage alone.

He indicated she approach the fire.

Isabella uncoupled the cloak, dropped it in a heap, took a small leather bag on a string from round her neck, and fumbled with the fastening. She extracted seed pearls, a baby's coral, and a brooch, put them down without histrionics on the table by Josiah.

"These are mine, from my mother. They were in my own room, not with the valuable ones locked in Father's box. They will fetch something. The brooch, see, has a little sapphire set in it."

She bowed like an effigy to Josiah, but recoiled (and he saw it) from Hugh. "Don't say nay. You must take them or I shall die for shame."

But they were already saying Nay, the old man quavering it aloud, Hugh shaking his head rejecting her.

To hide her face, she bent down to pick up the wet cloak. Hugh found himself so surprised at her daring their house knowing what Tom had done there, that he could not free himself from the nets he had cast over himself.

His expression was undershot with jeering at himself for having eyed the traitorous Royalist's sister.

He might have been turned to stone.

But within seethed a fountainhead, about to declare itself.

Isabella steered for the door, there looked for a reprieve. All she tried not to see, she saw, with the sensation of the moth at the candle flame: Hugh as if a tensed spring, eyes catching sparks from the light. And the old man had collapsed against his cushions, the skull that would claim him all too visible under the worn parchment skin.

She burnt, like the moth, but from shame. Tom's doing, her own brother. She gained the passage, wanted the open air, wanted oblivion, to hide in the dank outer air.

The door resonated shut behind her, a statement.

Within Hugh, the fountainhead rose and broke out upon him,

as if a black curtain parted. One moment standing rigid, next, he was rushing after Isabella, his crashing footfalls themselves an outcry. When he caught her in the passageway, under the flickering lantern on a hook, he seized her, clasped her, heard Isabella's gasp, and felt it too as his hands tightened upon her, overtaken by his madman's uprush.

"Forgive me, forgive me. See – I cannot part from you."

She never hesitated, yielded, met him in the embrace with which he circled her. In the truth of it in a sunburst he loved her truly, no matter what, no matter Tom, beyond shallowness. The sun of amazement shone upon him even as the little sun from the lantern by his ear lit a new world. Isabella read his ultramarine dark blue eyes in the candle's sun, never mind the lines on his face, only the living, breathing man.

"Oh, come," said Hugh, and, yet aware of comparison with Greateleate's serpent tongue, gave her his mouth to try, persuasive, gentle, until her arms tightened up round his neck, then willing, unrestrained. The bosom he admired rose against him. He leaned back dizzy under the lantern and drew breath, for Isabella was tentatively stroking his long hair. Was he sane?

The sunburst grew through him.

"Now kiss me, kiss me."

When she learnt what he meant, he thought they were only beginning – what would come, given a feather bed and a locked door… why had he thought what did life matter? Matter?

He would now be mad, and love Isabella. He bent his head again to taste her.

On the goads of Athalia, Tom and the Royalist nightmare, Hugh Malahide declared his true heart beyond pretending.

Then he said what he should have said somewhat earlier.

"I'd best get after Tom." He sighed. "Blast him."

"Look, she knows him."

Chapter VI

The wind blew behind Hugh to clear his head; leaves scurried like mice across the ruts of the road. It was, he supposed, not nine of the clock despite all the turmoil and farewells. It was, moreover, the right road. Tom had gone from Josiah's to Fentiman's, not vice versa, and must have continued that line.

Where?

Straight along lay Stonebury, the market town. He couldn't see poor stolen Bonny getting further, the state of her, all ribs and hard use – come to that, he couldn't see Tom was in much better shape, after his invalid weeks.

He might have overtaken them, had it not been for the glorious, amazing delay – and for comforting his uncle. But the events had paid their part. Hugh Malahide left the shelter of respite in his uncle's valley a different man to the defeated soldier of a month back. A welcome, and a breathing space under his belt, as a new breastplate might be, as protection.

Still astride the cart horse, he reflected, well if so it be, so what, it would not kill his dignity. Nor increase his speed. Kicking had no effect on the placid beast. He'd wear out his boot heels before the leviathan trotted. He wasn't at The Red Lion yet, though he could see an earthbound star tangling in the branches of the thicket at the curve of the road and that must be the beacon from their window.

He nearly rode on by, for Tom certainly needed to put more space between him than this, five miles out from Fentiman's. But

The Red Lion, which did no trade bar the farm boys or some traveller benighted, was humming with life. The star he'd seen wasn't the gleam of some bedroom candle upstairs, but was swinging in the hand of the landlord, a firefly of his gesturing, shirtsleeved annoyance.

The wind and a set of voices suddenly blew back upon the oncoming Hugh.

"Very sorry, sir, can't account for—"

"And what's in his stead? A fleabag!"

Hugh's ears pricked up. What stir was all this? Who'd stirred it? He needed to know.

He kicked his rustic steed vigorously into the lantern's yellow shaft.

"And who might you be?" enquired a 'that's all I need' tone.

"S Hugh Malahide, sir, a neighbour." The ham hand swung the lantern, artistically illuminating the landlord. The Red Lion was convenient near one of Josiah's tenants, and had seen, helpfully as it turned out, Hugh's custom. The other speaker proved a large, angry Puritan, a wrath of God expression writ in mauve (with gold highlights cast by the lantern at his ear).

"I care not who he is, what I want to know is, has he seen my horse."

"One thing's for sure, he ain't riding it." Thus the landlord, now turning his rays blindingly on Hugh. "Whatever you doing riding that old thing, an' this time o'night?"

"Do I understand you have, er, lost your horse?" asked Hugh of the cross Puritan.

"Lost? Lost? Do you think lost? Stolen, sir! And some knacker's-yard creature left in stead."

"I've passed noone," declared Hugh carefully, "is the, er, substitute a brown mare with a white star and off-hind sock?"

"Didn't notice. A poor thing."

"Bonny!" And Hugh throwing his leg over the neck and wide acres of the cart horse jumped down the lazy way. Not pausing to explain, he strode into the yard where the sad horse was hitched by the tavern door.

The Puritan seemed disinclined to give their reunion a smooth passage. "How do we know that's yours? You could say that—" (and to the landlord, "country's gone to the dogs when decent God-fearing men can't travel without rogues at every bend of the road...")

"Would I have ridden up here on the cart horse to steal this?"

"You can't just unhitch it—"

"Watch me," said Hugh Malahide, "Bonny!"

"Ah, look, she knows him. Poor old girl."

Bonny indeed. But Tom? Tom now galloping off like the wind on this fellow's blood horse! Tom had too many talents with other people's belongings.

"You are not the only man in the Kingdom to have had a horse stolen this night," Hugh informed the stranger, and was rewarded by his expression drawing itself up into a sniff, as if Hugh in his old cloak was not the sort of passing acquaintance in misfortune he chose.

"Describe your horse," he requested the other.

"Very nice type of chestnut, if you must know."

"A blaze? Socks?"

"What's it to you? None of your business if it has."

"Thank you. We may well meet in Stonebury," said Hugh, "you after the four legs, with or without socks, I chasing the two."

(To the landlord,) "Olly, keep Bonny, here's a coin for your trouble, until I'm back, if Ebenezer happens by, get him to take her home, I'm for town – no time for pleasantries, sir, I regret..."

He left the pair of them gawping, so keen had he felt to get him away now the scent was calling. Had he been a hound he'd have given tongue, he said to himself, the smile lasting till he was out on the high road again kicking at his cart horse; turning, he caught a glimpse of the stranded traveller whose self-importance had been wrecked on the exposed sandbank of Tom's need for a very nice sort of chestnut.

The traveller, in his Puritan black, standing there under Olly's lantern, looked punctured, like a preacher upstaged by the presence of a drunk in the congregation. His eyes, and those of Olly the landlord, were on the man departing on the carthorse. It had been some time since Hugh Malahide upstaged anybody, out in the world.

Now if Tom had kept going, he'd likely take a night's sleep in Stonebury, and he, Hugh, had better catch him there, before he went the four ways of the wind and was gone like the scudding leaves.

For after that – where? Not Basing House. Fallen. Not, surely, Oxford, for, thought Hugh, the very practical reason that noone there in that city of no hope had a brass farthing with which to buy pearls, or could be trusted to leave his uncle's rents unmolested in Tom's saddlebags.

No use joining the hopeless.

Perhaps Tom had friends? Within reach, now he was mending of his hurt.

Or would he make south, for the sea, a dash for France, or the loyal Channel Islands?

There wasn't much else left in Royalist hands.

Best catch him getting his breath after an unusual first day out for an invalid.

Hugh had been up all night before this; he settled into his

cloak as an old hand and smelled the damp autumnal smells of ditches running high, with their undertones of freshness. He wished he might add to these, the warmth of Isabella, the pang of holding her tight in front of him on the self-same horse, before he left her back at Fentiman's on his way out here to pursue her brother – it had cost him dear to give Isabella back to Block. Block had actually missed their drama. His need to know things had been caught flat-footed this evening. But to be fair, the old Trojan had chiefly been hopping with anxiety. He wondered what Isabella would tell him.

How much.

Don't… you'd best think forwards, he told himself sharply.

By breakfast time he had trod into a dozen inn yards in the town, calling cheerfully for sight of his old friend Fentiman who rode a nice sort of chestnut.

It would prove quicker than subterfuge, and he had no time for lengthy preparation of ground, in case Tom woke bedtimes and took himself off again.

"D'you know the rascal? Tallish, pale, bit horsey nosed…"

And whilst enquiring, his alert eye sorted out the weeds from the decent horseflesh in the line of stalls or tethered in the courtyard.

But no easy answer no, "That'll be the chap came in last night," no perky conker shine from a horse pleased to have riddance of its overbearing Puritan owner; no traces – not at The Fleece, not at The Rose, nor at – ah, they had changed The White Cross into, God save us, The New Tavern, presumably nervous of the good old crucifix now ripped from churches.

Hugh looked with disfavour upwards at the poorly repainted sign creaking above his head, and kicked the door as a gesture, ducking to go in and earning the gratitude of the tavern cat waiting on the step. He found himself leaning against a scrubbed trestle sipping his draught, wanting stronger waters than thin ale to set him right this morning.

"Seen hair or hide of my friend Fentiman?" he asked sideways of the hostess, she a barrel of moral rectitude and the sight to scare off any lurking crucifix, with her look at him as if beady eyes were a virtue. Hugh wondered if there was a Mistress Crop-Ears Prynne: the fanatical pamphleteer ought to have just such a wife.

"We only has gentlemen," she said.

Hugh accepted this rebuke. He was clearly not her idea of one. He hid a rueful grin in his collar and sank his tankard. Anyway, she was right, shabby as he was, standing there and he'd been up half the night.

He tried The Bear next, thinking of John Block painted swinging on the inn sign; then his spirits flagged a touch and his over-rehearsed question seemed stale as it came from his lips. The Bear was smarter, too, he had exhausted the back-street, hideaway places he had assumed Tom would choose.

But behind the pot-boy's shoulder (he had caught him passing the doorway with a big floret of pewter pots held finger-in-each) he suddenly focussed on the horse.

A chestnut, resting a leg, tethered under a half-roof. A beauty.

"Let's try..." he said to himself.

"That's my friend's!" he exclaimed, thinking pity it wasn't Bonny, who would whicker at his coming and give credence to his tale. But let's pray this is the right one.... "My friend putting up, is he?"

Or had he gone? By now it was mid-morning. But here was the horse.

"I believes you've just caught him," said the urchin helpfully, with an innocent if appropriate turn of phrase. "Said he'd be down to settle the reckoning an' then he'd be off."

Hugh suffered the inevitable vision of himself about to accost the wrong man who merely owned the second-best chestnut in Stonebury. But he marched promptly in at the door and headed for the stairs indicated to him.

At the half landing, a door latch quivered; the string jerked, and under Hugh's fascinated gaze, released first the catch, the door, and the emerging Tom two yards from his nose. Tom ought to have settled his reckoning ten minutes earlier. It would have come cheaper than the reckoning Hugh brought him.

This much his expression told Hugh by its open 'O', its sudden descent from pale to green, and the application too late of a false smile which vanished like a turned page as Tom turned and pelted down the open passage along the landing.

Tom was not fit and Hugh was upon him by the closed door at the further end. He banged Tom hard against it, whereupon it unhelpfully gave way behind him and caught Hugh the more unbalanced of the two because he had been pushing. He absolutely somersaulted in over the top of Tom subsiding, and landed, banging elbow and shoulder, against a cupboard. The crash was echoed by a shriek from the bed. As Hugh picked himself up and sprinted after his quarry again, he caught one glimpse of someone half-dressed, pink and affronted.

He owed it to the urchin and a stout type in an apron that Tom could not make good a departure. Perhaps these worthies were sufficiently roused by the prospect of a night's lodging leaving at the gallop, to block the stairs. Perhaps they were fool enough to poke a long nose to see what was disturbing the peace, but whatever it was, Tom collided with them on the half landing so all Hugh had to do was seize him, bend his arm painfully up behind him in a position that would pull his new scar if he lent harder.

"Got you," he said, obviously.

"I apologise for this disturbance," he then said to the stout type. It was the urchin who rebuked him, though.

"Have to ask you to leave," he piped. "We can't have brawling."

"Give me five minutes with this gentleman, and he'll pay your reckoning. And I'll pay it over again. I am very sorry." Hugh needed the five minutes. It was curious, he found, having to deal in the civilian world as a civilian; a private person, after years of giving orders with troopers at his back.

Yet he spoke with the authority that bred. It gave weight to his apology. The stout type came up a step.

"What is all this?"

"A private matter. This gentleman owes me more than he owes you. Now I will go in his room with him, and you can watch the door, and neither of us need to lose our fair dues."

Tom, still in his grip, twitched.

But the fellow nodded. "I'm not leaving this spot, see? Pay up as you come out. Bartholomew here ain't leaving neither."

Bartholomew was the urchin, who now squared what would be his jaw when he became a man and nodded.

Hugh pushed his captive into a little cell of commendably polished panelling. Tom had slept in a feather bed, which was more than Hugh had, there was the remains of a fire in his fireplace and a tray of comforts, without, clearly, the appetite to do them justice.

Hugh released his hold, standing with his shoulders against the only exit.

He leant back and watched to see if Tom might betray a hiding place by a glance, or by rigidly not looking at the spot.

That fire precluded anything being up the chimney.

"Decent horse, that," began Hugh Malahide inexorably.

"I'm – I'm—" said Tom feebly and his legs gave way beneath him. Hugh, watching the greenish features when he took his head from his hands, was thankful Tom had not eaten his breakfast. They would not have remained united.

He regarded Tom, spitted him with silence.

"You can have the rent money," Tom whispered in a rush, "I meant to send it back once I'd sold the pearls, I swear I did."

Hugh extended one hand in the universal gesture, palm upward. To Tom grappling with sore guts, sore scar and sore conscience, the stern man standing over him seemed larger than his usual size, the brown hand extended for the return of the money a giant's. Guts got the better of him and he turned away to retch emptily. He could not have felt worse.

Perhaps Hugh saw that, for he felt pity then and used the extended hand to pull Tom up so he sank into the feather bed, moaning. Hugh Malahide had practice (latterly, too much practice) at heartening defeated soldiers, getting what was left out of poor material. Applying this out of force of habit now, he told Tom in an steady voice to give him the rent money back.

He couldn't make out, for a moment, why the leather bag Tom had simply hung up on the coat hook, was heavier than he expected. "What's this?"

At Tom's weak gesture, he tipped the bag and a surprising tide of cash fell onto the bedcover. Then he understood. "You've sold the pearls."

A measure of bravado crossed the equine features. "That proves what I said, doesn't it. I meant to send the rents back once

I was funded."

What if Josiah had suffered, not a little turn, but a great big, fatal one? Hugh growled a low growl. Yet this intention might – just – be true.

"You've been quick about it," he returned. "How is it you got that price?"

"They're good," said Tom, tossing his mane.

"I would have thought." Hugh measured him with the blue eye. "That never mind selling them for money, you would have desired to keep them as family treasures; for your future family. You said Isabella had no right to them. Which meant, in place of yourself?"

"Oh that... no, of course, they are mine to do what I chose with. Father is to blame for all this, he has passed me off for dead. After that I didn't want anything he set store by, did I."

"Not even for spite?"

"I did feel bad about the rents," he said, hangdog. "Yes, of course I could have kept the pearls. But I couldn't sleep last night because of – doing what I did. So this morning I went out and meant to feel better by selling the pearls so I'd other funds and could do as I told you, return the rents."

The miscreant was sitting up straight trying to convince him. He didn't, of course, want to believe him, he wanted to blame Tom, kick him, make him suffer for all the wrongs of yesterday done to his uncle, done to Isabella.

But he found he might believe him.

Sighed wearily.

Got up, crossed to the door, put his head round it. Immediately the urchin and the big man leapt to battle stations, ready to claim their reckoning. Hugh made a pacifying gesture, put a small portion of Tom's booty into the moist palm of the urchin. "There's at least twice what he owes you, and what I promised. So you can fetch me something to break my fast – not yesterday's stale crust, either. And we'd better have a drop of brandy-and-water."

He rallied sooner than Tom, of course. New loaf, a mouthful of briney ox tongue, made hunger come rather than go. He cut a hunk off the bread, and spearing it on the point of the knife jabbed it at Tom. "Eat it. A mouthful of plain crumb'll settle you. Then you can tell me how you got that price for Isabella's pearls, and – more to my point – where."

"The goldsmith said I was fortunate, he said he had few clients these days who come in like this gentleman after a double row of pearls and declared 'only the best would do.' I did ask more than I got, but 'tis a fair deal. He must be an honest goldsmith."

Hugh was receiving this on two levels, as on the brisk summer days when two layers of cloud cross the blue. High up, he discerned the mares-tails of relief that his uncle could rejoice, restore vital solvency (this relief causing his nephew silently to toast the old man in the brandy-and-water) while on another level, darker clouds were traversing.

Like a simpleton, he'd painted for himself the scenario of return to cheers and smiles: he, Hugh Malahide, saves the day. But he hadn't saved Isabella's day, had he? The pearls were sold and gone. He erased the return of the family's heirloom pearls from his cloud-cuckoo vision of how clever he'd been.

Wouldn't old man Fentiman be back for Christmas? Back by Advent, probably.

"The goldsmith didn't pay much for the other bits," Tom was saying, "said there was no demand."

This was probably true. The market was flooded with every

117

gewgaw since King's supporters had found themselves strapped for cash, thought Hugh distracted; but he was not attending. He couldn't toss the shining pearls into Isabella's lap, couldn't anticipate her look of delight and gratitude – no clasping him in her arms to say so, no cries of 'I knew you'd do it.'

The gulp of brandy-and-water he took might have been hemlock in the sudden self-disgust at being so puffed up that he could think of these things even when there were no pearls.

"Come," he said harshly to Tom. "Get to your feet. We're going to see if we have enough here from the other pieces of value to buy the pearls back."

The stout man and the little lad were still outside. Hugh let the former bar the stairs until the quick child had darted in to check the room. No, they hadn't broken the furniture.

"He hadn't eaten his supper," reported the urchin.

"I should promote that boy," Hugh told the senior partner as they squeezed by his gravy-stained apron and went out into the draughty day.

The goldsmith was a little go-by-the-ground man hiding behind respectable shutters next to the church, down a little alley. His cramped green-lozenge windows looked out onto the graveyard, where, depressingly, six people in attitudes of grief were ushering a coffin to the grave, attended by a clergyman showing a rehearsed variant of the same thing.

"Certainly not," said the little man, politely. "I am very sorry, but I cannot help."

"You must," began Tom, too sweaty, too eager – This'll put the price up, thought Hugh, trying to look impassive and gazing past the goldsmith's bald head at his little scales and little weights.

"How much do you want?" asked Hugh indifferently.

"I perceive, gentlemen, that you have a predicament... but alas, I'm powerless to help."

Behind him the coffin had been lowered into the dark, and a middle aged gentleman burst into tears and despaired against the churchyard yew.

"...this has been a fortunate morning for me, if not for yourselves, for the client for whom I had been seeking just such an item called at eleven of the clock, by pure chance; we completed a transaction."

"You mean to say you've sold them already?"

The news seemed to put poor Tom into nearly as bad a case as the bereft gentleman now being led from the graveyard.

"Can you possibly tell us the name of the gentleman who bought them?" asked Hugh more practically.

"No, sir, I cannot," and there was in the air of the little goldsmith that which Hugh recognised as integrity. Hugh could physically have made mincemeat of him, yet he stood up to his full five foot two and looked Hugh in the eye, at the necessary angle upwards, resolutely. Hugh did not insult him by offering a sample of coin from the leather bag.

But the little man was thinking. Behind the grey eyes a shuttle of thought flew to and fro, shuttled until a decision had woven into throat-clearing, and now a little speech.

"I know who you are, Master Fentiman... I knew this morning when first you came. Mayhap I should have spoken then. But these are strange times, gone hard with me, too, for, sirs, I share your persuasion." He shrugged his fledgling's shoulders; the linen collar he wore flapped little wings. "I have not been a combatant. I cannot take pride in that. Hiding here. I may live out of the world, but I know the world. I am as true a King's man as you, Master Fentiman, and I daresay that goes for

119

your friend here also."

Friend? thought Hugh Malahide.

"So I shall break a confidence, albeit an implicit one. Something has gone awry with you, sir (to Tom), and you came here in straits, of a financial nature. Took your pearls and pieces. By heaven, I wondered if I should. But half an hour later while I was yet worrying, in came the gentleman who wanted... something especial, he is to be married, sirs, the gift is for the bride. I wonder if I could tell you his name. I wonder if I should."

The eyes shuttled again, this time not inwardly bent but on the flagging Tom and the ill-dressed, once handsome man beside him. The latter gave him look for look from deep blue eyes under scimitar brows; the goldsmith relented.

"You could ask if he'd reconsider..." he said, then, in a voice as low as a rustle, the thwarted man of action added: "or help him to. He is the Parliamentarian squire of Longstaffe, Peter Clayzell. There..."

"Help him to."

"Well, sir, I am doubting you'd funds to top what he paid; the pearls were at last what he was after. He has been looking some time. Much of what people need to part with is... not so good as they think it. I, er, took my profit on the transaction..."

"Quite right," said Hugh Malahide, abstractedly.

The little man watched him push back the hair from his brow and wondered who he was. Years ago Peter Clayzell had bought from him and failed to pay. Perhaps this man would be the one to give Clayzell one back. There was something of pent-up energy in him, anger, human feeling. A presence, in the low-ceilinged little room.

"Good luck attend thee," he uttered, surprising himself.

The blue eyes kindled. Hugh nodded back. "We're King's

men together. We'll keep your name to ourselves."

Neither of them noticed he excluded Tom.

Right, thought Hugh, shaking his mane, thinking hard: two courses urgently to take, firstly to give Josiah his rents back, then, seeing as I can't send back the pearls, somehow to get them from this Clayzell. How?

"Where is Longstaffe?"

Tom knew. "The far side of the downs."

"When's that wedding? The pearls were a gift for the lady – did he mention the date?" Hugh was after a timetable, for firstly and no matter what, he'd put his uncle's mind at rest with his rents in hand again. He hoped the nuptials were not for the morrow.

"Nay, I know not. You have me there. Before Advent, or is he holding out till Twelfth Night? Can't say."

He might give the gift in advance as a sweetener, Hugh thought, mightn't he.

"He might, but wait." The goldsmith smote his pate with his little pink hand. "There was something Clayzell did let drop, what was it? I know: the gift is for the lady's birthday."

"And that date?"

"Oh, sirs, he never said."

I've no time to lose then, thought Hugh; but what do I do?

"But… it can't be directly," continued the goldsmith, recalling, "can't be. For although he took my (your) pearls, sir, he needs to suit the lady and must haul up to London after all. He detests London. Full of fat Parliamentarians like himself, think he'd have no dislike of the company, but there you are. The lady had wind of the London plan. She hath love of London life, of course intends they take the jaunt. A stir, this match," added their informant. "One of those nine-days' wonders, for Clayzell's living example of men born to be bachelors. Snug in that house, running like clockwork, his sister attending his every want. There's a nose'll be out of joint. Now here he is, after some uppity creature half his age. Made a spectacle of himself."

The turmoil in the Clayzell establishment rose briefly before Hugh's eyes, with a sharpening of focus at the words 'half his age', touching his sensitive spot.

"You are a mine of information," said he, "I might say, a goldmine."

The little man blinked pinkly, and Hugh gestured to Tom, who had lapsed into a corner on a stool, that they would be on their way.

The goldsmith looked sympathetically at Tom. "A good thing I knew you, Master Fentiman."

"Why?" asked Tom, startled.

"Otherwise I would have hesitated to do business with so rascally favoured a chance comer..." And the owner of the rustling laugh ushered them to his door.

A catch-your-death chill wind assailed the sagging Tom, making Hugh somewhat cursorily push him into a pie shop, where there was a reviving fug. The game pie, when it came, was entirely rabbit, but hot and juicy.

The parting shot of the goldsmith had gone home. He and Tom were dressed like vagrants. The shaft from the fat harpy of the New Tavern, that she only served gentlemen, reinforced the message.

"Tom," said he, "you are a horse-thief, and moreover you look like one. I am about to turn thief myself, or foot-pad, to pursue those pearls. I believe it more probable that I will get me apprehended if I look the part, as now."

Tom, looking a trifle warmer, turned a pair of suddenly-broken-in colt's eyes on the speaker. He was ashamed and he was attending. Hugh therefore spoke urgently into his ear. Nobody heard their words, low over the meat bones which one diner had sucked and the other picked at.

"You have in that portmanteau that which we are not going to throw after Master Clayzell's birthday gift. It seems obvious he won't be bought off, from what the goldsmith tells us. Nor can we top his price. Right?"

Tom supposed so.

"Now wouldn't it be justice if by some – means, the pearls could be restored so Isabella isn't blamed, and you, who have had a harsh deal by my book, keep some of what is family money. Pounds, shillings, brass farthings. I mean what's in the bag."

Tom followed that if he was not in possession of the prize pearls, he had a hand on the bag on his lap, in which there lay a healthy asset. He had expected Hugh would remove this from him. As he felt too weak to run away with any hope of outdistancing him, he had despaired anew.

"Nay," said the other, reading him, "your father did you a wrong and I consider you should have the money, but not the pearls, because of your sister having to answer for letting you into the house when you made off with them."

"What can you do? Hopeless…"

"If the pearls come back there's no additional reason for your father to disown you. There are years ahead for chances to reconcile."

"Come back?"

"Yes. Which means you or I have to steal them."

"I can't," said Tom drooping, "not just yet."

"We can't exactly dawdle."

"You wouldn't do this for me?"

"No. But it is otherwise a trap for Isabella. As matters stand she'll carry the blame for letting the pearls walk out of your father's front door. He will believe you two were in it together."

Tom looked ready to sink into his half-eaten dinner.

Hugh regarded the top of his lowered head without allowing pity too great a rein. He wanted something of Tom, so must stop him fainting away, and would not reduce him further. True shame (he judged) had worked – and, somehow, the elder Fentiman's unforgiving attitude so antagonised Hugh that he found forgiveness towards Tom, if not yet absolute, at least beginning. Let's say, he might have meant that he would send the rents back to Josiah.

"Listen, Tom. I want you to do something to help us in this business. We need clean shirts and that which goes with them. You must remain in town whilst I return the rent money to Josiah..."

Tom moaned slightly.

"I'll say you repented, even. But we do not need to be taken for ragamuffin hedge-creepers. You must avoid The Bear, because that Puritan whose horse you borrowed will be searching for his fine ginger friend. Pity; you would have got a sum in hand for him had you gone about selling that item of goods instead of the pearls."

So Tom ended a twenty four hour torment by allowing Hugh to spend some of the pearls-money on clothes for each of them. Tom felt too much like a whipped dog to care much what he wore, but acknowledged his partner in imminent crime looked less of a vagrant than hitherto, and dimly hoped he did, too.

He grasped chiefly that Hugh had accurately called him a horse thief, but had run out of invective, or words had failed him.

"I require something of a nag which you shall pay for rather than steal, on which to speed me back to my uncle with his rents. Then I shall try for the pearls."

At this point Tom believed him.

Cantering away shortly thereafter upon that nag, rents in a leather bag bumping his knee with the stride, Hugh Malahide left Stonebury faster than he had come in. Had he the pearls in that bag also, his happiness would have been notable.

The positive general effect, and the smile he had allowed himself as he set boot heel to horse flank, faded in the autumn chill: what could he actually do to repossess the pearls, short of abducting the bride and recapturing them, before Fentiman senior returned?

Chasing him hard, riding his shoulder in the autumnal blast, was the wish he never had had a bride himself and could be free to desire Isabella.

Chapter VII

Isabella had been on blush and tenterhooks to see Hugh, wakeful in the night and assailed by his effect when he embraced her. Next, he returned, without her brother, but with his uncle's rent money and, at least plans concerning the Fentiman pearls, if not the actual shining double handful. Here he stood.

Hugh, newly better dressed at the doorway, swung a dark green half-cloak from width of shoulders, the hand which then lifted hers contrastingly brown to the bit of lace on the new shirt cuff; he wore the shirt, cloak and boots he had obtained in Stonebury. The general effect was of masculine energy. Without a word Isabella's immediate carnation blush informed the incoming Hugh that she welcomed him. He kissed the inside of her lily wrist.

Hugh was humanly keyed up. He saw her eyes flare and darken. The door opened on Block. She sidestepped away.

His impression was that of a young doe, all eyelashes, about to run. But she was, or was she? Sidestepping because Block's great feet were bringing him within a yard of Hugh and his intentions? Of course, a cold hand of reason undershot the moment, as Hugh failed to subdue the knowledge his spontaneous first embrace of Isabella had nothing, nothing of eligibility he could offer.

"The rents are safely back," he began, giving the easy bit first. "Tom says he would have sent Josiah's money back once he'd funded himself with the family resources." (Tom's word had been 'baubles'.)

Hugh had wondered if the arm he had bent up behind Tom hadn't been the best aid to conscience he had.

"'Tis the family pieces proved the challenge," he told Isabella and Block, in as light a tone as possible, "I've the little bits here, all of them, but the pearls…"

"Won't Tom give them up?"

"He's, er, parted with them."

"Tut," said Block, constricted with worry.

Isabella's valuable jewels, thought Hugh, were her eyes, shining at him. What could he tell her? "I know where they've gone, and to whom," he started, concealing he was about to do something less than lawful. "I'm off after them. No, I'll not say more, I intend to parlay or treat, or—"

He ran out of words, could see Block tightening his features with concern, couldn't look at Isabella. If her father returned to find pearls missing…

Inwardly he was cursing the circumstances. Why, fool he, had he pictured his return laden with rents, pearls, all – of garlanding Isabella with ropes of lovely moons – fool he. The prosaic reminder of Not Counting Chickens brought him to reality.

"No news of your father's return?"

"Not as yet…"

But coming shortly; coming certainly, unlike the Scots recruits.

Christmas is coming, said the chill in the darkening evenings.

Got to be quick.

He was glad of the old cloak thrown on top of everything else, disguising the new clothes, for the blow of the north wind.

Trotting through Overstaffe, the hedgerows awry with tatty old-man's-beard, he turned his collar up. For the rags of autumn leaf, the vermilion sealing-wax of hips and haws, his eye rejoiced. But there was a harsh breath of winter on the stone-cold air.

He decided to name his new mount his Winter Queen, for Elizabeth of Bohemia. The horse was warm beneath him, his spirits rose, he caught himself imagining warm Isabella unclothed but for the pearls. He shook out the reins, shook his head at himself, and said aloud to two magpies. "You'd better be two for luck" And did not contemplate Fentiman her father, not just now.

In earnest then, a glove on the Winter Queen's neck, crossing the old packhorse bridge at the bottom of the dip into Netherstaffe, he knew he was approaching not only John Block's niece, armed with an introduction to provide him with a billet, but the moment he couldn't put off: of finding out what to do about the wretched Fentiman pearls.

Netherstaffe began with a pretty mill house on the waterline of the stream, like an overloaded vessel. As if dashed from a jug of sauce, red creeper poured down the stone of the building; ducks below swam in the glassy flood.

The road rose and turned, the ruts of summer now too cold for mud. Here came the village of little humped cottages mostly under thatch. The creeper had furnished the last cheerful colour. It was as if the very realm had changed, with the season, to winter time. Where had King Charles's springtime gone, with women, and men too, flowers on the bough? Where was new growth of soldiery strong as oaks? Withered, as the times. In these very country villages, the Puritan winter beast was turning pretty maids into plain Janes, thought Hugh trotting up Netherstaffe village, eyeing a knot of maidens in severe cap and shawl at the pump with their pails.

The wider world had blown with the Puritan weathervane after the fatal field of Naseby. England had grown darker.

He asked himself whatever was wrong with Sunday sports? Go to church then play the fool or go courting: why be killjoys?

He wound himself up with the old infuriation, then presented himself politely, with his hat off, at the back door of Molly Whitehead, Block's married niece. It was by the church: Whitehead was vicar. She was taking her washing in, and he startled her.

"Well," said she, putting pegs in her basket, "I'm caught all unprepared."

Hugh Malahide couldn't have expressed better how he felt himself.

Early darkness found him, two nights later, spending a chilly vigil outside a hoary building, the squire's house. It was hung with stump-work of ivy and decayed roses; the last blooms had withered where they hung. Now, indigo had fully descended, these leathery bells were lost in the gloom.

Hugh was nerving himself to climb in at the downstairs window he had wedged from absolutely shutting the night before. He edged up to try the casement under-edge with his finger. Noone had noticed – it was pulled to, but not fast, and he could lever it with the blade of the knife ready in his other hand.

He felt very loath to do it, declare his Rubicon. Out here, he was cold and he was trespassing, but had done nothing culpable. Once that casement yielded, once he was inside the house, he was damned if caught.

It was unhelpful to consider the other world, where might was right, where troopers behind him seconded his every whim – the calm "Do this" of military authority. It had been recent with him, too.

Squire Clayzell's home was in the back of beyond, with the building sheltered under the great arm of woodland behind the hill. Hugh postponed the awful moment by admiring the stars, then by looking up at the tall house, telling himself he must pin-point which windows showed a gleam of yellow; above the roofline, tall chimneys were hatched like a woodcut by the bare branches of trees.

There must be incessant down-draught, thought Hugh, or they'd no need for stacks that high. Why do people choose such places?

The hoot of an owl made him jump.

It resolved him. It was bad enough standing out here. He'd insert the lever of his knife and pull – and here it came, without a creak. So this is it...

Feeling as awkward as a great cormorant in his cloak with the dark lantern underneath (better not set fire to himself with the thing), he got himself in over the sill, and stood silent as the Seven Sleepers, listening.

It might have been a vault.

He risked the lantern, its door spilling rays like a painting. He was in a library, with a neatly laid, unlit fire in the fire basket, the row of fire screens standing like battledore bats at one side. There was writing equipment on a desk, pens, ink-horns, what – not; he was lucky he had not wedged the other window or he'd have arrived with a crash on all of those.

He crept with exaggerated care to the internal door, thinking he must have got howled off the playhouse stage had he essayed acting; a vision of his tiptoe-ing, lips'– pursed, self- shh-ing self threatened (as moments of crisis will) to set him laughing.

Acting's banned now, he reminded himself.

Cold sober anew, he tried Block's method at the keyhole. There. He couldn't see more than a peep of a hallway and stairs – but he could hear.

Music, to charm the heart.

In any other circumstance he would have listened transfixed, for music was much to him. Even here, he had to pause as a silvery voice and accompanying lute carried to him through the keyhole. A cadence died away and there was a rustle of clapping hands, a murmur of appreciation, then another song began.

Which was helpful. The household had its attention fixed, and the music makers had closed the door to the rest of the house. Hugh opened the library door, and urgently bethought him where first he should try for the pearls.

He soft-footed it down the hall, as if stalking the music, to ascertain whence it came. The music makers were in the chief room of the place, which he had pin-pointed the day before. It fronted the building with a great window like a waterfall of greenish coloured panes like rainwater, floor to ceiling.

Stalking music and pearls in a strange house… what a strange occupation. How different to the last time he'd circled a house. He'd had his troopers at his back, a pot helmet on, and the object of flushing Roundheads out. Now he had none of the soldier's supports, or excuses.

Had he sunk so low as a common thief?

The alternative was Fentiman shouting, "Where are the pearls?" at Isabella.

Gritting his teeth, he essayed the staircase, reasoning that trinkets would be in a bedchamber. A mighty wooden fortification, the staircase ascended three flights round the three sides of the hall, wasting a great deal of space in the centre of the building. A galleried landing occupied the fourth side, continuing the last-century flourishes of mermen and sea creatures with massive twisty tails, accompanying Hugh up the stairs as balustrading. Moonlight swam down from the top of the house above the stairs under a lantern window.

Hugh took his hand from the scaly wooden tail. He'd better be swift, for all that he felt as one does in a nightmare, rooted to the spot.

He tried the wrong room first – a quick glance showed a room disturbed by refurbishing, lengths of bed-tester material rolled out for cutting, an embroidered bedspread half sewn with fringing cast over a sewing table and dropping its skirts to the floor. Colours glowed like church windows in the passing sunbeam of Hugh's lantern.

Of course, these were the preparations for receiving the bride.

Hugh slunk back along the gallery. The best chamber, that'd be the one he needed. That'd be over the music, finest chambers over one another.

Well, at least he knew he wouldn't be disturbed by the squire himself. Molly was Block's true niece: she knew things. Molly's cook knew the cook at Longstaffe House. And thus, Hugh knew that Clayzell was from home with his betrothed, whilst the preparation fitting the house up for her as the bride was completed. They would be back in a week to celebrate her Birthday, the gift day for the pearls.

"Got to say it." Molly Whitehead chortled, "Noone'd credited Master Clayzell with blood enough to rouse himself and get himself wed, he such a little newt of a man – and then, of course, falls the harder because he's not used to it. He's got himself led by the nose by Goody Two Shoes, mind. Won't know what hit him once he comes to his senses."

Hugh found another bedroom awash with changes. What nuptual anticipation did to Squire Clayzell's pocket, he did not like to think. Here was a tapestry, evidently old hat, thrown down. A pair of steps stood with a basket of nails ready to tack up its replacement. Furniture was covered by dust sheets.

Aware of the dangers of making a noise, the risk of a spark from the lantern, "Let me try next door first," he said to himself, "they'll not have left valuables in the rooms with workmen in."

Then hope struck, for the alternative door opened into an inhabited chamber for the first time. From below the music rose, like the spirits of the house.

And here was a big square bed with hangings tied back in swags onto the posts. Tables with twisty legs were burdened as if baggage animals by a heavy cargo, stump-work boxes, fancy dishes, trinkets – you can tell the Parliamentarian houses, thought Hugh, sourly, by their still having their plate. A good Royalist would by now have seen his gone to the King, swallowed by the hungry Mint, like Moloch.

He opened drawers, prised a chest, but they were full of bed linen. The sound of the lute below died away, and he froze. Why was silence so loud?

He awaited footsteps on the stairs, waited whilst pips grew into apples, cities decayed.

A hand below rippled lute strings and a woman sang.

Hugh felt ashamed of his nerves. He had to be a burglar, so he had better be a good one.

Then he found a key, an ornate, Spanish looking handful (Toledo steel?), inside a vase. He looked swiftly about him for what the key might match.

There!

In a stride he reached the chest in the corner, twitched off the embroidery cover, threw the peacocks thereon to the floor. He was puzzled for the orifice for his key. Then, running his hand over the steel embellished lid, he found a place to slide, and the well-oiled cover yielded.

In with the key.

Here were a row of little boxes, some flat-topped, two domed; he feared these too needed keys, which would defeat him, but the little keys were in some and others did not lock.

A ring of rubies, first, set in a floret. All on its own on silky stuff in a square boxlet.

But now? Could it be? No. Corals.

Ah. Here they were, in double row. He calmed himself, replaced all the containers in sequence shut the case down. Dropped the key, the sound though slight, a check. Then he retrieved the key, fitted it, turned, withdrew. Hugh threw back the soft peacocks-cloth. Done it.

The key went back in the vase, the double row of pearls in his pocket. The absent Clayzell had set up a store of treasures for his bride. Hadn't he heard all this had put someone's nose out of joint? The sister...

Who must be downstairs now, soothing her ruffled feelings with a little lute and voice. The house, as he again crept through it, was so quiet he assumed she'd had the servants up to listen.

He removed the wedge from the library window, took a quick swing out, stood carefully easing the window back so this time it actually clicked shut. A hideous discovery burst on him that he could enjoy burglary, which he hastily battened down and denied as he made his way back through the cold woods.

While he rode back, the hedgerow hips and haws seemed brighter, the berries red as garnets, then the moon rose, lighting his uncle's beckoning doorway as if the best pearl ever.

He gave the Queen over to Harry to rub down, feeling his new life mattered. He'd been hiding his head in a haven, taken a respite. Rural isolation was as secure here as if no outer world existed.

But thieves stole pearls, and maidens hearts, where ever.

He felt a shiver. The old Hugh, who rode Bonny, not the Winter Queen, would not have trusted elation.

But Josiah was propped up beaming, his whiskers a-tremble with welcome. Luisa, stately, silent, allowed herself her rare, sweet smile. Brownie, and then Harry's baby, came pattering and staggering up. It was all hock-carts home.

Tomorrow he'd have welcome from Isabella, the very picture he had painted. She would say, "I knew you'd do it! Father will never know. Saved the day!"

He didn't sleep, though.

There he was in the morning, facing John Block, thanking him for so jolly a niece to make him welcome; while facing the doorway to the big bleak room at Fentiman's where he had given her the dancing lesson.

At the one moment, he wasn't looking, Isabella came in and Hugh's pulse jumped. There she stood in a grey dress which a sunbeam through the window had lifted from dull to silvery, the sloping shoulder line softened by a cobweb of delicate lace. She had tied a smaller cobweb most successfully in her hair, and curling tendrils tasted freedom at her ear. She was a little shy of showing Hugh these improvements, so also showing eyelashes.

"Good morrow, lady," he greeted. "Advance, and be recognised…" Why couldn't old Block evaporate?

Isabella, inhibited by Block plus natural blushing, came forwards to him. The sudden colour demonstrated cheeringly to Hugh she had not forgotten when he had been spontaneous and his heartfelt kiss had conjured up probably the first kiss she ever returned.

Did shy forest deer blush? The fancy made him smile. "Come," he urged, and Isabella's answering smile entrapped him.

He bid her look, thus their three heads, bronze, Block's wisps and hers Van Dyck's colour, bent over Hugh's clasped hands, which he spread, and requested she part the tissue round the pearls.

Isabella gasped. To his confusion, she lifted the double row of graded moons, ran to the window. There, she scrutinised what she held, and he saw her shoulders and the lace droop.

"Isabella?"

"These are not our pearls."

Block stumped towards her, hid her with the bulk of him as he too bent over the pearls.

Hugh stood there for a moment as if he heard a foreign tongue he couldn't understand.

"See," she was saying to the tutor, "look at the clasp."

John Block reared round, little eyes lacklustre. "She's right. My boy, these are the wrong ones. How could this happen?"

Hugh, somewhat aghast, rearranged his features. "They bought our pearls. These are the pearls of the house," he heard himself say.

Isabella must be wrong?

Then Hugh knew this was idiotic of him, of course she would know. Block knew. But – he put his hand to his head. How would he, Hugh Malahide, know them? 'The pearls.' 'The pearls.' There were pearls in many and many a family. They were purity, they were tears. They ornamented the fair up and down the land (unless beggared to the King).

Damnation take him, he'd never even thought of not knowing the right ones. These must be that sister of Clayzell's. He was a fool. Good grief, now he thought calmly, he'd never set eyes, not once, on the Fentiman double string. When they had decorated Isabella he'd not been privy to the sight. If not decorating Isabella, they'd been shut up in that casket Tom ransacked.

"O, no," he said aloud, and banged one fist into the palm of his other hand. "And that's that."

"What, oh heavens, can I tell Father now?" she asked the window, the wainscot. "This is desperate."

"We had a line this forenoon," Block growled. "Be with us this day sen'night."

At least he didn't say Fentiman was due this afternoon, thought Hugh savagely. He was beginning to emerge from his daze. He was about to ask if old Fentiman would recognise the clasp, but stopped himself: yes, old Fentiman would.

Why didn't she rail at him? He couldn't bear the turned head, the limp cambrics, the disspirited new curls.

The goad of his imagination pictured Isabella exultant in his embrace, saying she knew he would do it – Hugh threw this strongmindedly from him, and straightened.

"You must draw me that clasp. Tell me, are your strings the longer or the less? Or differently graded? Does the quality compare?"

This, in the army, he would have named retiring to rethink: strategy, save-the-the-day.

An automatic process came into play. Without being aware of it he was ready to act, no army but one man caught disadvantaged. To re-deploy... to get back lost ground.

He'd had practice at that.

137

But it meant returning.

Returning to that house with its downdraught and its bower of trees, turn thief again (O no, said a weaker voice within, which he strangled): could he?

He'd better.

Or old man Fentiman would get here and find false pearls, Squire Clayzell would wonder why his second-best pearls were chosen by a curiously unselective opportunistic thief – and Isabella would still be blamed for aiding and abetting Tom.

"John." Isabella turned to the tutor. She had not called him John ever before, and this fixed his steady old presence a half turn upon her. "I beg thee, fetch me paper and quill, and I will try to draw the clasp. It hath our Fentiman 'f' on a silver disc."

He went with alacrity, though rheumatical.

Did she do that on purpose? Hugh hoped, and crossed the gap between them, wanting her to want him, show warmth, forgive him, all in the little space of time before Block lumbered back.

It was impossible – for Isabella, so close to his masculine strength and devastated by his failure to save the pearls, needed to gather up. She hadn't his military training. Militarily, he might have resolved to get back lost ground but humanly he was miserable.

Did nor show it, but in the moments before Block returned, clasped her, and Isabella realised from contact with his rib cage, flat waist and below, what would follow kisses. A privacy might have allowed her pleasure without baulking at that new world. But she was very young and sheltered, and she was overwhelmed.

She half turned as he set her back on her feet, he couldn't see her face, only that the turn was not towards him.

Block, with equipment, lumbered in.

Isabella drew the clasp as best she could, gave him the paper. "When you compare, I think these will not look as good."

At least she'd said when, not if.

He could hardly bear to go, which made him look stern, and so anxious to conceal his feelings that he went at once.

John Block sighed, and set about being kind to Isabella. He couldn't know how matters would resolve themselves. But he had applied his eye to the keyhole, before bringing in the ink and paper. He'd nearly spilt the ink when he saw Hugh embracing his lamb. He had comprehended as clearly as if he'd seen babies in the eye. Pshaw, trumpeted Block to himself, crossly.

The two people he cared about, thought Block, even if Hugh Malahide came newer than his Isabella over the horizon. It was worse for him seeing her with a man who should have her than he expected, for if she could not have Hugh, it might break all three of their hearts, including his own.

And of course she could not have him, Block knew that, even though as yet he knew not of Athalia. But he was riven by his peeped glimpse. He kept reviewing, painfully, the strength of feeling Hugh Malahide had let show, and how Isabella had only not been ready.

Chapter VIII

It was peculiarly akin to those sensations of somewhere familiar in a dream when everything was askew.

Hugh wished he might wake up two days ago when everything was going well. It wasn't the Puritans who had made the berries dreary along the same hedgerow or distorted the reflections on the millpond, he could blame noone but himself.

Today's magpie was, naturally, a singleton. The Plain Janes had fled the village pump. And Molly Whitehead, quite definitely, was not quite so jolly at the twice being caught unprepared.

But he'd nerved himself. He'd not waste time or his nerve-endings. Since Molly assured him there'd been nothing out of the ordinary in the village (no hue-and-cry then, thank goodness), he concluded that noone seemed to have sought for the pearls still in tissue in his pocket.

Surely, he could get in again? Make restitution. The challenge was the switch. Why hadn't he looked in all the little boxes? But how would he have known which to make off with? Now at least he had Isabella's drawing. Look at the clasp he reminded himself, as he had a half hundred times.

And went up again through the woods bent on housebreaking. But everything seemed different, as if the fates were against an easy test this time. Before, the black twigs and flapping wet-rag leaves had been as deserted as a winter Garden of Eden after the Fall. But here and now – Hugh stepped hastily off into the undergrowth behind a substantial tree girdled with ivy – he heard voices, cheery with anticipation, and impatient footfall of passers-by. He saw a firefly swinging, and another. They carried lanterns on crooks, seven or eight laughing, happy people clumping down the path arm-in-arm in twos and threes.

Was there anyone else up at Clayzell's? Possibly not, for as they passed him someone told him of their destination.

"I does love the days of a-wetting the baby's head. 'S proper joyful."

"Ah, here's blessings upon him."

"Let's hope 'e don' resemble Ned, that's all."

They were past Hugh in gales of laughter. The contrast to his wretched purpose and solitariness could not have been keener. It took determination to overcome the sudden low pitch of feeling an outcast. But he walked up the woods and got the bulk of the big house in his sights. Action was the only cure for his predicament. Get on with it, he instructed himself.

No one had obligingly left that window not quite to, this time. He doubted he could get in that way again. The light had faded fast and stars were out, with the Moon and Venus by. Venus; Hugh shut his inner eye to his picture of Isabella and walked blinking round to the frontage of the building.

He realised the gaggle of cheerful people hurrying down the woods must have come from the house. Could luck have sent the house servants off for the evening? He'd have cause to thank the ill-favoured Ned for so timing the celebration for his infant.

That still didn't get him into the house. What to do?

Along the house front, light spilled from the tall window and cast a silvery patina upon the ground. Hugh advanced very cautiously outside the rim of illumination to look in.

Two people were there. A thin English gentlewoman (Ah,

thought Hugh, she's the sister!) was talking and nervously gesturing at another, whom Hugh took for a child sitting with her back to the window with only her cap showing above the back of a settle.

He beheld the other lady clearly in the illumination of plenty of candles and a brisk log fire. Evidently he had been right about the provision of those tall chimneys, for even as he watched a sudden downdraught sent a billow of blue smoke the wrong way and misted his view, but those within took no notice bar a bit of fanning, clearly used to it. There were smoky stains to the left of the chimney breast, giving the general tendency.

Yes, that will be Clayzell's sister, for sure. She's the age to feel threatened by brides, thought Hugh somewhat compassionately, drawn into the scene despite himself. The object of his scrutiny was twitchy, taking up a book, putting it from her, rushing about the room whilst turning to converse. It was as if she, not himself, was wrought up to go a-burgling. It was all rather strange.

She was very well-dressed for an evening in, skirt and bodice costly in two blues as dark as the sea, and the lace drawing unfortunate attention to her salt-cellars was beautiful.

Had company been expected but not come?

Not that, or she would have kept the servants from their junketing.

Was she expecting a (Hugh baulked at 'lover', looking at her) private friend?

So many candles...

Clayzell's sister dropped a sheet of what might be music, snatched it up and gestured to the other to come closer, evidently considering a trifle or two would pass time. There was the lute in a corner, tied with a knot of ribbon.

142

A fat hand rose above the settle, waving. "Nay." The sister rushed at her minded to give a good shaking, restrained herself and backed off, fiddling with her back hair and jabbing at it with hairpins.

He'd freeze out here. His hands would be too numb for opening window catches or fumbling upstairs for pearls. He must do something.

But he didn't have to.

Even as he stirred, the downdraught blew, the candle flames leant one way, a stronger curtain of smoke rose. and drew the lady to abandon her unco-operative hair to give battle with the poker. There was a shower of sparks and a crash. A brightly flaming log, three feet long, fell rolling out onto the rug.

There was a shriek from the gentlewoman and the panic of trying to prod the spitting, smoking dragon back onto the safe stones of the hearth. The other woman joined her cries, into a duet, and for the first time threw herself from the settle into view. It gave Hugh a shock to see she wasn't a child but a middle-aged dwarf, her misshapen limbs in a dance of fright and haste.

The dwarf was wearing the pearls. Hugh was rooted to the spot.

She was wearing a double row of obviously superb pearls as if she were a Queen. A three-foot, squat little Queen, presently hopping in and out of his vision and attempting to kick at the burning brand, get it back to safety before the rug took light or its smoke choked them.

It was out of hand.

No matter his purpose Hugh did not hesitate. Too many houses, great or small, went up by immolation. A candle, a chimney fire; even, too truly, by his soldiers' torch.

Those women could not contain it.

143

In the instant Hugh saw the rug had caught and taken flame he ran forward by instinct, seized the ring on the studded great door, and by simply turning and a push, entered the fortress.

He'd girded himself with difficulties about getting in till imagining the house as locked as Queen Bess's maidenhead, and now by six strides and a firebrand, here he was. In!

He stamped, beating at the fiery shooters, coughing in the hot and acrid smoke from the bough in a black nest where it sat and burnt the rug – it would burn them all unless he dealt with it.

"A traveller passing," he shouted at the women as he took charge, energy a tornado. Into a melee of skirts, the rug bonfiring, in the tail of his eye he saw the table-hanging catch with an upwards run of tongues of flame. He hauled at the tablecloth, discharged a shower of books and combustible sheet music, bundled the lot underfoot, stamping. Fumes announced success, but a shriek swung him like a weather cock. The dwarf had stepped back on the log itself. Wearing his pearls as she was, she opened her little round mouth in a primitive O of despair.

My heavens! There goes her petticoat.

Hugh flung himself upon her, involving dwarf, petticoat and child's proportion skirts in a bear hug. He crashed within reach of his cast-down cloak, caught it up and over them, then, extracted his own two yards' length from the dangerous parcel, rolled her along the floor, excluding the air. He smothered the flame to the detriment of his cloak, straightway cast aside lustre in peril so he could attend to the brand which nearly had sent the unfortunate dwarf up like a torch.

Thrusting aside the major outcry of the full-size lady getting in his way, he turned to deal with the log itself. Behind him the dwarf was crying with pain and the distracted lady bent over her, but Hugh could not pause.

He caught the half-blackened rug up in a shower of loose charred bits, but they weren't alive, now to blanket that log, trying to save his hands, shovel the whole lot out of doors.

He rushed out of the room, crossed the hall like a cook with a hot pot, out of the front door and threw the whole lot into the frost.

It was rather like casting out the Devil: a spitting black presence fell out of the rug. He saw it writhing, then satisfactorily dead, out upon the cold frost.

Hugh rubbed a black hand at a sore eye and rushed back in again, for he feared the floorboards had caught; he stamped like a dervish upon the place and realised a scorch mark was the sole wound. He stopped, and fell over the gentlewoman, who had crept up behind him unheard in the din he had been making. The impact knocked him off his feet, and he collapsed as if sitting familiarly with a trollop, across her lap, and thus discovered her face for the first time, a long face worn perhaps by more summers than his own, the age at which it is said one gets the face one deserves. And Hugh saw a kind one, with wishy blue eyes opened wide by the suddenness of their crash. Pepper-and-salty hair had come down all over her shoulders.

Behind them Hugh beheld the dwarf examining her nether limbs for damage; she rent off a blackened set of shreds that had been petticoat, was about to do the same with her skirt itself, had suffered a sore patch on her stout calf. Gleaming at Hugh still, round her neck were the most beautiful pearls in the world – to him, at least.

He looked back to Peter Claydell's startled sister whose lap he was sharing and whom he had trapped beneath his thigh, so she was unable to escape him. The crisis seemed gone, the fire was out, his pearls were safe, and indeed he was smiling as he

"I'm as clumsy as a horse."

came to himself.

Mistress Clayzell's eyes, a mere foot from his own, eased from alarm to a sense of ridiculousness at her present position. "I'm entirely to blame," she assured him. "I'm as clumsy as a horse. I tripped you up."

"Yes, you did," he agreed; now he found himself sitting firmly on her spreading silk skirts in a tide of the two tones of blue, preventing her from rising despite maidenly heavings, but she had a keen sense of her awkwardness and burst out laughing in nervous relief.

Which made him laugh, and first kneel and then rise to help her up, sit her on the long seat, stand back – the while, warming to the gawky creature for laughing at herself.

She was concerned about the dwarf's sore shin and hopped up again, bent down like a gannet fishing to see the damage. "Oh Katty," she exclaimed. "This calls for goose grease. You stay there. This stranger gentleman shall bear me a candle – (will you?) – yes, we'll fetch a soother. Rest you there."

Hugh trying to fabricate an alias thus found himself instead bearing a candle with exaggerated caution, as though he feared setting light to every portion of the house on the way to the still-room.

By the time, he had answered her call to, "hold high," or, "this way," round the still-room, they had banged shins together and opened every container bar the right one, united in the phantom intimacy of the candle's reach in the springing shadows. He had better knowledge of the lady, too. A nervous talker, in rushes (who could blame her, he thought wryly, and she'd be even more agitated if she knew him for her burglar): "Squire Clayzell's my brother; I brought him up. He's no credit to me… I am Eleanor Clayzell, of course; he says – used to say – he'd be

147

lost without me—" Here, she caught her lace on a projecting drawer, which braked her as if shot and Hugh walked straight into her again. The candlelight threw one shadow with two heads as a monster on the wall. He steadied himself with one hand to avoid running aboard her.

"This is blind-man's buff," he said, put his candle down so he could unhitch the bit of bobbin lace and free her.

"I'm in such a bother! Where is the grease? I cannot see it."

"These would seem to be – Imperial Water, tested, it claims, A Water for Ulcers, for The Fret, and here's Our Panacea."

"Oh. All out of order. This is she! I maintain the best still room in the county yet she comes, 'Oh, this won't do! I'm to be mistress, I shall have matters run my way.' She! She is to wed my brother. I am not myself from it all, I'm not, I'm distracted."

She wheeled round recklessly to face him, serious, quite unaware of the state of her hair, of the lace collar hitched half around, charcoal on her face. She needed someone to talk to. Had Hugh vanished, distilled himself into cough remedy or the house Panacea, she would have talked to the wall.

They discovered the grease where She had set up an alien row of jars. "Oile of sweet roses," read Hugh, whose focal length seemed better than hers.

"Oh, no; but here! Look, this is it, next to the rose oile. All out of order." Her tone summed up desolation. It seemed the incoming Mistress of Clayzell had taken away the joy of life, as one's still room was no longer one's own.

Not if there were no status of marriage bed or nursery.

She was kind, next, if clumsy whilst dabbing black hatching from poor Katty's face with a rag and bowl. She reared upright. "Katty, you've had a near squeak. We'll take a restorative."

This inclusive term resulted in Hugh sitting most improbably

148

drinking with the pair of them, the dwarf and the lady to whose house he had come to lighten of the pearls now around the dwarf's neck. Their gleam was as far from him there as on the moon. Resigned to a stay of his plans, he met the ruby glint of their raised glasses with the glint also issued to him, aware of the gratitude in their eye.

Hugh had beheld Jeffrey Hudson, no, Sir Jeffrey, indeed; the Queen's dwarf, a manikin in a big hat, but never had seen a female before. The solid bun face above the rim of Katty's vanishing restorative showed upturned arcs with the smile of relief she was giving him. A lesser man would have felt a Judas.

"I'd have gone up in smoke," said Katty, "but for the rolling."

"I'm thankful I put you out," he told her, quite truthfully. "Is your leg dreadfully sore?"

"It is a bit, but less hurt than your cloak, look, that's wrecked."

"Never mind the cloak. It was not this year's mode," he assured her.

Mistress Clayzell let out a sigh. "We were but trying to cheer ourselves, weren't we, Katty, it ends like this…"

The dwarf bridled. "And why not? Why not, I say." She addressed Hugh, "We don't sit and mope, we don't. Cause enough. But not us! We've had music, brightened ourselves up while he's gone. To show him."

Him would be the prospective bridegroom. In whose absence these ladies had dressed up and lit candles. He remembered the silvery voice. "Music? I see the lute, there."

"I play," the dwarf asserted.

"I sing," the other allowed, "a little."

He couldn't admit he'd heard her.

149

"All finished." Katty's crescents and chins turned towards the floor. Mistress Clayzell hastily poured some more restorative, spilling, and chinking the glass.

Hugh got the same treatment, from the trembling hand, and to apologise, she looked straight at him: "I realise the whole house could have gone up in flames, if that rug, the hangings, all the sheet music, had taken – and all down to my clumsiness with the poker."

"Put it from you," he told her, "the only way is to say All's Well."

The dwarf snorted. "Only till She comes."

Hugh wondered whether he ought to seize the little thing and carry her off like a Sabine to ravish her of the pearls. He was running out of inspiration.

But he would have missed his moment, for in the next moment Katty put her stout arms up round her neck, undid the clasp. "Time I took them off."

"Oh Katty, perhaps. I'd forgotten."

"'S to cheer us up, we have them out for the evening," Katty informed him, "we take turn about."

Hugh remembered to look at the clasp she had just undone. He had come through the conflict refusing looting, taking nothing of that from his men, let alone himself. And here he was, embroiled. He blamed the blind boy.

He had Isabella's scrawl of the clasp in his pocket, together with (he came to himself with a start), the other pearls. He'd forgotten this in the drama.

Those must belong to this unhappy lady, who had presumably not missed them because she and the dwarf had been keeping the bride's better ones warm.

"I am for my bed. I've collapsed." Katty announced.

"Can you manage the stairs? I'll light you?" offered her mistress.

"Nay," said the dwarf stoutly, "I can manage."

Hugh assumed that life at the height of a child had taught her every scrap of independence so as to be seen as a grown woman. It was a brave effort he watched as the squat little figure marched away clutching the ruin of her skirts around her. The rents showed her balustrade legs with each step.

The pearls however still dangled from the grasp of the unhappy Eleanor, who clattered them down on the tabletop. They drew Hugh's eyes like deadly sins.

"Please take some more wine," she was saying, and trembly as she offered it.

Hugh therefore suggested she sat down, fetched her some, and put the decanter down, trying to distance himself. He surveyed the dishevelled figure that was his own in the glass on the wall, liking it not.

Recoiling, he tried the paintings. Every picture in the place seemed to be of playful monkeys pelting dogs with fruit or nutshells.

He must talk to her whilst considering whatever else to do.

Take her hostage? Tie her up? Vanish with the pearls in a puff of smoke? Who was it who drank off a powdered pearl dissolved in a draught of wine?

He was stuck for a topic he could mention.

But she had one. "Are you married to a wife?"

He turned back to her anxious, inward-looking eyes that dwelt on new wives, jerked back with pity to her world. "Yes," he told her. "Hearing about your brother made me think Was everybody about marrying the wrong wife? It does seem we are."

The wishy blue eyes exuded a pang. Had Hugh put a finger

on her wrist, he must have felt the pulsing emotion. "Poor lady," he said softly, "you feel as we King's men must, that we are loath to give ground, yet have to."

"That, indeed; and I am ashamed, too. But She could share! I would… it is the dear little goodwife, clinging to Peter's arm so he feels six feet tall, whereas it is for me, 'How ever can you manage like this? We'll have to see about all that needs doing.' I know I'm outmoded, I'm dull, I'm old. So does She. 'Poor Eleanor'! How dare she? She is one of those little women with self esteem."

"She sounds dreadfully like my wife."

"Oh," she said. Another pang communicated from those eyes. That each had been ironic in their admissions resulted in a shared smile. He rested one hand on his knee, they looked eye to eye. What could he say?

"I wager She can't sing."

Eleanor hastily drank some wine. "Ah, but you mustn't say that. You haven't heard me."

Her brother ought to have praised her all these years, boosted her worth. He ought to have found her a husband. What had he heard? 'Ran the household like clockwork for him.' Peter Clayzell hadn't let her go, until the dear little goodwife had netted him, his Manor House and the prospect of lovely birthday-gift pearls.

"Your brother seems hell bent on decorating the bride with, er, pearls."

"Oh, he is! I know Katty and I had no right to put them on, but, well, they stuck in our craw."

He laughed aloud at her choice of words. "Well done, why shouldn't you? You should, as thanks-offering for putting up with her."

"He's been re-making every chamber, hangings, chair covers, every cover. When he came home with the pearls ready for the birthday, well, it was too much. I feared I should shriek."

So had Hugh, over Athalia, but differently.

He looked quietly back at her.

Would this be Isabella, if he could no way claim her?

Athalia existed. Would hole-in-corner kisses be enough for a lifetime? Isabella, his desire, arrowed him, blotting out the room, a new rose, Isabella who had turned from him because she wanted to love him. The circumstances bit.

Had Isabella this to come? An unwed, unclaimed maiden forty? But her father would match her in the end. Was that better? Hugh knew a pang: choked on his raw patch. Scarcely.

If he had thought, a minute earlier that he was unhinged, now he was not exactly unhinged but too aware of truths. He had to utter one.

"When I stamped your conflagration out, I did myself a disservice," he essayed. "I cannot do what I came for. You've given me the best of welcomes – 'tis appalling that this is the house I entered to lighten of the very pearls." He set his wineglass down as if it was as fragile as the bubble he was about to burst. "Naught else, I do promise. I'm not the usual thief: look, I've even brought pearls to return—"

He drew them forth, tossed them into her lap of blues with silk scorch marks.

"May I tell the story?"

"There is a story to tell, clearly. Yes." She fastened her attention, and wound the pearls round her thin wrist, unwound, wound again, all the time he spoke.

"All I thought was, you'd not given a name," she told him when he had told her. He was stranded until she reacted. Now she'd risen and was marching about with her back to him, so he couldn't read her face.

Hugh, thinking that the account of Tom Fentiman stealing his own heirloom to spite his father would cut no ice, having said his say, had better get him gone, he'd pick up the remains of his burnt cloak from the floor – nay – it was beyond hope – and depart, still nameless, without either double rope of pearls.

Not blameless, but with restitution.

"I had forgot, lady, that beating a fire to bits engenders fellow feeling," he said, and trod to make his exit.

Eleanor Clayzell interrupted him with a physical collision again, all elbows, then got between him and the door panels as if she desired to turn into a draught excluder. It was his turn to be surprised.

"Don't go," she cried.

He stood off, reluctant to force her aside.

"Don't!"

She was suddenly vehement. "What about the promise you told me you made to that Tom? What are these pearls to me but a crown of barbs? Oh, I could have hurled them out of the door, personally!"

"I shall say two men came in to help us fight a fire and they – helped themselves. All our people are off tonight at the celebrations for the new child: Katty and I couldn't help what happened."

He was open mouthed. But she hadn't finished.

"You can have the pearls. If you stay."

He knew what she said, he knew the meaning. The very monkeys and flop-eared dogs in the paintings seemed to freeze and attend, so sudden was the burden she flung at him.

Poor lady, not even with bravado.

154

Had Eleanor Clayzell thrown a dash of cold water at him it could not better have cleared his head from the muddle of rights-and-wrongs with which he had been struggling.

Whatever remained best in him prevented him, by a hair's-breadth, from letting his mouth utter the O of astonishment he felt rising. He managed to look levelly at her.

"Please," she said.

"You do not have to bribe me, lady. Liking hath power too."

Why had he said that? What basic other voice had told him to say it? Maybe he should have uttered a shriek and run for it, like a nervous virgin – but nay, nay, that was she! She, she was wretched; the instincts in him had answered. He led her back to the settle, placed her. Now, of course, she couldn't look at him.

Could he?

He usually could.

He wouldn't get her with child, he thought, practically; not at her age, likely.

There again, he hadn't got Athalia, had he? But he had not had much encouragement to attempt it, either. If Isabella... but he choked that one, hastily.

"Why?" he asked, conversationally.

"For the once, the once. Or go to the grave, cold," she said, vehemently.

"You are in the doldrums," Hugh said; but then she looked up and the nice person she was won over the long face and the complexion fading like the roses on the winter house. Her eyes met his and transformed the plain lady, sufficiently.

"Also," she told him honestly, "you have a birds-off-the-trees smile."

He began to think how to make it good enough for her, how best to bridge the awkwardness, practicalities, where would she be warm enough, least inhibited.

"We are spotted like the pard from the smuts," he said, "let's have more warm water in that basin you brought for Katty. We don't want to spread charcoal."

He found his apparently famous smile had provoked hers, at least.

"Is your bedchamber warm?"

"Oh! The fire's laid. I am the only one not dispossessed by the refurbishings."

"Weren't you going to get any? Or did you refuse to move out?"

"The former, and my chamber is consequently laden with every knick-knack out of all the other rooms whilst they undergo splendours. I can scarce move in there."

"I hope we are getting the bed clear to ourselves?" he said quizzically. "We'll light your fire, fetch a drop of warm water—" and led the awkward lady to see to both. She now jumpy of him – had she been a bluebottle, he could never swat her, he thought. But why shouldn't she be jumpy?

He wasn't, not now. It was so obvious she wanted him and he must help her, that Hugh found himself lighting the new fire in her bedroom, smelling its pine-cone warmth, saying encouragingly, "You can do it," to sit with him in the growing warmth, then getting her for the first time to touch him, by sponging charcoal from his face.

"Do you answer to 'Nell'?" he asked. The bowl in her hand jerked, but without the crash of smithereens.

"Why not!" she allowed, recklessly.

He tried seriousness. "Will I do, or is beauty beyond me?"

"No, yes—" But the nervous lady smoothed charcoal from his cheekbone.

By the time it took for him to do something of the same for her she wasn't as twitchy, they were warm by the safe little fire, she let him stroke her, encircle her waist, bridge her isolation towards what he would do, which she desired, as maidenly reticence began to go hang.

"Cleopatra rolled out of a rug," he said, "but I've passed Katty up, for thee."

He was peculiarly stimulated by the unusual situation, and that she had wanted him. Possibly he was hallucinating. Or Eleanor was.

"You'll have the advantage of She. When's this wedding planned? You'll have days, weeks, of knowing what this is, before she does." That'll cheer Nell along, he thought, and it looked like it did, as she rewarded him with a surprised smile.

She's lonely, he thought, that's all it is. Moved by the smile, he put his hand to tilt her chin, kissed her, not acting. "Let's test the feathers of your bed, come."

She might likely buck him off or kick him, such were her movements when upright. It might all prove a fiasco. However here he was, to earn his pearls.

He enticed her to sit in her shift in the feather bed, found a silver-backed hairbrush among the hundred oddments on the nearby table and began to brush her hair, sitting behind her to remove his breeches. Here he was, he'd make her like it. Feared she'd prove dry as a biscuit. The hairbrush dropped to the floor.

"Tell me your name," she asked, suddenly baulking.

"It is Darling," he said laughing, "say it!" and she clasped him, and said it.

Chapter IX

Hugh trotted cloakless astride the Winter Queen over the frost, his way paved by silver-edged leaves and grasses as beautiful as emblems. The hedgerows might have been dipped in chipped sugar, the air he inhaled tasted clear as he patted the horse's neck, astonished yet over the night he had spent.

He would have one half of his tale to tell Isabella, and he had the Fentiman pearls this time, which was enough for the Fentiman ear. He had that which is conventionally termed beyond price, of Eleanor Clayzell's, and that was his secret.

A robin on a twig sang like she had, and caused him to smile in the silver morning. One burden he did not bear was guilt. She'd needed him, she now could look the pert little bride in the eye with 'Beat thee to it' in sounding inner triumph. He'd certainly pleased her, and by that, she'd given back that which he, too, had needed.

He would remember her awkward elbows, the wishy blue eyes, never added her to the list of things he was ashamed of, in a lifetime.

Stonebury's towering church crowned the rise, in five minutes its attendant roofs and gables would surge over the brow as if he was a mariner riding a long wave. Stonebury always seemed to hide in a trough, then one was upon it.

The cold was still keen, as it had been when he left Molly Whitehead's at first light. The horse's shoes struck iron on iron. Advent was cold and upon them.

Hugh shivered in want of his cloak, which would tell what Nell would first inform her servants, then Clayzell: deserters scurrying down the woods had stamped out the fire but snatched the pearls. The scorched floorboards, burnt rug and the remains of Hugh's cloak would confirm the fable.

"I can't tell you the satisfaction this brings me." Eleanor had the expression of a for-once naughty child: "I know 'tis wrong, but, my word I have to live the rest of my life and this, this gives me the joy up my sleeve I know and nobody else ever will. I also would have preferred to throw those pearls in her face. People think I do not have temperament, but, oh, I do. I don't have courage, that's all."

"You've plenty," he'd said, "and an admirer."

So here he came trotting into Stonebury, slightly somnambulant. The Queen was awake, fortunately, and Hugh was now cold enough to think of a tug at a hayrack for her, a bite for himself, and a half hour in the warm.

For all his need to ride the north wind to Fentiman's and drop the pearls Tom had stolen like a conjuror upon his sister, he'd been up, one way and another, all night – there was time for an interlude.

He had his boots up on a fender, comfortably warm again and reading a broadsheet in the inn parlour. A gulp of hot mull was in him, to go with somewhat better tidings in the crabbed imprint. The Princes, Rupert and Maurice, had reconciled in cheerless Oxford with their uncle the King. That at least, thought Hugh to himself. Though it was better than the King deserved, and could not, now, save more than their own feelings not the realm; the Cause was lost.

The King forfeited too much with the capture of the damning correspondence after Naseby... what Englishman would stomach Irish Catholics making the army of the King up to strength? Desperate bedfellows, thought Hugh Malahide, King's man, unproductively, as he had a thousand times. He gazed at the page he had just read without reading it anew, and then his unhappy vision of the past was removed by a hand descending to whisk the broadsheet away, revealing the unhappy vision of the present. Tom Fentiman, evidently still haunting Stonebury, had found him out.

"You don't waste much time," avowed Hugh mildly. "I only blew in five minutes since."

"Ah, didn't you let drop that The Feathers was your usual hole in Stonebury? 'Tis the old story, look for the horse. I've been glancing about for you on the off-chance, and I know the mare. Should do, I paid for her. Saw her outside."

"Wanted to catch you."

"Have some mull? Overspiced, but you can spit out the cloves."

"Listen, will you? I haven't come to dog you, this is important. Got the (he paused, and sank down to Hugh's level, the better to hiss), PEARLS?"

"I have," allowed Hugh.

"Are they chasing you for them?"

"Damn it, no."

"That's a relief."

"So it might be, seeing as I did the, er, tricky bit for you."

"I know, I know."

"What's so important?"

"God alive, yes, I must tell you – I thought either I'd missed you and you'd already gone, or Father's beaten you to it. You'd best get a move on. He came through Stonebury before you. Half an hour since, he finished a meal at The New Tavern and set off homeward. There!"

Hugh uncrossed his boots, lowered them from the fender and sat up, casting King Charles's shortcomings aside with the broadsheet.

"You saw him?"

"Large as life. I was held up in the press by the bridge there, where a carter had dropped his barrels, his horse had slipped on the icy bit, and that held up all coming along the high road from London. I thought, *That can't be Father*, but it was – sitting there in the coach drumming his fingers on the door, you know how he loves waiting. I slipped down Church Alley and waited till the press cleared, and I heard him call the man to pull into New Tavern Yard."

"But he's early."

"Well, wouldn't his London cronies have had enough of him," said Tom uncaringly, "and by pure chance I skirted round this way and said to myself, 'if that isn't the mare.' And it was."

"Good, good." Hugh scalded down the mull, got to his feet, threw coins to the boy. "By heavens I'm glad you found me. I didn't go to this trouble to get the pearls back for him to beat me to the house to find they're gone! He wasn't expected yet, and that's a fact."

Tom tagged out into the yard with him, as Hugh required the mare give up her hay net for the bit in her mouth again. "You look a touch worn?" he enquired unknowingly, and Hugh glared at him. Got his toe in the stirrup, settled astride, mastered himself.

"That's my line I say to you," he responded, "save that you look the better for the few days – what cheer? What will you do?"

"Oh," said Tom smugly, "fell in with a comrade going home, made us a little sum at dice, next we're going to his place at Avenhill for Christmas together."

"Good news," said Hugh abstractedly, "good fortune, Tom."

He wheeled the Winter Queen and clicked to her, went out of the yard in a clatter.

Worn indeed, he'd got out of bed having not been asleep in it, to get him gone before the servants straggled up the hill full of wet-the-baby's-head drink; he'd spent filling-in time at Molly Whitehead's, still sleepless, and had ridden out through the frost, and now, with a pint of mull jumping about inside him, was riding as fast as the ground permitted after his unfavourite Parliamentarian gentleman, with the pearls, Tom had stolen in his pocket.

How far ahead could Fentiman be?

He must both overtake him and avoid him.

"Ho fellow – don't I know you – and dislike you—" wasn't going to help, exactly.

He passed an old man leading a donkey laden with firewood; a mile along, two beldames in the bundle-of-old-washing costume of their kind. Then a long bleak chase, the fog gathering like wraiths in the churchyard around man and horse, a shroud, thought Hugh shuddering.

He was not fearful – not after the army! But gripped by the chill. The mull inside him had gone cold.

He drew rein at the brow of the hill past The Red Lion, and saw his quarry: half a coach, pulled by half horses, such was the effect of the rising vapour as if a barque floated on the billows. A clearer patch preceded them, and then even as Hugh watched, the tide rolled and enveloped them.

It was good chance he'd come up the rise when he did, or he'd never have sighted them. It was now nine tenths winter dark, to add to it. Well, he'd know not to run into them. He would circle round by the little path he used from those tenants of Josiah's, and outpace them. The vanished Fentiman, in state, in his conveyance, could only crawl the last mile homeward, whereas higher up where he was on the chalk path he trotted the mare.

Thin air…

Nothing of Thin air about tonight, thought Hugh, touching Winter Queen with his cold boot heels, patting her neck.

He had further to go, of course, circling on the shoulder of the downs, but better that than sink along with his invisible quarry in the featherbed depths.

Then the horse stumbled over a tree root. Close home by now, time to be careful. He must skirt Sammy's lodge cottage and its shut gate, make an extra half mile of it to where Josiah's boundary wall had come down, but would spare him jumping a tired horse in the dark.

He dismounted, feet numb, to encourage her over the two-foot heap of stones. Close by her head their combined exhalations made personal fogs. "Come, good girl," said Hugh in her ear.

He was above the ford, but the vapour off the stream threw up a curtain to his view. He must have outpaced Fentiman, he must have – down in the fog, perhaps the coach driver would have dismounted to walk with his horses, for safety, with the ford in his path.

Fentiman wouldn't want to follow the Greateleates in a spill, thought Hugh smiling insofar as his cold face could frame one.

As he swung up again on the warm mare, ready to make the best of his way to the house, over his shoulder he glimpsed ears, then horses's heads, then the top of the coach with baggage lashed upon it, and, yes, there was the coachman on foot, struggling with them at the ford.

Hugh therefore dashed his last dash of the night into the trees girdling Fentiman's. Down from his mare, with a crunch into the

163

frost – his hands were nearly too cold to hitch her. Clumsy, aching from his long night, he ran round the tall flint building, most of its eyes blind and dark. There was a yellow gleam from the kitchen. He couldn't assault the front entrance, clearly. He had once only, in the wake of Tom's pillaging.

It must take Fentiman what? Ten minutes at least, to grind over the ford, round to the lodge and roust out the gatekeeper.

So you've five minutes, to deliver the pearls! Don't dither… Hugh gripped his cold wits. In truth he could have done with a shining window, within, Isabella like Juliet… was there nothing? Wait – that upstairs window had a line of candlelight round its closed shutter, hadn't it? He rushed down, leaving footprints unavoidably in the rime.

Hear me! he willed, aiming gravel. Threw again, hoping he hadn't targeted the old-crow housekeeper's cell.

A third time.

When he heard the shutter squeak he stood under the brick and flint precipice. A brilliant square leapt out upon the frost. It was not the housekeeper. It was a stout outline.

"Block." Hugh stepped into view.

"Good Heavens! Is it you?"

"Certainly."

"I'll come down."

"Nay, do not! I am possibly five minutes ahead of Fentiman, that's all – I chased him out of Stonebury and overtook him on the way. I have what you're short of, have them here."

"Close finish, hey? He's not due, you know. Not due… Can you throw our pearls up?" Block's cannon-ball skull rotated so a profile showed. He was turning into the room behind him, and Hugh heard him call to Isabella.

Whilst he got his freezing cold fingers into his pocket to tug out the little burden. The pearls, last ornamenting a dwarf…

Hugh had concocted a story. He had Block's attention: "Say I'm Tom, say Tom brought them," he urged. "Say he restores them—" Then Isabella was there behind Block, in the act of throwing a wrap round her shoulders. Candlelight threw an amber highlight upon throat and rising bosom before she hugged the wrap against the chill from the window. Her hair was loose. She was as out of reach as if upon the moon.

"Catch," he called, "on three – one, two—"

Isabella, expression concealed by the candlelight behind her, breath snatched by the cold night air, looked down at Hugh's foreshortened figure, where his expression was revealed as urgent.

His eyes gleamed, his parted lips framed. "Two, three." And threw. Somehow she clasped the leather pouch with its amnesty for her brother within. Held it safely, gasping. "Oh," never looked within but passed the cargo without a backwards glance to John Block. She was looking at Hugh.

"Nay," said he, "you cannot ask me in…" and stood there, in the square of light from the window, smiling, a touch worn, flag of hair on his shoulders, a cut-out figure against the silver frost.

"You have done it!"

"Check the clasp," he suggested. "Put them straight in the casket. No time to dawdle, your father's rousting Sammy out this minute. He is, is he not, an unexpected pleasure. I'd best get me gone…"

"Then why are you loitering? Are you silvered from frostbite or is it a trick of the moonlight? 'Tis a new look…"

"'Ill met, Titania?' – you've got the wrong season."

"I wish you could come in."

"Lean forward." And with a quick step up onto the downstairs windowsill he reached the silk tips of Van Dyck's-colour dark brown hair.

"Oh – I hear the wheels!" and she withdrew with an intake of breath.

He jumped down, stood back. "I've seen Tom. Stronger, and somewhat contrite."

"Thank you beyond words."

"That's later…" And he laughed, cold as he was, dishevelled and elevated. In the outer dark the rumble grew nearer.

"Begone, begone!"

"Intended to bring bays and holly—"

"Get you away!"

"Yes, lady…"

The near spark of a close finish acted as stimulus: Fentiman within an inch upon him, the draughts of cold air, the informal tassels of her loose silky hair. Withdrawing seemed an anticlimax; Hugh was a different man to the dispirited soldier of the autumn. Inertia, like convalescence, was long gone. He'd had an illness from the King's defeat, and he had recovered. Under Fentiman's window he'd had not a King's victory, but his own.

Apart from that, exhaustion and an energetic night were not far off pouncing upon him. The realisation he ought to get to Josiah's and lie down, suddenly became imperative.

Curious, that he'd robbed one of Parliament's supporters to restore the prize pearls back to the fat fist of another.

The frost became an enemy then. The novelty of silver mornings, flowers on the window glass, wore off rapidly in the house where there was an old man to keep warm, a winter to surmount and farms to run.

They carried in the great Christmas log trussed captive on a sledge. Luisa's maids decorated the rooms with green swags, set up holly boughs. Hugh came in rubbing life back into his hands to find the little child Luke trying to eat holly berries while his mother and young aunt were up the stepladder; or trying to give them to the dog.

"You're a pickle," said Hugh, restraining him. "How's Josiah?"

"Not leaping and praising God." Luisa sighed. "Could you look in and tuck the rug?"

Josiah had gone to ground like an animal, under a heap of blankets and rugs. The primitive urge to survive which had seen him through ninety winters was nearly snuffed out. Hugh found his hand was as cold as the Crusader's in the church, but, thank heaven, not as lifeless.

"We'd best dig an ice-house," he said. "I've been lifting blocks of ice from the cattle troughs at Hayman's. His poor boy on the peg-leg is unhorsed each time he tries their frozen yard. I've shifted ice like great half barrels. There's enough for all summer's creams and ices."

Josiah twitched, beadily, and Hugh talked to divert him, keep the spark going. He didn't dwell on the farm people he had visited who huddled over an insufficient fire smoking their eyes out, missing their young men, saying, "Our Will, he'll be back…"

It wrung Hugh's heart, for all the Christmas show of cheer-up at his uncle's, whether he was tacking up the mistletoe he'd found sprouting like a great hairy armpit from an oak tree, or warming his muscles out in the yard splitting logs.

What he said only to himself, was that with the farms as they were, they'd never pay the rents come Lady Day. How could they? If this had been a mild winter – if he were ten men, and been here these past summers.

Athalia's land had prospered when he ran it.

Something about the dead end of the year required souls to cheer it. The sour old Puritans say Nay to Christmas! He trusted they would be miserable.

He wasn't miserable in that way. He would not brood on the might-have-beens.

On Christmas Eve, he came into the kitchen clumping the snow off his boots to find a stranger supping broth at the fire; a soldier making for home, even as he had.

"There be naught left," said this man, fumbling his chilblains round the bowl, "save starving in Oxford. That won't help my kin at home. What's left to do? Yet damn me, for all strife, King's King yet, and they can't change that."

The maids were absorbing every word, oh – and ah-ing sympathetically.

One could only do so much. Hugh had vowed not to spend the rest of his days maundering over might-have-beens. He would throw all he could into saving the day here, for Josiah, stave off his personal disasters while he was about it.

"Dunno if I can get on tonight," the wanderer was saying dolefully, "s hard to be near an'yet so far... but the snow's drifted. I'll see in the morning, if that's all right by thee?"

"Where's your home?" asked Hugh, stretching thawing hands to the fire. "Are you far?"

"I be a mile or two out, know the lane branches off at The Red Lion? I lives the Avenhill side o' there. Dad's the miller."

"You'd best put up overnight, then, that lane'll be blocked."

"You're kind, sir. The bad joke'd be, if after all

168

campaigning, a bullet-wound, three sword cuts—" (The maids tutting sympathy, earned his nod) "if I got me sunk in a snowdrift or that foot-pad got me."

"What foot-pad?" Hadn't the club-men been bad enough, back in the autumn? Why hadn't the foot-pad got Fentiman?

"There's talk they're a pair, troubling the highway now King's men be swept away. I thought I'd go the roundabout way an' avoid them, but here's the snow."

"We can keep you from freezing to death," Hugh said, thinking, where did I hear Avenhill mentioned? Avenhill – "Where did you hear the foot-pad was?"

"Done their act twice on the lonely bit. Somewhere between Swinburne, Avenhill and the five-ways."

"Won't get you this night, anyway. Probably tavern talk, anyway."

Grappling his usual pang to embrace Isabella, he and she far apart behind separate bedcurtains striped with cold starlight, he had the sudden realisation. Avenhill! It came to Hugh as if a banner unfurled. AVENHILL! What was Tom doing for Christmas? He was at Avenhill with a crony.

Chapter X

Men who dislike waiting mislike uncertainty. Tom and Isabella's father Fentiman liked his life cut, dried and apportioned. In the autumn, he had anticipated the prospect of the Greateleate acres, a congenial son-in-law, and the pleasure of telling his daughter what to do in her new circumstances. It had been no part of Fentiman's scheme to withdraw under a cloud directed by the clearly unappreciative family he had been beneficent enough to favour – in prospect at least – with his daughter.

Tom was dead to him; what more could they want?

What he, Fentiman, needed was a quiet Christmas, where the wounded feelings of a man unused to the truth might be soothed.

London had been in an unsettled state still, with great defences marring the approaches, sea coal scarce, every man in the street hearing a different voice from God how to run the realm; and no certainty as to how Parliamentarians could come to terms with what God had given them.

Inwardly, Fentiman felt there should be a man at the head of affairs with qualities, he in all modesty acknowledged, not dissimilar to himself. Pity was, that he hadn't been in a position to come to prominence. When he saw jumped up soldiers! Strutters! Fanatiques! What was needed was level-headed men, men who knew what's-what.

Lacking a sympathetic sounding-board amongst those with whom he did business, his thoughts had gone back to his tall brick and flint house in the country.

A retreat, good word, that, he reflected. He'd been upset by the ungrateful Tom spoiling prospect of Greateleate acres. At this rate, he'd be taking physic.

London had irked him. Why delay? He had set out. Thus Isabella found her father in conciliatory mood once the journey was behind him, allowing his household hastily to welcome him.

He commended the housekeeper, refrained from his usual cross-questioning of John Block, and was affable to Isabella.

His manner was of a preacher with more cheery a text than usual; he required Isabella to devote herself to him. He had decided to favour her; he had a little surprise.

"There!" announced Fentiman, mock jocular, twitching a cloth off a little painting.

Isabella faced two fathers, the sitter and the portrait. Two sets of jowls, two impressive noses, and that look (more recognisable in the breathing parent than in the oil painted one), to make the wrong sort of dog wag its tail.

"Impressive, father," she assured him.

"Fitted me in, of course, I told him I hadn't time to wait on his leisure."

"Of course…"

"Thought you'd like it."

Watching him summon the servant to hang it, she thought he was like a child wishing to give its grandmother a hobbyhorse, or a gallant presenting a Toledo blade to his inamorata.

She was the excuse for his gift to himself.

The gift she wanted would have given him apoplexy.

Isabella counted the frozen days. The unrelenting winter frost, dead cold, leaden, made the very skull ache, turned Fentiman's into a fortress and incarcerated Isabella, whose skirt tails would declare any sortie as plainly as a trumpeter from battlements.

She was jailed; she was gated.

I shall go mad, she thought. Is this normal?

Each morning white light reflections danced on the ceiling telling her before she was out of bed that the frost endured. In Fentiman's parlour, she sat in the window to catch the light, obeying his instruction to read aloud to him. He had enthroned himself in a large wing chair. Only his large crossed feet were visible, extended on a stool; she assumed he had fallen asleep.

She hoped so.

I shall go mad, she again thought; is this normal?

Her mind had not been on the page she was reading.

The cruel arrows from the blind boy, the old entertainment, had pierced her, the effect of a man who shouldn't want her.

But because that man had wanted Isabella, showed it, clasped her, kissed her, in an unexpected sunburst she and the man old enough to know better had declared themselves.

No maiden should admit anticipation of pleasure, but Isabella knew it. The spark in the blue eye, Hugh's alert cast of countenance in her mind's-eye, tossing back the sweep of bronze hair, was furthered by an inevitable unseemly thought of this of that man with his shirt off. She had not got as far as any image of Hugh with his breeches off.

By Candlemas Fentiman began to feel country retreat palled. He too felt mewed up, and began thinking he might take his daughter back to Town with him this time, get her presentable as an adjunct to himself. 'Credit to me,' was how he phrased it inwardly, pleased with the idea.

He couldn't think of going yet, not with the country roads dripping with melting drifts and mud to capture him. Reflecting on this, his dignified nose thrust against the window pane to check for incoming frost, Fentiman's eye ranged over the view more freely than his feet presently could. In his imagination he soared over the valley, up to the downs, away, away. Acres, acres.

He sighed aloud, reminded painfully of the Greateleate lands. Strongmindedly though, shut down a barrier on what he'd lost, irked he'd reminded himself. It was just that he'd been snowed in. He was tired of it, felt shut in, yes, and it might feel less tiresome if the valley acres were his acres. Own the view, cried Fentiman, to himself. That's freedom.

Yes...

He must get on with what he'd temporarily lost sight of – buying up his neighbour, the struggling old Royalist.
He suddenly didn't feel so mewed up now the idea had come back to him. As he recognised, thinking of it had done him good. As much good as a strong dose of physic, and without the inconvenience. When the frost lifted would do well enough; now he'd call for a hot toddy, and be snug in his castle.

The eventual change in the weather, when it came, released the thaw and foolhardy snowdrops, and in Fentiman, a mighty head cold occasioned by the sudden shift in temperature. He felt so ill his mind was totally taken up with the perils of survival, a bursting head, a bursting nose, and a lost voice. This last would have allowed the Parliamentarian plaint of, "Where is the God of Marston Moor and of Naseby now?" but his throat was too sore to voice it.

In the outer world, the stream, hitherto frozen into a solid ice serpent of unusual shines and gleams, began to yield and mope tears at the edges. Icicles brained the unwary. The few with leisure to slide on the frozen flood and the tuggers of sleds carrying wood for their fire, lost their glass footing. Eaves dripped like ticking clocks, and in Stonebury mangy foxes slunk round the back alleys. The horse doctor came in with a broadsheet, giving, unsurprisingly, little hope of the Royalist last-ditch in the West Country. Ebenezer found Hugh with his shirt off in the kitchen, towelling himself down after a struggle with a blocked ditch.

"Hopton's'll never hold out." He spread his hands. "How can they? Out on a limb... even the snow hasn't stopped Cromwell. I would that we were back in the good old days of saying, 'Who is this Colonel Cromwell?'"

"Ar," agreed Ebenezer, "thass too true."

"How are the roads? Apart from filthy? Anything stirring yet?"

"That footpad's out. Had a go at some traveller up the high road. Didn't waste time, did ee?"

"Near Avenhill, was it?" asked Hugh.

"Nearer the bridge a mile out, I believe. Don't hear they got away with much. Gave some souls a fright."

Was it Tom? It might not be – yet – O, thought Hugh, throwing his shirt over his head, were they reduced to this? King Charles's army, defeated, unpaid mostly, on peg-leg like Ginger Hayman, or disfigured; proud men, decent – were all brought this low?

Gentlemen, too, as was Tom, none of your worsted-stocking man about him. And what about himself? Hugh Malahide, muddy from an actual gutter. He had a glimpse of himself falling, falling. It was the other gutter. He, too, had been out thieving – pearls. Common criminals. That low. Must Tom court the gallows this way? Yet what else could Royalist gentlemen turn to?

Hugh looked round the kitchen, acknowledging warmth and

"Was it Tom?"

a cut of mutton beginning to charm the air. He had a roof. He had his uncle, by a thread. Tom, wretched Tom, what had he?

He knew in his bones that it was Tom and this crony who were out as these wayside vagabonds. They were the ones talked about. But how long could they last? Gallowsfodder...

He found himself banging his clenched fist on the dresser so the plates jumped, bringing himself to with a jerk. Breaking the crockery wouldn't help.

Why couldn't Fentiman father and son be reconciled? He'd see Tom dead in a ditch otherwise, and that worse than he deserved. He owed Tom the peculiar debt of fellow-feeling in adversity. Perhaps he could think of some way to help.

But for his uncle, he might already be a foot-pad.

Fentiman got up too soon, detected relapse, and went back to the big bed which had reminded Hugh of a tomb. Within its curtain wall, he allowed himself to be in a fragile state and decided to take more hot brandy-and-water.

The scald of it going down his red lane was first heating and then sleep-inducing, to which he gave way, gratefully.

Dare I? wavered Isabella. She assembled a jar of suckets, some cordial, tail end of a pie of mutton into a basket, and went imploringly to Block. He gave her a sharp look but surprisingly agreed they might take the basket down to Goody Jenkins at the lodge cottage.

"The way's not so foul underfoot now," he allowed, "that you mightn't step out for a breath on my arm."

She nerved herself. "And maybe to enquire how the old gentleman doth, up the valley?"

Aloud, he agreed, as if it were nothing whether she did or not. He knew things. "Why not."

Hanged for sheep as lambs, he thought. Isabella brightened.

My lamb, he thought, she is.

Anticipation was the one thing, what is to happen, another entertainment entirely.

She could see Margery and Jane hanging the flapping sails of wash-day. The kitchen itself was empty, no Brownie, no little Luke playing tambour-major with a pudding basin and old spoons; like coming for an invitation on the wrong day.

"Would you wait a moment?" she asked of Block, who eased himself into a high backed chair by the fire. As he held out his hands to it she went on into the house.

Where was everybody? Winter sunshine weakly patterned the wall, there was a candle dripping away last night's cold wax stuck awry in the passage. All told Hugh was from home. The canary, perhaps feeling the unaccustomed sun through the window, began to sing. Isabella turned in that direction, saw the door through into the larger room to be half open.

She'd go in and give Josiah a greeting, with a handful of snowdrops she had found braving the tussocks on the way. Would he be asleep? If he slept, she would go away like a mouse. She hadn't called out, in case.

Then she saw Josiah and Luisa. It was a scene of such private and comfortable intimacy that she blinked at sight of the pair of them in each other's arms, in the big chair, the wasted old man and the handsome woman, his head on her shoulder, her features relaxed and calm, skirts covering two sets of feet, her shawl draped round them both. They were accustomed to what appeared the most natural behaviour in the world, living and breathing kindness with one another.

Isabella picked up her skirts and fled. Her mother was long dead, her father the man he was; why did she feel overcome to see before her what caring about another meant? That it didn't need youth and beauty, nor, most certainly here, marriage bonds.

"We'll not disturb the old gentleman, I think," she murmured in Block's ear, tied the snowdrops into a posy and left them as hostages on the table.

Fentiman, blowing a righteous note on his nose for days, rallied, revived and with a portable desk on his knee by a roaring fire, attended to the household accounts, small payments due and what-not that had accumulated while he was not in the mood over Christmas. Finishing these, he let his thoughts rove again outdoors.

He'd cheer himself up by setting in train the course he'd settled on before struck down by his great cold. He'd neglected his best interests too long.

The necessity was land to bless him.

He penned a line to old Josiah again.

Wouldn't demean himself by an interview (his previous encounter with Josiah face-to-face, when that party had still been up on two sticks, he remembered too well. Had Josiah been Henry V encountering a less desirable specimen of French peasant soldiery shortly before Agincourt—): the man's naught but an unworthy old malignant.

His land lay ready for a well-judged offer from a generous neighbour. The acres of the Greateleate had evaporated, castles in Spain. Fentiman drew a new desire from life. He was a practical man.

"Nearer home," said he to himself, squishing his seal on the wax.

Josiah dismissed Fentiman's man without a ha'penny, read the missive and threw it on the fire. An afternoon's growling to himself sorted out his reactions, mostly un-Christian, directed at the other side of the valley. He was glad his nephew had not got to the messenger first.

Hugh was currently feeling more cheerful, the physical effort needed up at the farms an antidote to fretting. Clearing a ditch, blocking a gappy hedgerow, were the up-and-doing part of encouraging the various tenants. Beyond that, what could he do? He bustled out Harry, the ex-sergeant of pike, to lend his strong arm.

"Hear the King ain't the only one don't pay his army," Harry was saying as they peered over hurdles at Hayman's ewes. It looked warmer in the woolly fold than it felt like outside in the damp.

"What? Are not the Parliament reliant on Almighty God for largesse?" Hugh turned up his coat collar, interested in rumblings of troubles for others.

"Seems thass it: the earthly reward is what they ain't getting, then there's this Irish business, the regiments not only don't want to go, they won't go. Poor old Cromwell, ha ha."

"Mutiny? That bad?"

"Looks like."

"Would they'd fallen out sooner, done us some good..." It was no good chasing might-have-been, thought Hugh. More flesh and blood might-have-beens were the number of aborted lambs after the harshness of the weather.

"They've got falling-out all right; them Levellers..."

Hugh was looking at the ewes. "They're ready. Are you willing to camp up here?"

He left the Levellers for Old Ruby Nose (Cromwell's salient feature) to deal with.

However this very subject was rise up at Fentiman's two days later, between its master and John Block, who had brought up letters from London, the carrier's gossip, and the recent crop of pamphlets – more this day because of the backlog of the long freeze.

"Tut—" Fentiman's frown contracted his features. "Tut—" He held the first of his letters up to the light as if he detected a forged watermark.

"I trust no bad tidings, sir?"

"What, Block? Only that this is weeks old, from Croxley, my man of business, or, from his unlettered clerk by the scrawl – Croxley's ill. This is too bad. I must return. He says—" Fentiman stopped, bottling what the clerk said, none of Block's business. He focussed on the Leveller pamphlet in Block's hand, seized it, glanced at the gist, and looked not kindly on the bringer of such stuff into his parlour.

"I'll no more o'this," he trumpeted, setting his jowl. "Sedition, that's what we have here! Sedition. The place for such men is behind bars."

'England's New Chains' rapidly went the same way as had Fentiman's letter to old Josiah. Fentiman followed up this one with the poker. "At least our good Cromwell loves not the name of Lilburne. Loves the Will of God. Quite right."

He beat a tattoo on the firedogs with the poker whilst John Block reflected that Oliver ought to love the Will of God because it told him whatever he wanted it to. "I do hear these Levellers have little love for the army," said he mildly, didn't add that nor did the royalists in Ireland, whence the more prudent of this selfsame Army of Parliament seemed most reluctant to take themselves.

His master had thrown aside these lesser points. "This talk of mutiny? Stuff and nonsense. What we need to do, is silence these printing presses. No substance in these pamphlets save ungodly rumour, shouldn't be allowed."

The ash-grey flakes of the pamphlet had dispersed satisfactorily. Fentiman straightened, his neck band flapping.

After all, pamphleteers were miles away from events, holed up in their rats' – cellars, not out in the world like he, Fentiman.

He was considering whether or not to allow his daughter Isabella the privilege of accompanying him back up to London.

As the righteous had beaten the Royalists, that was that! And Royalists were kennelled up in Oxford, therefore it was safe for decent men to be abroad. Wasn't it! Thus Fentiman, and he carried on directing Nan how to pack his shirts, and spoke reprimandingly to her for showing too much of her ginger hair under her cap.

But the regiments that had harkened to the voice of John Lilburne fermented still, wanted the miserable equivalent of what they would have earned as labouring men safe at home paid into their hands, without delay.

Fentiman informed his daughter that she was to come with him to London.

In the kitchen, Nan, the housekeeper, and John Block discussed this.

"He'll not go?"

"Will he?"

"A regimental mutiny'd stop me going abroad," said John Block, "but he's made his mind up. Thinks if King, Prince and all left in Oxford city can't harm him, noone can."

"Do he mean to take her?"

"Isabella? What do you think?" said Block tetchily.

"But—"

"She ain't overjoyed, seemingly," said Nan tossing her head. "Be better than sitting here, London town."

"What can I do?" Block asked rhetorically; "can I turn his coach and horses? Intransigent, that's what."

It was no use saying so to Fentiman, but trouble there was. A couple of regiments had declared themselves risen up – for their money, for freedom to think as they chose, and reluctance for Ireland. They were for getting together. They were for a move now.

John Block consulted the horse doctor, who confirmed matters. Block thereupon stumped upstairs. If it cost him his employment he'd say a word to his master. 'Reconsider taking the young lady,' he'd framed, hearing in his head Isabella's single cry. "I can't go—" She'd hidden her face, but he knew why.

Block's regular tread, and rehearsal of his 'Reconsider' speech, was suddenly interrupted by a messenger with a letter. Brought out, the man said, especially.

Fentiman, hearing a strange voice, emerged and took the letter, withdrew it from an oilskin packet and began tutting.

"Croxley'd rallied – now he's died," he announced, as if complaining of inconstancy. "Fetch Isabella, I would make haste. The office will be in chaos."

So John Block was upstaged and never gave his speech. The matter was settled. They were for London, and that was reality, unlike all these empty rumours.

Chapter XI

The countryside was empty of all activity save the water-tap drip of twigs and hedgerows, the rushing of ditches and the crunch and sway of the coach. The roads were barely fit, of course – Fentiman's optimism, like Canute's, was in expecting what he wanted and then being insulted at difficulty.

Isabella held on to the leather strap as the body of the coach heaved. Her father held the opposite strap radiating ill-humour. For herself, she wished they had simply overturned in the ford half-a-mile from their door, like Greateleate – and never moved a yard after that.

As it was, the poor horses toiled past The Red Lion. She felt for them; felt for herself, half hoped for the footpad (but this wasn't the road), wanted a step back for each one forward because of the man she hadn't seen since before Christmas.

Stonebury reared as slowly as if it fought them off, such were the conditions. Fentiman had no choice but they must rest and eat. As he would take his own horses back up to Town with him, they must rest also.

What was the confounded matter now?

"The ground's that deep it's sucked two shoes off the bay, sir."

"You'd best find a farrier then," said Fentiman resignedly.

He hadn't intended to spend the night in Stonebury's flea-ridden inns, but they had made such poor progress he could see he was baulked of his favoured hostelry in Marychurch further along.

"Isabella! Fetch your bag," he summoned his daughter. "We are benighted."

Out of Marychurch that evening came one mutinous regiment, and tramped through the mud and ruts to take its grievances to meet up with those of the likeminded, wrought-up soldiers of Parliament that had come up to meet them from the west. Their crossroads was upon the common at the bridge-foot at Stonebury. There, where lately the townsfolk had been skating and sliding and eating hot chestnuts in the freeze, they spent the night, arriving at the time decent folks were abed, indeed, in The Feathers were respectively heaving rhythmically in a large bed or cold and wakeful in a smaller one.

Fentiman's daughter, without grounds to defy him, felt much as Walter Raleigh must have done on his long haul up from Devon to the Tower.

Neither of them felt the slightest presentiment of outside interference with Isabella's introspective misery or Fentiman's vision of Parliamentarian Utopia.

He made his dignified ascent to bed, full of fritters; Isabella crept to her cell, glad to be rid of him.

Half a mile away the common was getting a mud-churning, from a newly-come number of booted feet.

The Feathers faced the market square, as did the better rooms let to guests, so the surprise was soon disclosed. The united forces of the mutinous regiments came in to pray in the morning. The different buzz brought out every eye in Stonebury to a shutter, every bold spirit to stretch his neck round a corner.

There was a bravado show of sea-green ribbons in hats worn by the Levellers, a self-consciousness of posture – and a looking over the shoulder, just in case. Soldiers sauntered in twos and threes, aware they trod the boards of their play.

Isabella, peeping, counted them, tried to discover what was up. The serving maid, eyes popping, put her head round the door. "Look, Miss! Here's a pretty pass. They come up in the night, they're the MUTINEERS!"

"Does the gentleman next door – my father – know?"

"Dunno," shrugged the servant. "But there'll be no moving off early, the bridge'll be stopped."

Oh good, voiced one basic layer in Isabella on that one. But she was prevented from further speculation by the loud tones of Fentiman as he progressed from his bedchamber down the corridor to his daughter's wide open portal. There he stood, fully clothed, even to his hat, rammed levelly over his frown.

"Daughter," resonated Fentiman in his best parson-in-the-pulpit bass, "there are misguided men abroad."

"There would seem to be a number of—" and naughtiness made her to substitute, "church-goers" for 'men', "in the square, yes, Father."

"Church-goers! Churchgoers! Those are seditious men, that's what they are, agitators against authority. Look! They are trying to influence decent townsfolk! There, see?"

A knot of timorous local citizens were accepting the approach of a calm soldier in his buff coat, gathering round to hear what he had to say.

"Look at that! Can't go on. This has to be stopped. This is an infection, an infection, I say." Fentiman stepped back from the casement, pulled down his doublet, settled his cuffs.

His rear view filled the doorway, marching out. The servant shot a scared glance at Isabella. The measured tread departed down the stairs.

Instinct told Isabella. She turned to the window again to see the top of her father's hat, his grey-cloth doublet, foreshortened banister calves and buckled shoes emerge out of the front door of The Feathers and carry him straight up to the nearest soldier with a sea-green favour in his hat.

A rattle of musketry broke out from the direction of the bridge-foot, seconded by cries, then one further shot – nearer, this! Fentiman, by now the centre of his group, paused in mid gesture. The whole throng of townsfolk, mutineers, turned as one in that direction.

And were fronted by the onrush of—

Who were they?

It had to be the loyal soldiery of Parliament, here to finish the dissenting element within their ranks.

A bullet richocheted with a sharp crack off The Feathers' swinging sign.

Isabella hid her head, gasping. There had been a panic. The mutineers had been taken unawares. Perhaps their lookouts had been silenced. At any rate the pattern of first-reaction resistance, weapons grasped, a group hacking swiftly at the newcomers, was brushed aside by a salvo of musketry and then the clash of hooves announcing loudly on the cobbles that horsemen would ride down men who had not had time to go to church.

The mutineers had not all fled. Isabella daring the window saw that a score of them had enveloped her father and a knot of Stonebury people like the tide – a tide with sea-green spume, very visible at first floor vantage. This tide swept them in spur-of-the-moment flow across the last dozen strides into the church door.

Up the steps.

The door opened, blinked, shut fast behind them. Isabella heard it crash.

Her father had gone to church with the mutineers.

They'd kept the presence of mind to grab hostages as they dashed for sanctuary.

Isabella was betrayed by surrendering ankles and lapsed onto the bed. One moment the strong thundercloud presence of her father had filled this little room, the next it was as if the cobblestones in the square had parted and swallowed him up, hat, buckled shoes, and all.

What ever ought she to do?

She waited for her wits to tick. Her father's departure, as usual with thunderclouds, induced relief; which in these circumstances, she had no right to feel.

Would she have to ransom him? Would the Parliamentarian loyalists rescue him? What on earth was to be done?

Wavering downstairs, she recognised their coach driver at the doorway, back turned.

"They've got the old sod, then?" he was asking of the landlord.

"Dick," she remonstrated, and he jumped and turned.

Outside, the church's flint with brick banding looked as impregnable as a castle. Isabella saw human gargoyles up on the tower: mutineers with matchlocks, pointing long barrels. Their intentions were not innocent. Below in the square a prone figure lay in a spreading pool of blood. Someone hurt outside Isabella's line of vision was cursing and wailing with pain.

The horsemen had swept on by to take panic-stricken mutineers as they ran. Temporarily, the square was clear of all but those who could not move.

Isabella recoiled from the sight of the blood.

"Your dad'll be all right," offered Dick, "you mark my words, he'll talk them out of shooting him."

"Oh." At the new thought Isabella possibly blenched, for the landlord took her elbow and got her to sit down. She couldn't bear the thought of her father dead in his own blood like the man there in the square. She'd rather he walked out fulminating under his familiar thundercloud.

"They've got the Mayor! Troops have to flush them mutineers out," the landlord was saying.

Soldiers began drifting back, some on foot, some on horseback. The gargoyles withdrew until only their heads protruded over the crenellations on the tower. Another matchlock came poking from one of the smashed church windows. Stained glass meant idolatry to stern men.

Isabella realised the mutineers had nothing to lose. A man in a sash came striding across the square, took a quick look and withdrew under the overhang of the market building on its pillars. He gestured to subordinates, conferring.

"This'll take some time?" she asked the landlord.

He pulled a face. "This'll ruin my trade…"

"Dick." She tugged at the coachman's sleeve. He turned from gawper's ease.

"Find me a horn of ink, and a quill and bit of paper as quick as you can."

The one thing she could do freed Isabella's chains. No longer was she stunned into compliance not knowing how to defy Fentiman's heavy authority.

Not knowing where Dick's loyalties would first lie, she enclosed the note inside another for John Block, and instructed Dick to ride one of the coach horses home with all speed bearing it.

"I ent got no saddle," he said, unhelpfully.

But the landlord overheard, recognised a crisis and offered to find one; and chivalry brought him to stand up for the old sod's daughter. He brought her a flagon of his best. "Keep your heart up," he urged, "an' I should let you have the back room, in case they soldiers come pestering."

When Hugh arrived, he shouldered his way through the crowded tap-room calling for the landlord, who emerged rubbing his hands on his apron, exclaiming. "What a day!"

This was clearly the best seat in the house from which to watch the half-completed play, over here opposite the church. Would it be a comedy or a tragedy? But then he saw a lady weeping with two half-grown girls clinging, and altered his cynical assessment.

"They've taken the mayor, sir, that's his lady and the maidens. Bad do."

Overcoming his natural resentment at the square full of Parliament's soldiers, he enquired for Isabella.

"In our back room, sir. Safe and sound."

The door Hugh flung disclosed calm after the hubbub outside. The landlord asking behind him if he might fetch them anything, prevented all but Hugh's eyes leaping upon the graceful column that was Isabella.

"Praise be it was not you they took. Tell me, are they still holding him?"

"They've been there all night, now, father and some half dozen others. At first light one of the mutineers came out on the roof and threw down terms. They want a safe conduct..."

Gone were the days when the Prince might send a trumpeter and require terms of Parliament. Hugh wryly shrugged. "What a pass, that we have Parliament fighting mutiny, with your father, their champion, in danger from his own."

"Will they shoot him?"

"Half a day of your father's company would compel most hosts to shoot him," he said, "I thought the besiegers looked unready to rush the church as yet. They're showing a presence hoping their numbers will daunt the defenders."

"We may have a long wait?"

"I hope so," he said, "I came to rescue you, not him."

Isabella rewound the flutes of her skirt by turning away, she now pink rather than pale, looked back at him over the curve of sleeve and shoulder, showing the faun's eyelashes. "Oh, you must think I only require you when in trouble—"

"Pray continue." He spread his hands. "I'm thinking it would be a dull life, without you and your betrothals and brothers and pearls. Now we are reduced to fathers, that's all."

He was aware, very aware, that the sudden rose of her cheek wasn't for them. "'Twas due time you had a crisis. How are the pearls?"

"The pearls! I've yet to hear how you managed it."

That was the tale he would not fully tell, when it came to it. "Never mind how." And he brushed a dismissive hand (that had been his crisis, for a change.)

"I would like at least the once to see you bedecked in them, though, to demonstrate my efforts."

"They are now in father's custody, I fear."

"What a pity, to live under his bed in the dark."

The landlord put his head round the door. "Seems they've sent out for food. Not getting any. Soon starve 'em out."

Hugh turned like a weathervane between them. "I'd best take a look. See what I can find out. No, you may not come!"

"But it is dreadful waiting here!" she would have followed him, but the crack of a matchlock, cries, rang out, and Hugh pushed her firmly down on a chair. "Stay! Promise—" And went hasting out through The Feathers' yard at the back, round behind the market building to approach the town square without dashing straight out into it.

"What's to-do?" he enquired of a spare little man sheltering behind a pillar.

"Seemingly," said the fellow, not removing his gaze from the interest of the foreground, "thass to get the soldiers to stand back – ah! Look."

Across the square, the church door suddenly shot open, a figure came stumbling out and the door shut with a crash of bolts. They'd let one of the hostages out.

It was a small, round gentleman in a broadcloth suit, his hands up to protect his head as if that would save him from a little lead sphere should the ominous gargoyles up on the building decide to shoot him.

It was neither the mayor, then, nor Fentiman.

Hugh couldn't be entirely sorry – well, not sorry at all, really; had it been salvation, what was there for him but to give up Isabella again? The mutineers had got Fentiman, they can keep him for a bit, he thought, moving to a pillar of his own as it had become apparent the little man beside him had recently been engaged in the carting of dung.

He made his way back, behind the soldiers, past the house windows lining the square, towards the inn. In every window heads crowded, watching. He was in the middle of a nine-day's wonder.

The hostage had been let free in order to bring out a second demand for safe custody. He was groggily having a restorative, his brother's arm round him, in The Feathers. He happened to set down his pewter tankard, with a hand which quivered still, as Hugh came by. The army officer, his lobster – tail helmet in his hand, was bending over him, and Hugh heard the hostage tell news that fixed his attention.

"If they don't get what they want, they'll shoot us one by one."

"Is this your opinion, or did they swear they intend it?" asked the officer, determined to get it correctly.

"Nay, see for yourself, 'tis writ here. You must act! Do something!" Hugh left them reading over the paper the hostage had been sent to bring, and, for the first time seriously concerned, returned to Isabella. He hardly could soften the message. There it was.

"I hear," she said.

"They could leave them be, call their bluff, or maybe the army'll storm the place to rescue them... I think them unlikely to be throwing safe-conducts around, because they daren't have this carry-on be seen to succeed."

"Oh, they'll shoot him."

"They could shoot him. Let's hope not. I'm here. You be brave."

What he'd give for his troopers, good and true! But they'd hardly be out rescuing Fentiman, the Parliamentarian.

"I wonder, if I should find Tom?" he asked suddenly.

"You mean, if it comes to the worst."

"Not that yet. But, if your father gets out safely, mightn't Tom—"

"They might make it up!"

"Now, tell me, Isabella, what do you wish? What do you truly think's best to do?"

"Oh, we must try. But do you know where Tom is?"

"I've a general notion," he didn't add, I think he's the local footpad.

"Could you find him?"

"If he's where I think he is, it won't take above a couple of hours to get him. Will he come, though? I don't like to take him hostage in these circumstances."

"Tell him, please, to come for my sake?"

"I'd come for that," he said, and as she raised her clearing amethyst eyes, his faun came out of the forest and his heart beat for joy.

He took her hand up, her wrist a slim stem within the full sleeve, bent, and put his lips to her hand.

Every hair on the back of Isabella's neck curled, she held his hand against her face. The barriers was gone, he breathed and gathered her against him, she sighed and raised her mouth, giving, so the little room they were in hummed about him until he had to tear himself from twenty Calypsos, all sweet; he paused at the door, smiled over his shoulder with the blue torch eyes as he caught up his cloak again.

For two pins, he'd have shot Fentiman himself, to stay and taste Isabella.

However, as he had been fool enough suggesting finding Tom, he'd best do it, and get the ruts of the Avenhill road under him. The sooner gone, the sooner back.

What had Tom said? His friend was the Avenhill connection, had a home there, that was it. Avenhill was a poor straggle of farms, nothing much. He'd need to unearth the local Royalist. Not easy, as sit-on-the-fence folk were now discovering they'd always felt the King was ruining the realm.

However, there couldn't be that many of the King's allegiance likely to be Tom's friend in a place that size.

"The Manor?" snorted a labouring man up to his knees in muddy ditchwater; he looked at the mud-splattered traveller and mud-caked horse, unimpressed. "You ent been along here lately, then," he said, leaning on his spade, "thass for sure. There's the gates. Go an' look for yourself."

Hugh wheeled the Winter Queen and trotted as indicated. The crescents she left merged with the puddles like footsteps when the tide comes in. Here was the gate, left open, a hinge gone. Maybe the Royalist friend was out of funds, needed wayside clients. Hugh sighed, overcome by the melancholy of it all. This place did not smell very cheerful. Up the rise, the good mare trotting well, and here was a left-hand bend.

Then he knew what the old man had meant, for before him was a house with a burnt roof and dead windows. He'd startled two black crows into flight, and that was all there were for occupants.

What in summer might be a pretty cottage came next in view under a hat of thatch. If there was a cottage woman, Hugh would ask her if she'd heard the name Fentiman hereabouts, seek Tom out.

He was halfway out of the saddle when the door opened and a man with a very black beard stood in the shadows with a pistol and demanded his money.

"I'll be damned if I will," bellowed Hugh, nettled. "Get me Tom Fentiman at once, or you'll regret it. I'm known to him."

A shutter opened in the dormer in the thatch, disclosing Tom himself, startled. His partner in crime below, distracted, looked innocently up, so Hugh rushed up the path and seized him by the wrist. The pistol now pointed at, in turn, the sky, watery sun just emerging, and the white face of Tom.

"Drop it—" growled Hugh.

"Will! He is a friend of mine: at least—" (As Hugh glared at him.) "At least, I know him."

Hugh successfully turned Will's wrist and the pistol fell in a puddle. The black beard was a scarf which had been tied round his face. It collapsed round his throat to reveal a boy's thin face, with freckles.

"Good God, Tom, get your friend to choose his victims with more selection. I've not two groats to rub together. Also I have disarmed him far too easily. I thought this Avenhill footpad was a desperarado."

"Sorry," said Tom, "it was a misapprehension."

They looked a miserable pair, thought Hugh; and recognised nobody would be that inept from choice.

It must be desperation.

"Was that your home, back a way?" he asked of Will with the freckles. "Burnt half down?"

"I never thought to find it so," said the boy.

"Will's had the most sorry homecoming," Tom put in. Too true.

He's not alone, thought Hugh. He went to hitch Winter Queen on the gatepost. "You're living here in the cottage?"

"Scratching along," admitted Will.

"Far be it from me, but don't risk your neck until you're better at it."

"I-I must have funds," said the boy, hang-dog.

Hugh hadn't come to pass judgement. Was he above reproach, himself? "I'm so sorry," he heard himself say.

"What do you want of me, to bring you out here?" Tom demanded. "How did you know it was me? I've plans too, you know. I've only to find a few guineas, then I'm for Holland and a new life."

"Before you set sail for Holland, or the gallows," said Hugh less unkindly, "I've come to ask a favour. Will you accompany

195

me back to Stonebury? 'Tis important."

He had to talk Tom into it, but then, he had caught Tom at a disadvantage.

The hostages spent a dull afternoon, time as a sunless sundial.

Hugh's army instincts were of nothing about to change yet, a lull; the dumps settled over Stonebury – if but for half an hour. And he was urgent for a meal, another instinct from campaigning days: never lose a chance to eat or sleep.

It would liven up sooner or later.

At The Feathers, the landlord had the whiff of drama under his nose by now, took the principal players into his kitchen there to wield a fork and sinister black pan and made an omelette.

"Eat up," he urged, "what a day! I'll put all ee care to name on your father's reckoning, Mistress, that'll show I believe he'll be spared."

Tom rolled his red eye at this; but, even if Hugh always saw a horse with flat-back ears when temperament bit Tom, at this moment Tom wasn't kicking.

He'd come into Stonebury almost as if what Hugh proposed might be a relief.

Hadn't it been Tom's wish to be reconciled, to come home, that began all this? It had only been intransigent old Fentiman's rejection that started Tom on what was by now a distinctly downward path.

"What do we do now? Wait?" asked Tom, through crumb. He turned and smiled weakly at his sister, not noticing she had become left handed; Hugh had her right hand under the table and each was eating with forks in their free one.

Hugh, variously fortified, had an idea. Immediately wished he hadn't. But once thought, there the notion stayed, as these

196

things will.

Why wasn't the force of soldiery out there trying something? In their place – again, O for his heyday with the men to do his bidding – he'd have had faggots at the door, smoking them out. He'd had that work! My word, he had – and bagged the lot of them as they came choking out. He conjured up the memory of his enemy sitting on the ground flapping their hats for air: and he'd laughed, and rounded them up.

He allowed himself to tell the tale, rewarded because it made them laugh.

Unfortunately, telling the story didn't make his idea go away. It swelled and jogged his elbow and insisted he heed it.

What they needed, practically, was not merely that Fentiman emerged (in whatever mood took him in the circumstances) but discovered Tom under his nose, instrumental in the rescue.

Saying in effect: "Look, father, I am saving your hide."

Having got this far, Hugh and his thoughts galloped off. First of all I need a peep into that church to see the lie of the land, where the hostages are, where the soldiers. It is full daylight some time yet.

So, what I want's a ladder, round the back. They've look-outs on top of the porch round here at the front, I don't believe they'll have felt the need to do that at the back while the army's sitting this side.

"More?" asked Tom, pushing the bread board. Hugh focussed on him. "Where do I think I've seen the graveyard? I know I have—"

"Not that bad, is it?"

"Dolt, think—! Wait. I have it. Recall the goldsmith's, round the back. His window gave onto the graveyard."

"Yes it did," Tom remembered, and the painful occasion,

"but?"

"Get to your feet, we're going to visit our goldsmith. I want a look in the church from a different angle to this public one."

There were a couple of soldiers at the back, where the graveyard gate let onto the alley. Tom and Hugh sauntered past. The soldiers were tired of waiting, one perched on the railings looking the other way and his comrade smoking a clay pipe. Neither of them looked interested.

"What cheer?" asked Tom.

"Bad do," said the pipe smoker out of the other corner of his mouth.

His companion shifted, to tell him to shut his mouth on the pipe.

"S all very well," grumbled the first. "They aren't paying us, are they?"

Hugh pulled Tom's sleeve to get him to drift away up the alley.

"Dissent's wonderful," he said, "would that they'd show more of it."

He tapped on the goldsmith's door, hoping that man hadn't gone to watch the excitements at closer quarters. But here came a shuffle and the sound of a latch. A length of chain prevented the door from opening more than three inches, but in that space the goldsmith's nose appeared.

"Ah," rustled the voice, the chain was released and himself disclosed, small, precise and quicksilver eyed. "I know you gentlemen. Slip in, slip in. Perhaps you would be good enough to use the boot scraper."

After the hurly burly outside it was like being in a maiden aunt's parlour.

"So that's the way of it." The goldsmith tapped his fingers

"The soldiers were tired of waiting."

together after they explained. "Have I a ladder? I think I must have. Do I want you to use it? I think I do. Though, Tom Fentiman, I would that your father were a King's man like yourself, if you must rescue him."

"I'm not sure that I want to, myself," admitted the truthful young man, "however, my better nature will get so far as a look in the church to see how he does – from your ladder, if we may."

The yew trees in the churchyard, ancient, mighty, must block the view of Parliamentarian soldiers, and there were substantial tombs; the goldsmith's house next door had a wall to its garden. Bent low, the ladder between them, they scuttled past a pair of barrel-topped last resting places to a singleton protected by iron railings. Crouching behind this, breathing hard, Hugh found himself eyeball to eyeball with a grinning skull carved in relief by some grisly mason.

"Last dash," he encouraged, "come!" and they were then protected by the angle of the church from any sighting.

They were now under the fine west window.

There was a hand's breadth break in it.

"Never thought to be glad of window breakers, Tom – did some oaf take a pot shot at it?"

"They've shot John the Baptist's head off."

Hugh set the ladder beside the window. The sun had helpfully found a cloud. His head wouldn't be as strongly a shadow outline against the opening, and, unlike the Baptist's, he intended to keep it on his shoulders.

He needed the shot-away peephole. Grasping one rung he put one knee on the stone sill, applied his eye.

There were two groups of people and one single figure. The hostages, save one, were slumped together. He counted six dispirited heaps sitting under the rich curls and decorative infill of medieval stonework; above, a small carved creature squatted, hoof in mouth, most unfeelingly.

The remaining figure was sitting apart on the steps to the font, giving every impression of having been ostracised by his fellows in distress, like a guest at a party who has told an unfortunate joke at which noone has laughed. It was, of course, Fentiman.

In any other circumstance, Hugh would have relished the moment. Had Fentiman tried haranguing his companions? Probably. He hopped down from his ladder and told Tom what he'd seen.

"Now what?" Their eyes met, considering. They looked about them.

Peeping was the one thing, action another. Shortly, someone would be shot; Tom's father, first? Or second… couldn't know – or, as with most threats, would the mutineers haul off?

The two soldiers who had been in the service of the King conferred in whispers, their backs to the church wall.

"For sure the army—"(Parliament's Army, need he say) "must rush them, bound to be casualties, d'you think?"

"Probable," Tom shrugged.

"I wonder if we can get into the belfry above. There was a little door, to one side of where your father's sitting. If he doesn't shift—"

Cricking their necks they considered the vestry roof, thence a step along the leads.

At this moment though, a familiar sound to army ears came through to the graveyard. It announced the arrival of Parliament's reinforcements in the market square, come to swell the ranks and storm the building. It was no moment to be a hostage.

The mutineers must sell themselves dearly if they couldn't

hold the door. There was the rattle of gunfire. Hugh rushed up his ladder onto the lead roof, raised his boot to crash the window in like any fanatique, pulled Tom in over the gap-tooth remains.

There they stood in the great chamber with the bells tremendous beside them: great primitive sounding-vessels. Was it true, Hugh thought disorderedly, the sound up close could kill a man?

He hurtled over the dusty floorboards, found the descending narrow spiral. At the bottom, through the panels he heard a heavy splintering crash. Whilst blinded by the descent into darkness he tried to pull the door against the bottom step rather than push the thing; he steadied, pushed cautiously and looked out at the crisis.

The reinforcements must have a great ram at the church door. A second crash and it gave, whilst men shouting, outside, became in the instant, men inside, cramming in at the church door and spilling into the aisle.

Fentiman standing as if turned to stone with the font he was clutching for support, his back to the belfry stair, faced what instantly became bloodshed. One of the mutineers shot a shrinking hostage with his pistol, yards from the Army storming party. Another, his sea-green colour visible in his hat-brim, fired at one of his own. The very doom painting might have come to life, with screaming figures, and a lost soul – another hostage – praying on his knees amid explosive flashes and powder smoke.

The plan became imperative. The watchers quit the belfry stairs, took running strides and laid hands on Fentiman, who, deafened and unsighted, jumped as if struck by lightning. But he comprehended their urgent mime and began to impede Tom back to the open door under its serene little decorative arch. Tom virtually kicked him through, leaving Hugh to the split-second realisation that they made a large target together and they had been seen.

Would his adventures end now, at the hand of a disaffected Parliamentarian? He saw the fellow, bandolier jumping, steady to get his aim, saw the glow of the match, the round mouth of the weapon.

He'd not choose that to kiss him, and flung himself bodily into the doorway, grasped for the door latch to pull behind him, had it nine parts to, then the crack came and the impact drove the splintering door shut upon him. Thank the Lord whose house this was, thought Hugh fervently, for fitting a good stout door. He'd had a horror of splinter wounds, always.

Shuddering from having felt the bullet spend itself so closely, he shot the bolt and clambered up the spiral stair towards daylight.

The extra regiment had cut it fine, towards day-end, and they finished their business. They shot the mutineers, though Hugh Malahide and the Fentimans missed this. They heard, though, that three hostages had died.

Chapter XII

It was a curious situation. Fentiman found himself back at The Feathers. To come in, he had to pass the tear-streaked family of the late mayor of Stonebury, hear their primitive wails. Their husband and kind father had not left church this day.

That Fentiman had, made his heart pump with the realisation he might well not have. This was a simple emotion, chiefly felt at the pulse and behind the knees. He squared his shoulders, true, threw out his stout chest – but the knees were human, and demanded he sit down.

Thus he discovered himself grounded, in the landlord's back room. Give him a minute.

He couldn't ignore the fact that he was presently seated facing his son Tom, Tom who lived and breathed though in want of a shave, despite what he, his father, had given out after Naseby. Tom might be an inconvenient fact, had ruined the match got up for Isabella – Tom an annoyance to his father's self-regard; but, but, Tom had just saved his life.

Tom with, who was this fellow? Fentiman bit his lip on the rim of his tankard, swallowing down a gulp of some fire-water of the landlord's. He gulped again, telling himself it might brace him up. The fire-water made his eyes spin. He knew he'd clapped eyes on Tom's companion somewhere or other; in his diffused then clearing focus, Hugh Malahide multiplied and blurred before reassembling pin-sharp as the man who had appeared uninvited to argue for Tom, aeons ago back in the autumn.

Hugh was that moment thinking the last time he had encountered Fentiman, that gentleman had required that he left before he had him thrown out.

I suppose these Royalists have to stick together, allowed Fentiman, dimly admitting a concession.

Then came a prick of his inner self, and did him credit. More than this was called for. He might be dead this minute if – if – he shuddered, and took another swig at the fire-water.

A truth had surfaced. O, for all he had declared he never desired to set eyes on his son, ungrateful, disgraceful King's man Tom, it now struck him painfully that for the past thirty-six hours he'd been prey to company he'd been compelled to keep, and now that he was in the presence of Tom he infinitely preferred that.

He cleared his throat, and cautiously reached out to pat Tom's hand.

The three people who had anxiously been watching him heaved separate sighs, prayers of relief the game had swung this way. Under the table two of those present found themselves glad of the other's hand.

Thereupon Hugh rose, resolutely murmuring some suitable disclaimer, this being the time and place for the Fentiman family, not for him. He bowed formally at the door, and received Fentiman's stiff-necked nod as a gesture which it must have cost that man to do.

Thus Hugh acknowledged the nod, formally hatted, withdrew. It would have gladdened him to be included, acknowledged, drawn in where Isabella breathed, had things stood differently. It caused him an unfortunate grasp of reality.

In the stable with his face against the bay cheek of Winter Queen, fitting the bridle, he was all rubbed up the wrong way, sore, for two pins would be offering to join her, share the haynet and the warmth, such was the exclusion from the Fentiman family – how ironic: he'd been instrumental in bringing them together. A triumph. But a Pyrrhic victory.

It had all worked like a dream, even the nightmare episode in the church was awakened from safely. Tom was reconciled. Fentimans were restored to their rightful relationship. Even Fentiman himself was not entirely a monster – he'd been forced to acknowledge Tom, yes, but he'd done it.

They were going to be happy. Well, happier. She could do well now on her own. She would forget him. She must.

A pale moon swam on its night sky.

He was left with failing farms, a loved relative not far from the beckoning hand of the next world, and King Charles's ruination.

Then he cursed himself for self deception. None of these things were what was amiss with him.

None of them. His hands which he'd clamped to his head, he put to throwing the stable door open wide, so as to sting himself into honesty with a douche of cold air.

He knew what it was.

He'd known sitting there in The Feathers.

Nor had he needed to leave that precipitately. He had been quite welcome to stay, united with the rescue party, then slip away later.

He'd denied himself proximity to Isabella – even that, he'd fled.

Was it the rub of beholding that Fentiman, proud and self-righteous and Parliamentarian, was capable of changing? Not changing far, perhaps. But sufficiently to acknowledge his poor son Tom. Nor had he a second time asserted he would have Hugh thrown without doors.

Hugh grit his teeth. He could get round old Fentiman. He might not like him, but then, there in The Feathers, in accepting Fentiman's nod he'd found himself able to tolerate him. That nod had cost Fentiman dear, but he'd done it.

Given suitable circumstances he'd be prepared to get by with Fentiman, after this.

And groaned aloud, because by 'suitable' he meant if he could court Isabella.

It was not Fentiman he was resenting, but Athalia.

The severing of one day, start of a new, came welcomely with the routine actions of seeing to the horse, putting leg astride her, turning her head for home. Perhaps he would subdue his ache by setting his back to Stonebury, never looking back – never to look at the tower of John Baptist as it sank slowly into Stonebury's receiving dip, nor think more of yesterday's drama. Fentiman and his children were journeying to London, where they would rest, gather up, would say, 'Life goes on; what plans have you, Tom?' and they would now look forward together.

But he couldn't dull his ache.

Few things are as absolute as the judgement of an unhappy man.

Actually absolute was the death of Fentiman's man-of-business, and this fact had jogged Fentiman's elbow when everything at The Feathers had calmed down. During his evening of freedom there, he cogitated. He had got out of the habit of Tom, and was unused to the Prodigal sight of him like a suddenly replaced piece of furniture. He did see that Tom's version of how he'd spent the Conflict serving King Charles might prove a bone of contention between them from their differing viewpoints.

An evening of managing to bite his tongue had rubbed Fentiman's fur up the wrong way. And yet; he did want to agree with his boy. After all, he was not a stone's throw from his place of imprisonment, and Tom had got him out.

"I'm for bed," he announced in best pulpit tone, but, with the arms of his chair still in his grip, didn't rise, for an ideal solution presented itself.

"Tom, my boy: did I not hear you say, that your plans would be for Holland? As the climate here in England might prove a disadvantage now, er, to men of your persuasion, you might..."

He backed off from provoking one of their old arguments. Were they to be closeted too much, too soon, they would be at the cudgels. "In other words, I propose to get you safe overseas and started upon whatever life you might wish."

"There," he said.

Tom gasped. It was a good evening, after all.

Unless one were Isabella, outwardly serene, like one of those smiling cut-out figures placed at table should there be a vacant place. She nodded at the prospects for her brother. Yes, that was the answer for Tom! As if a magician pulled the trick out of the hat.

But in the morning when she found the bay mare and Hugh had gone, Isabella felt as if she went over the weir, came sleek down the flood, drowned in a whirlpool of un-maidenly emotion.

Fentiman declared himself fit, his mind made up. Croxley, poor man, was no longer breathing over his affairs. The sooner he got to his office to set in motion the business of Tom's passage beyond seas with that shipping acquaintance, the better.

Tom would have agreed with him there.

Isabella heard her father calling for the coach driver. They might be in London weeks, months, for ever.

She went to her bedchamber, strapped a pad round her ankle with her handkerchief, sprinkled cold water from the ewer on it, called the maidservant.

"I fear I've turned my ankle on the stairs. 'Tis swelled already. I feel quite sick with the sprain."

She couldn't go. She must defy her father, would present a story that she could not stand, nor bear the jolting of the coach on the long haul ahead.

Fentiman might be sufficiently diverted by Tom's plans. He'd be lecturing Tom the whole way up to London on how he should proceed. Thank heaven, he had the new preoccupation large in his sights. He was already beginning on instructions to Tom as the maid tugged his sleeve with Isabella's fable of misfortune.

Fentiman ceremonially climbed the stairs, inspected his recumbent daughter, thought her subdued, felt put out; but not crucially. He supposed that jolting in a coach wouldn't do. But he couldn't delay here. Been delayed already, shut in the church by seditious mutineers, starved, parched, forced to drink disgusting font water – he'd be away from here!

"How did you do it?" he enquired sternly of his daughter.

"I think I stepped on my hem," she told him. "I'm so sorry, I've no wish to hold you and Tom up."

"Quite so. That landlord seems to have taken you under his wing, so, confound it for a nuisance, girl, you've imprisoned yourself: not like me, I was forced to it."

That's his nearest to a jest, she thought, weak with relief – he's in a good mood still. I'm going to get away with it.

When the coach wheels had rumbled away, Isabella rang the brass bell to ask the landlord to step up. Shamelessly she paid him the sum Fentiman had entrusted to her for a few days' stay, if he would but keep to the tale that she'd stayed a-mending for the time paid for.

"This is market day, I think?" She heard the bleatings and the bellowings outside and the hum of yesterday's tidings being twentyfold re-told.

"The livelong day," he beamed.

"I expect your people know our horse doctor?"

"That's not a hock you're mending, lady." He shook his head, fingering the purse she had given him,

"Nay; but Ebenezer will get me transportation homewards."

The ribbon of the highway that Hugh Malahide followed rose under the hill where trees called The King and The Maidens crowned the height. The married man, weary, neared the landmark thankfully, reflecting the events and their outcome. All was well, Tom reconciled.

He made the account brief when he gained his uncle's house, he was fatigued and travel-stained, and then went to the lengths of calling for water to be heated that he might take a bath, gain solitude, in the kitchen.

Perhaps it demonstrated he wasn't as young as Tom. The hot water would soak bodily pains away, the other pain maybe would dull.

Steam rose, the maids, bedewed and rosy, poured hot rivers from pails.

Thinking wearily of next day's clean shirt, he stepped out of stockings, breeches and sullied shirt, sank him in the tub. The maids, half peeping, scuttled in to throw towels over a stool within reach. He lay back and shut his eyes.

From its pen in a corner, a Roman-nosed ram lamb watched curiously, unused, at its age, to dipping. Every cottage wife gladdens when her charge strengthens from tremulous bleating to butting and baa-ing. This one, Fleecy, was a Tartar, due back in the wider world now he had discovered he could charge the maids to great effect if caught behind the knee when stooping to the hearth or dustpan.

"Lamb collops," they'd warn him.

Hugh rose like Neptune from the water and realised why he'd felt himself overlooked. Even he smiled, towelling, hair seaweed.

Got him to bed, too tired to resist sleep after all and in the morning there was an eggshell blue sky. Everything was behindhand after the frosts, but in the first warmth the small birds mentioned spring.

Josiah commented his nephew looked rested, and were there any daffodillies yet? He liked a daffy. "A target, see: got to last till them." He cackled, "Been saying that since the Prince's mother was Queen of Bohemia."

"Keep saying it," said Hugh, "I'll see if the maids can find some ready." He would take the day as holiday, be at home, so he would. Chasing round the farms could wait. At home, that best of phrases, surrounded by home comfort, homely voices. The full sleeves of his clean shirt were galleon sails as he stretched his arms.

"I'll go and check my mare, give her a lead out perhaps."

"Don't let her eat the daffodillies then."

He wandered out with the bay on a halter so she might pick grass from the untended bowling green by the house, turning to raise a hand to Josiah within. It must be years since bowls was played of an evening, he'd like to see that again.

It was almost warm today. The Queen was mowing steadily, pulling Hugh like a somnambulist. He looked about him. Josiah's vanished heyday had run to a gentleman's amenities. The topiary had been a row of pyramids, globes and fan-tailed birds, they'd lurched, sprouted and gone lop-sided now like drunkards, the effect was of grandmother's footsteps, movement caught surprised.

Didn't Luisa tell of a bell-tower, in Italy, more aslant than they?

But he wasn't rational, a blink would bring back a nightmare.

He saw Isabella, who was in London, under heavy guard, coming towards him in a blowing cape.

Hallucinating, he saw a cumulus of springtime colours. Her clothing had been dark clouds. He saw cream-coloured full sleeves, skirts, he saw these.

It is Isabella. Or am I mad?

The forenoon became a better place. Athalia was far away, he with his pulse beating stood there, melancholy stripped away.

Let me not wax foolish.

He rejected, "Not gone to London, then?" in favour of foolish song, handstands and daffodil garlands, heard his normal voice. "Good morrow, shepherdess," he said calmly, "we are rearing this wild lamb in the kitchen in order to test those such as thee, who are come about the post."

He regarded Isabella over the down-arched neck of the grazing horse, saying his 'why not gone to London?' with a lifted eyebrow.

"I was Father's hostage; I escaped also," she informed him, "and without bloodshed. I obtained terms."

He looped Winter Queen's halter over his arm. "What terms? They mutineers who wouldn't go to Ireland, you who refuse London town—"

"I sprained an ankle."

"But I see they match, lady, neat as twigs." Her skirts, at last not mud-heap brown, were tucked up out of the dew so he could see petticoat and ankles. "Are you a deceiver? For shame."

"Only of father," she assured him. "It was a crisis, and after all, he had come unscathed from his peril, so his sights are set on telling Tom how to make his way in Holland. Thank the luck I had, his mind was on that."

"I declare when you smile, with those crescents, you're a Turk. Are you indeed here to share my day?"

"I am now let out from jail." She advanced a little, close enough to smooth the horse's warm neck. "Jailed since Christmas."

Not Christmas now, he rejoiced. No, Isabella, a little flustered, stood near him in the springtime grass. She had failed to tuck up the buttermilk coloured skirt securely, and the ribbon which should have clasped her sleeve had come undone. She must have run down the meadow.

Not bad, on a sprained ankle. She must have wanted – he couldn't have claimed what, in case he burst the bubble of hope rising to choke him under the clean shirt.

"My jail was in your going," he said, giving himself away.

Isabella's bodice breathed and tightened. Hugh, distracted, overrode his despair, threw aside circumstances.

"I'll put the mare away."

She walked beside him, willing him to comprehend that if she was a Turk as he'd called her, with crescents when she smiled, she had come to surrender.

What, he wondered, could he possibly say? He had begun with easy desire. How to explain it was more, meant more, following that spontaneous embrace he never should have allowed himself to give. He wanted to give her what he couldn't offer.

Oh for Isabella led to him on strings to what he wanted.

He began, naming truths aloud, hurtful truths, as they must be to her, "I've thought, if only; it does me no credit, to have you learn I'd think of bigamy, to get you…" he was tying himself in knots from which she unexpectedly released him.

"Athalia is not here," she said, "would you have her spoil this day? You do not need to say aloud what we do not have. I am glad you have – talked, the once, but you need not again. I know it. Say what we do have, rather…"

It was her turn to see his eyes clear, see his once handsome face handsome still, lips parting, "Ah—" as he absorbed the sunburst warmth of what she told him.

The rude lamb in the kitchen, the canary singing from the parlour, the sense of warmth and welcome, his hand on hers, accompanied them into Josiah's lair. Isabella saw him after the interval to be frailer against his bolster, thin as an autumn leaf. She slipped her hand from Hugh to clasp skeletal fingers. At his elbow a brown-glaze jug held half a dozen daffodils, furled. "First Luisa could find. They'll be trumpets this afternoon, they're ready. Now you're come that's two pleasures."

"I see I've lost you," murmured Hugh behind her.

"Have you avoided that sprig of mischief in the kitchen?"

"That ball of wool and hooves?"

"Yes, and look at poor Brownie, forced to retreat in here with me. That lamb thinks dogs only pester sheep if they think they can get away with it."

Brownie raised red-rimmed eyes, heaved a sigh and laid his nose back on his paws.

Josiah wished Fentiman wasn't trying to buy him up, wished

it keenly. At his age, while he had breath in him, he'd play for time. After that, it wouldn't matter, but for Hugh. Why must it all matter so sharply, at ninety? He weighed up Fentiman's daughter, weighed up Hugh, thought his conclusion most unexpected.

She'd torn the fastening on her sleeve.

"You'll be losing that ribbon." He quivered at the place with a forefinger. Hugh watched her try to pin it. "Where are our girls? 'Tis but a moment to find a needle before you unravel."

"You'll think that rampant lamb butted me," she said to Josiah, but the old man had gone off to sleep in a blink, dropping the two little shutters over his eyes.

Hugh indicated they withdrew. "We can leave Brownie on guard," said he, then, returning to the fray. "Do you wear a sash with that skirt? You should persuade that father of yours to indulge you."

"With Father's views on raiment? He is for naught but that the hair should be strangled flat, and that should one fall in the mud noone'd notice because the clothing would match it."

"Then how did you lay hands on that you're wearing?" He held out his hand to her. "That is no mud colour? Curds and cream colour becomes you. I am opposed to mud colour."

"Don't laugh. This skirt was a put-away bed hanging I cut up, and these sleeves and bodice are remade and it nearly killed me to do it, from an antique style put away. I have been sewing all winter. I am not good with a needle, I can't have done the ribbon tie firmly. 'Tis tacking at best."

"Noone's tacked up anything for me to see them in that I can remember," he informed her, "come with me, the least I can do is fit you out with the bits and pieces you hadn't time to, er, finish off. There's a great chest of lawn and tiffany and what-not, where

I shall also find you a sash."

He had the immense good fortune to see out of the window that the maidservants were sunning themselves in the garden; Luisa stood leaning in the archway, the basket she was weaving on the paving by her stool.

He shooed Isabella through the tumbled nest of rooms upstairs, beyond the room Tom had lain in, wounded, into another where an alcove disclosed a vast domed chest when he twitched the curtain, the lid of its mouth half-eating a neglected petticoat. He opened it wide, found lace collars put away from the light in tissue, a heap of crumpled tabby silk, escaped tails of unrolled ribbon. Lawn, cobweb lace, that'll make a show – "Hold still!" and flung a cloud over her shoulders, got a vermilion tail, pulled, but it was too short, teased a coral snake out of the tangle, ah, better, a broad silk band. "Try this, turn, now wind around." Pushed her as if trying to be captured at blind-man's buff and tied a ribbon knot.

"Let me see…"

"Ah, vanity – I hope. There's a mirror, well fogged. I'll wipe its face with this bit of old finery, I think once a kerchief."

The glass gave the illusion those reflected there might be in a picture frame, an oil, perhaps, that needed its varnish cleaned from hanging in the smoke, the mirror's silvering not being what it was.

In the illusion of a painting, Hugh and Isabella were framed as he embraced her, reflected in each other's arms, suddenly a declaration. He kissed her in the actuality and the reflection, simultaneously. In the recognition of themselves together, he taller, strong, grasping her, she responding to him, it was memorable, it was stimulating.

Of course it was. It was wrong, it was forbidden. By the pull of her innocence, he had enticed the newly ready maiden, he knew what he had succumbed to: the faun in the forest, eyelashes, she half aware and he, overwhelmed. Was it wicked? Dear Heaven, never – apart from the circumstances. The Puritans would hate him.

In the reflection in the mirror, a man in a loose-sleeved shirt pulled down a lady's tresses.

He threw the cobweb lace from her shoulders. Isabella hesitating was then tempted, willing, the wavy tresses now upon her exposed shoulders. There she was, he had gathered the dark hair in one hand, bending to taste her. In the mirror night descended, because she closed her eyes as secret places responded, smiling with the pleasure. As she opened her eyes again, clasping him, Hugh's face planes were on hers, she knew the texture of his long hair, the blue eyes, laughter lines hatched deeply. "Ah." She sighed. "Ah."

What did she know of what he was about to do?

Now; but did she think it was poetry? What would she expect, lacking girls to chatter with? He knew what he was about, too truly. Yet, this was much to him, and he told her all it was.

"Oh, Isabella, I cannot bear not to have you."

He half released her, snatched crumpled tabby silk out of the jaws of the old chest. There was an unmade, ready tester bed. It had curtains; would she baulk in the moment it took to draw them, run from him? He risked it, drew the curtains but for the side next to the sunbeams from the window so it flooded them in a pool of warmth.

Sitting, he enfolded Isabella, lifted her hair against his face. "Undo me," he suggested, to see if she might unbutton his shirt. Lunatic that he was, even as she began to comply, he conjured up a vision of John Block mounting a ladder to that window armed with a perspective glass this very moment to know what was afoot. He told this, cheerful, sitting in the sunbeams with one sleeve off, and when Isabella laughed too and forgot herself, he threw his shirt off, its billows subsiding to the floor, a galleon foundering un-noticed. He had her against his strong bronze chest then, his eyes sparking ultramarine lights, gathered Isabella up on the tabby silk over the mattress, encompassed by the man she was kissing back. Her arms were clasped around him, he had got her near to the surprise.

"Come, Venus," hadn't he been wondering for months past if she'd prove rose or cinnamon, at last began to suck her, not cinnamon, rose. He felt her sigh against him, then that she was stroking his hair, his back, his sensitive spine. Drowning like a tippler in a lake of brandy, he came up for air, found her amethyst eyes, sank into those, too.

Her smooth skin, her delightful bosom, produced the sensation bosoms do, beyond this, more. He wished for the elusive qualities that came and went with the light and shade in her eyes.

Hugh, about to claim her, inwardly urged, want me, give me; aloud he heard himself risk telling her, "I love you beyond words."

The blue depths of his eyes seconded his words.

"… beyond words…"

He had the place, then the moment, he would enter.

"Will you? You can stop me." The ultramarine of his eyes were close, his arms about her.

"Don't stop." She cried, and he had entered, claimed, seduced her. He gave her what she wanted.

Chapter XIII

The delight of her saved the spring. Take that away and the wider world gave the inevitable body blow to the two Royalists, one so ancient, the other rootless before finding sanctuary in the valley under the downs. Hugh had pretended the farms were not failing, he resisted looking the facts in the eye. The winter, the lambing; rents? What rents? At Michaelmas, got in by scraping. At Christmas, oh, the frosts. By Lady Day, the lambing.

But after Lady Day, Isabella kept him sane, or crazed by the amours. He wondered which way round it was.

When she could visit.

"I like thee well enough, Ebenezer," he said exasperatedly, "but I would have thy company without your cargo of bad news. Never do you cross this threshold without a paper up your sleeve, 'tis the Dry-vines, the Priest-biters, or John Lilburne, I want no more of him, either, for all he loves not old Crop-ears! I want no more of any of them. I care not a fig—"

"But, listen, the King hath—"

"I care not what he hath done or not done. If he hath made a pact with the Barbary pirates, I care not. If the Hottentots have made up regiments, are disembarking at Tilbury this minute to seize London back for him, I—"

"I get thy drift," said Ebenezer, a calm man, "don't ee get heated."

Of course, the trouble was that every moment he fretted for the next time, sharpened by longing. Of course, she couldn't step down the valley too often, and then they mightn't be private, if his uncle didn't cat-nap or the house was astir, or if John Block armed her in. About once in six times he could be himself and hug her off her feet, waiting, waiting for her to tell him she loved him. Yet, hadn't she showed him? Oh, but she couldn't trust him to love her, could she, with Athalia an utter, granite fact. He couldn't pretend about that.

"Let us have pleasure, then," he told himself grimly, when low. "For all the circumstances." He was making hornets for himself. She was so pleasing to him and he so unavailable. He went on with the hornets. It was the circumstances.

It would be rank sham and fraud and deception to harp on to Isabella that he wanted her to be led on strings to him at the altar, in wedding array. It was wishing for the moon and he had seduced her instead.

Even so, when she did make a safe passage to Josiah's, it dulled all else with the uplift every time. She would salute Josiah, and when he dozed they held hand on hand. It was as if the recent solder had come home to court the young lady who was just ready, and he marriageable. He played that part, perhaps out of the blinkers of longing.

He had existed in the midst of turmoil or boredom in the army, solitary; in the civilian doldrums Athalia had nothing much to say to him. The new charm of human warmth had banished loneliness.

Here was Isabella regretting she had not gone to the play, but only knew the printed folio. Block, no actor, had not made the pages live when he read aloud with her, it seemed.

"Would I believe in boys that took the parts of the maids?"

"They've been hissed from the stage, there are no performers now. The boys had a short stage life, of course, then early retirement upon becoming a bass, with whiskers."

"I can but read on the page, so no squeaking boys have come my way, and Block reads in the same steady bass, whatever part."

"He is made for the nurse, that's the part for him. You must get the Montagues and the Capulets." He had a further thought, "As for Desdemona, for all she was innocent, she kept a-harping on the one string too long. She would have irritated Job."

"Perhaps, Job would have suffered it, rather than strangling." Isabella, now easy with him, gentle, eyelashes. "We talk of the stage, the play world; you do not talk of the campaigns?"

"My heavens, there lies a pitfall. I don't mean to become one of those old pains who run ruts in the road of one old track. I have our Harry, who is years younger than I am, narrating how they held off Ireton, blow by blow. I know that one off by heart, had not the plays got banned I could assume his part and tread the boards this minute. I restrain myself from prompting him when he falters, as it is!"

"I miss you of an evening." She suddenly gladdened him. "I might bear an old tale once or twice."

Ah, that was sweet. He vowed not to test her on that one, it was the mark of being older.

Josiah was asleep. Hugh led Isabella into the springtime day.

He had to face the straits the farms were in all too soon. He'd known but not dared to look. Then he happened on Luisa turning out cupboards, ransacking drawers. Disquieted, he enquired. "You're not spring cleaning?"

Then, "Tell me what's amiss?"

She looked levelly at Hugh, shook her iron-grey head, shrugged. "I am going through pockets for stray coins. If I find a sixpence – I rejoice…"

There was a small heap of coin on the table. He looked a

question.

"That is all there is. Alas, I mean ALL."

"You mean?"

"I am afraid. We are reduced to such straits for paying our way that I am reduced to searching like a thief. Josiah should have the apothecary come, but I am in want of flour milled, and there is the cooper due."

"I've seen it coming." He dashed a hand over his brow. "Luisa, we are come to this. Now, only now, do I feel, we have lost in the conflict."

She failed to smile. "I thought we'd hold out, but for this winter. I believed, when you came—"

"Don't, don't. Come and sit down, we mustn't hang out the white flag..." He seated her, his spirits a lead plummet. Of course he knew. Why had he fooled himself that it must get better? Thus he had thought during the conflict, till Naseby. Was this their household Naseby?

"I thought I had long learnt," Luisa was saying, "not to pray for a miracle but for fortitude. Fortitude has let me down. Josiah, oh, I cannot bear it for him."

"The rents – they can't pay up, 'tis not that they wouldn't, except old Hodge, who's a no-good. I've got to know them now. Oh if we'd had a better winter, some luck."

"Tenants can get a new master." She sighed. "But Josiah!"

"And you, Luisa." Then he remembered. Josiah and old Fentiman: Fentiman was for taking on Josiah's house, tenants, land and all: 'Get a new master, get a new man.' Josiah and Fentiman, daggers drawn. Fentiman, who loved acres. Josiah had said, said! Back in the autumn.

Hugh had not so much forgotten it, as thrown a cloth over it, as one did with the parrot to stop it squawking. It squawked now, loudly. Fentiman had, what had Josiah told him? "Been wanting to buy up my bits of land… liked my southerly aspect…"

The solid house in which he sat seemed suddenly fragile, as if those in Jericho noticed the approaching Joshua.

"You said, the apothecary – is he worse?"

"Always weaker." Luisa looked him in the eye. "Now we have begun, we must talk."

"Yes."

She had waved the hand that told one she wasn't English, the only sign Hugh always noticed: she would wave 'no' that way. "What's best, Luisa? What do you think?"

"He knows. I wonder, if worrying is not worse for him, than the alternative."

"Which is?"

She couldn't frame 'selling up'. He had to say it for her, whereupon she bit her lip.

"That Fentiman, he is his enemy, always. Always. I know he tried to make overtures to buy. Josiah put a flea in his ear."

Who else would want failing farms, all let go, but Fentiman? Buy us cheaply, throw out his frontiers, bag us, net us, shoot Josiah in his gone-to-ground hole.

"Would that I could steal the rent money all over again."

"I am unable to steal the money unless Hodge hath it for me to steal in the first place, he hasn't, so I am prevented."

She made the disclaimer gesture. "Or you would."

Frustrated to the soul at the siege of survival, Hugh rose and stalked up and down, a cat on hot bricks. He wheeled, clapping a fist in his palm. "One thing to start with, I'll go and fetch the apothecary. Then I'll sell Winter Queen. She's worth a handful of guineas, small beer. But I must do something. Or explode."

What's a whirlwind but an interruption? It only cast a

pretence on rescuing the day, hardly stilled his wretchedness. Of course neither brushing out the polished-oak coat of the Queen, then riding her into town, with Bonny on a lead rein so he might ride her home, took his thoughts from the chasm into which he, a dullard, had dropped because he'd refused to read the signs.

"She's never six," haggled the new mayor of Stonebury, tempted to buy the Queen and cut a dash.

"She is – look at her teeth," persuaded her present owner, trying to get her to open wide.

"Ah, well, perhaps, then."

Hugh watched the Queen's handsome hindquarters striding off with a stranger as if he'd sold his own friend.

Bleakly, he trudged back to lean against Bonny's withers, nose against her neck. The guineas weren't enough, by a long, long chalk. He'd asked the apothecary to come out, he'd sold his Winter Queen – what next?

Tell yourself the Queen's departed, the Winter's over.

"Liar," he told himself.

Bonny whickered, and he could have cried.

Lose the valley, lose Isabella.

"Will you weaken?" he asked himself. "You've backbone somewhere, find it." He set his jaw, and straightened, as if to show himself and the old horse that he was resolved, hadn't weakened, that whatever it cost he would put a face on disaster for the people he held dear.

He had to go home slowly, for Bonny's sake, she wasn't fit. At The Red Lion, he dismounted to walk her down, she'd come on so well he wouldn't ask more of her than he should.

The cheery landlord called to him as he dismounted, "Not bringing me that old lady again, are you?" He'd kept her for a week, with sugar chips, after Tom abandoned her for that high-stepping chestnut he stole from the Puritan.

"Never mention a lady's age. She's not that old, look at her, in the pink."

He found himself glad of five minutes gossip with someone unaware of his state of mind, nonetheless by his next visit he'd need the landlord to stand him one.

What were coins, but the bricks in the everyday wall? No wall, no house, no—

"How's trade, now the roads are open? You must have had a slow winter time," he asked, goading himself to remember ill-luck was not confined to his family at Josiah's.

"Not that bad," said his companion, bandily straddling the bench of a trestle. "I got some folks stranded in here Christmas Eve, they stayed near on a fortnight, kept me ticking, that did. Then souls put up rather than travel on the ice. There's always some makes the reason to turn windy. If t'ain't the deserters they're fearful of, 'tis that footpad."

"Is he still abroad?" Hugh pictured the poor lad in the cottage doorway, as raw as his recruits had been.

"Been quiet lately, thass a fact... maybe moved on."

Hugh felt a cold voice at his inner ear.

Which suggested a footpad could lurk in that thicket a mile back, make light work of travellers on the high road... if the Avenhill boy had packed up for the sake of his hide, wouldn't his patch be empty and waiting?

Wouldn't he, Hugh Malahide, make a better fist at men's-work than that whippersnapper?

He heard his own voice mock in his ear: 'Gallows'-fodder.' Had he said it aloud, or thought it, of Tom's unfortunate companion?

Would that help? Having Hugh's neck stretched for him

would bring his uncle's white hairs with sorrow to the grave. What would Isabella, so gently reared and kept so closeted, think of him? She'd be ashamed, dismayed.

But he'd stolen pearls for her, in order noone would accuse her of being in collusion with Tom. He had tried at being a thief the once – hadn't he?

He strode homeward leading his brown mare, unseeing of the evening twilight, the sun declining behind The King and The Maidens topping the hill.

He might have compared the twilight with Isabella's amethyst eyes; but instead wrestled with right and wrong, and where he could get ammunition for his empty pistol.

The vital voice in the future of the valley lands was absent but not silent. Fentiman himself, a man who liked matters settled, cut and dried, had turned his thoughts to the problem.

He'd dispatched Tom to board a vessel bound for The Hook, with letters of introduction to get him a toe-hold with an English-speaking Dutch merchant he knew, and he had allowed himself a sigh of thundercloud relief as he stood waving his handkerchief at the wooden walls and pillow-case canvas of the merchantman sliding away from the jetty. As always, giving the strange optical illusion for a second or so, that the jetty was sliding off and the vessel was anchored.

Whatever man thinks desirable, thought Fentiman in philosophical flow, is till he is closeted with it. Such had been his experience of married life, of his son Tom, and his aspirations. He didn't include Isabella, for he would put her to the test when next he determined to match her.

But, really, the trials attendant on his return to London! His man-of-business dead, his affairs in an unsatisfactory state due to

Croxley's illness before giving up the ghost; London still fenced about by the mud-heap defences, sea-coal only now getting into decent folks' grates again to warm chilly evenings. Had he never before noticed how pungently London reeked of closely confined horses, privies, and the common man?

But one wasn't close confined when one had acres. That was the point. He'd enough of being landless. Yes, he had his town house, the bustling wharves, and the office where he went to oversee business, but felt mewed up. The feeling had crept upon him. A man like himself needed the freedom to let his eye range, comfort himself with what was his!

He sat twiddling the lid of his little pot of chocolate, one Thursday mid-morning. In three minutes, he would begin checking the time by which his visitor was due, in seven minutes he would either be here, or late.

His place in the country. This was his habit to say to people. But the whole story, the genuineness of this, was flawed in Fentiman's mind by its being the rump of an estate, not the setting he deserved.

He marched up and down his room with a regular tread, applying a thin brown moustache every time he tipped his cup to take a sip when he passed it on the table.

It was sheer bad luck that his place in the country had come to him as the legacy of a profligate uncle; the house was stranded like a whale on a lee shore. That's all a house with no land was. His uncle, of whom Fentiman as a sniffy youth had disapproved, had been in the habit of staking a farm here, five-acre there, and had only died just in time, to his beneficiary's mind, to prevent him sinking the house at the card table.

Drawing a mental portcullis over the name Greateleate, Fentiman now drained the dregs of chocolate and set the cup down. He didn't want to wait for his acres any longer.

The country was ready to settle down! Prosperity, Parliament serenely at the helm, the King humbled: just such times in which a man could sit back and enjoy his acres. He wouldn't have minded, had Parliament brought in again that iniquity of the King's, whereby every gentleman whose land was worth forty pounds per annum to him was compelled to become a knight... for which advancement his present position did not qualify him.

The expected knock came at his door. Fentiman turned, settling his cuffs. He'd decided what he was about, how to deal with that old fool and malignant, Josiah Malahide.

After The Red Lion, the highway sloped gently into the valley and turned to the left, behind a tangle of hawthorn and hazel in new leaf. The intersection of the lane to Avenhill was hidden until travellers were upon it, and when they overshot the overgrown milestone they had to struggle back up the incline. Something of the sort must have happened that evening, for shouts rose on the breeze blowing back up the hill to Hugh descending.

Was a farmer that impatient?

Then nothing of the sort would answer. Hugh and Bonny walking down the hill like man and wife together, he with the reins in one hand, came round the bend. The last rays of sunset illuminated three rough men besetting a traveller on a stout horse, carrying a woman pillion behind him. Naturally this arrangement rendered him as clumsy as an unarmed knight in armour caught unawares.

The woman gave a shriek and let go a basket she had been nursing, from which, unexpectedly, a piglet burst and dashed squealing between the horse's hooves into freedom in the hedge.

The rider beat ineffectually down at the trio hauling on his stirrups and his legs. They'd unhorse him! – Hugh hopped with one foot in Bonny's stirrup, hopped again, she stopped wheeling about and he swung into the saddle and put his heels to her flank.

It wasn't the footpad, his first thought – nay; he recognised the species as men from some regiment, yet more deserters, falling on a farmer coming back from Stonebury market.

Bonny went bounding forward as the first man on foot saw Hugh and threw up his hands to guard his face, but too late. Hugh freed his booted toe from the stirrup so recently gained, raised his boot and kicked the man in the face.

Even as the man sank, his accomplice unseated the farmer with a crash, and fell upon him.

Bonny hurdled three prone bodies and came back in a tight circle, whickering loudly. The third man ran off shielding his head, and the farmer's horse bucketed off for home with the unlucky farmer's wife bouncing and wailing.

The farmer had sat up and hit the man who'd unseated him smartly in the stomach. The other, whom Hugh had kicked, was fountaining blood between his fingers, clutching his hurt nose.

"God be praised," bellowed the farmer, "we've routed 'em."

They had indeed. It was a little Chalgrove.

Hugh circled Bonny round the remaining fat or beanpole dregs of the army.

"What were you?" growled Hugh, hoping in the half light he and Bonny rearing above them looked larger than life.

"Hopton's," said the nosebleed thickly.

"Hoptons? I doubt it," he said contemptuously. To the farmer, now on his feet brushing himself down, "What shall we do with them?"

"Josiah quite naturally refused to see reason."

"Chase them off for me," requested the man. "Will ee ? I'm mortal obliged. I'd best get after Betty, my wife, horse'll take her into the yard I don't doubt, but I'd like to get me back and call out me boys – give these dirty bastards a drubbing if they show face again—" He glared at the now hangdog captives.

So Hugh and Bonny drove them away, made them run and stumble and then when he could see they were done, shouted them off towards Avenhill with the cry if they showed hair or hide this side of the hill they'd regret it.

Bonny and he came home in the dark, in the end.

Darkness was welcome to him.

He couldn't live with himself if he turned robber. The sight of the three men hanging like savage bull-terriers on prey to break it, tear it down, repelled him. There was not that in him to terrify innocent people, passers-by, chance-comers – not in peacetime, unconstrained by demands of military need. He could not cold-bloodedly set himself to lurk in those thickets, hide his face, see their fear, exploit it to carry off their cash or gewgaws

Hardship would make strange doings in the lives of men. That was the fortunes of war.

Would Josiah, in straits even as he was, be glad of money got that way? How could he lie to Isabella? ('Lucky at cards again'?)

He sneered at himself, paused shuddering with his elbows on a rough farm wall. Then he shook himself and patted Bonny. The cold moon rose behind the downs, as ever it had.

Josiah quite naturally refused to see reason, whatever state his coffers might be in. He was not going to sell up.

"If you think I'm content to be carried out feet first, you'd be right," he growled. "But I won't be carried out still breathing to die in some almshouse in Stonebury. I refuse to sell out to

Fentiman, that's what. Have the old reptile triumph over me? Never."

Nobody wanted him to have to say otherwise. Luisa and Hugh, like parents with a fractious child, had put what was sensible to him, what might be best, but with no conviction. They didn't want it a jot more than Josiah did.

It would be like accepting Judgement Day.

There was an interchange of glaring, chiefly from Josiah.

But how could his dear ones bully him? Luisa and Hugh retreated to the kitchen. The only bright spot was a pot of primroses on the windowsill. Primroses were at least free, unlike the cooper, or the fodder they had to buy in during the hard weather.

The next large outlay would undo them.

"The worst of it is, who but Fentiman would buy these lands? He has tried his several times to buy us up, but who else would?" Luisa sat drumming her fingers on the trestle, while Hugh, as ever he did, walked up and down.

The curious thing was that even as she spoke, two separate gentlemen unknown to them, were trying to find them on the map.

"Lost in the wilds like this, who'd want to acquire us, but Fentiman? We are neither large nor famed; by God, if we could but scrape by!"

It felt too closely as if he had lost the Conflict anew, that tug of no hope.

"We must keep that expression, what is it, 'Never say die'," Luisa asserted, "I mean to keep it going just so long as Josiah does not die. Oh, though every day I see him grow less. He was fired up today, because of saying no, but tomorrow, and the day after, it will be less and less."

"Oh Luisa."

"After that, let what will come, come."

"I think we can scrape, until…" He couldn't say it.

"Say live day by each day, for his sake." Luisa gripped his hand.

And it was their world too, Luisa's long adopted, Hugh's the haven come by lately. "It is his little Kingdom," said Luisa, drooping.

Hugh thought this sufficient low ebb, fought back. "Every day we're breathing and still here, that Fentiman hasn't got his foot in the door, we chalk up," he encouraged, "come, we'll tell Josiah we're damned if we will have him sell up. We will keep the 'while there's life' side of things strictly between ourselves."

"A pact," she agreed.

Josiah began to sleep and wake in the past, when his old age had been remarkable in that he'd lived keenly in the present. For a few days he wanted to tell of the journey he'd made long, long ago, to Venice, where his father in the train of old Queen Bess's Ambassador, had been assailed by a fatal malady.

Josiah was a last link to days not only long gone, but far flung. Hugh sat beside him holding his old hand, half harrowed, half fascinated as the old man harked back.

"Venezia seemed a rare show, as I approached, it sat on the water, like a treasure chest They say all strangers are amazed…"

"But, your father died?" Hugh's grandfather, in this exotic place.

"What a landfall, there I stood on the quay dazzled by the light, found I was surrounded on the quay by bravos and Levantine Jews in yellow turbans, think of it… stayed three months. Yes, my father died."

"Came back, with my aunt, and Luisa?" but no explanation

of that was ever forthcoming; Hugh rather respected him for it.

Josiah came back to his surroundings, normally beady, to regard Hugh from his nest of pillows. "Came back to make my home here. I don't want the valley to outlast me. Not a dream, like Venezia in the past. One can place a finger and pop the past, 'tis gone. But, Hugh, I wanted the valley, the house here, for you: once you came home I wanted it to be yours."

Hugh told him it was naught to him if he couldn't have it, but, "I value that you wanted that, and feel as you do," he said, choked, "and that you told me."

Josiah nodded. The two little shutters dropped and he was sleeping.

The centre of the universe is wheresoever one may be, Venice in all her glory or an unconsidered valley; or where one's thoughts transport the mind. Josiah lived out of the world, unconsidered, usually. Yet at that point in chilly springtime, his roof and the place he had in the scheme of things bulked steadily larger.

Fentiman, who could find Madagascar and the varnished oceans by rotating the big globe which stood waist high in his London office, was, however, considering Josiah's pretty brick and flint house, with its acres. His agent, with whom he had just concluded an interview, would shortly convert his idea of a journey thither from his frown and forefinger above the inadequate map, into the reality of wet chalk roads and thin spring drizzle. As instructed by Fentiman he was to present himself as a purchaser in his own right of Josiah's Royalist acres, with no connection to Fentiman.

"You've to keep my name out of this," Fentiman had declared, "no word that you act for me, or the matter won't go forward. You are to state you are a private gentleman interested in settling out of Town. Say that chance affairs during the late conflict brought you through Stonebury. Liked the look of the area. That kind of thing. I want those lands of old Malahide's. Understand?"

"I could be free this day se'nnight."

"Not sooner?"

"Sir, I have my own affairs in hand, which I must settle."

"Mmmph," said Fentiman, but what was a week? The old adversary couldn't run away. Why hadn't he thought before of sending an agent to conceal his name? That'll net the bird, if old Malahide would think he had dodged the inescapable, Fentiman congratulated himself. Fate? No. It was his reward for perseverance.

"I'll put a steward in the house," he mused, "do the place up, put the farms in order."

"Yes, sir," said the acolyte, nodding well.

Hugh Malahide, his uncle's heir, a gentleman, if ineligible, pledged himself to keep the roof on for the little time his uncle had left. He could manage that, perhaps. But then! Then the moment of reckoning. As if the Last Trump sounded here below. Then the farms, valley lands and the house itself must be sold up. He would be banished, not only from his life here and what Josiah wished him to inherit, but, inevitably, from proximity, from his very status in Isabella's eyes. He'd be a down-and-out as sure as if he'd never come home here.

But yet he had her, clasped her. Because of the dragon knowledge of impending disaster breathing fire upon him, all he did with her was heated, sweeter, because it was not to last. He couldn't tell her, couldn't say 'when the farms fail, as in an eye blink they will – when Josiah dies – I'll lose all this. I'll lose more: I'll lose you.' He might have asked the Almighty to give him an extra half-hour, had he been a praying man. Or an hour, or…

The sun shone in a corner out of the breeze, where he sacrificed his better cloak to the damp grass and once its seventh-wave billow subsided, picked Isabella up hand under her knees and floated her on it. Deafened by the blue butterflies of the uplands, drowned in the daisies and harebells, he convulsively clasped Isabella's unspoilt maiden textures. She was murmuring pleasure he should not be giving her. The price he feared to pay was when he would have to watch his faun go back in the forest, away and lost to him.

But first, let her tighten on him, let him smile and have the pleasure.

Chapter XIV

The centre of the world about to end in the valley, as Hugh thought, was that above his head in the big sky of the downs – but there existed another besides Fentiman striving to reach it from the outer world. Fentiman's agent was still three days from packing his saddlebags when a letter arrived, not for Josiah at all, but for Hugh.

He thought, Was it from Tom?

It sat, a plain folded sheet with a sloping superscripture, on the kitchen table. He came in with filthy hands from a task in the yard, and found the pale rectangle grew in size with his puzzlement whilst he soaped his hands and forearms and rough-towelled himself dry enough to investigate.

If it wasn't from Tom, perhaps some comrade who'd wind of his whereabouts.

It took him two re-readings. It came from Athalia.

But not from, precisely. Hugh read it again, witless.

It addressed him formally by name, then ran, rather briefly, as follows: 'your presence is required, with such speed as convenient to yourself.' His informant, Hugh's obt. servant, was Athalia's steward, whose likeness, that of a stiff-necked, bald turtle, rose un-dusted from the back shelf of Hugh's mind.

It said so little it was difficult to ignore. Was Athalia ill, or had she burned the house down? Was she hoping he'd died so she might take a new husband? Had she heard he'd come into money? (Never believe rumour, said Hugh to himself wryly.)

What was it? He wouldn't go, of course.

Luisa thought he should. "Who knows?" she shrugged. "It must be of some moment or she would not have sent. She must have hazarded you'd come to us here."

Hugh threw the folded sheet. "It can't be of much import as she hasn't troubled to write herself, but has had Treliffe scratch a line." Athalia picking at the everlasting stitches whilst telling her steward what she wanted writ, rose from that same back shelf of Hugh's, the one he had thought cobwebbed for good.

Thus prodded into recalling a whole other life, it wouldn't let him forget. Perhaps that was what the letter by its brevity, meant to do. It was intended to fetch him.

Whatever was that important? It had been three and more years, a thousand days. For ever.

Josiah had slept and woken and slept for a week, steadily, as if he would hold that course for months.

"You should go and see," re-iterated Luisa. She thought he'd been fretting so over the straits the farms were in, that action might be preferable for him. "So long as you don't stay long away from us."

On that, he bowed to it, like a man who tries to put off his dose of physic, he'd have to do it, he supposed. Or it'd go on eating at him.

"But very briefly," he conceded, stuffing a saddlebag. Isabella, John Block, the sporting dog and Luisa came to bid him God Speed – what else could they do? Isabella experienced the considerable pangs of unwed lovers of dissembling. She hated his going.

The two pairs of newly packed saddlebags thus passed each other unknowingly on the Stonebury road, one coming, unannounced under a nom de guerre, for Fentiman; the other,

Hugh Malahide, going, to see his wife.

It was irrational, but it felt uncommonly like heading for the prison house to give himself up. It wasn't the crime that lowered the spirits, it was the jailer... after freedom and escape in the meantime. Freedom, even the freedom of King Charles's army, had come sweet.

The discovery he could lead and command men, that he could pull round a setback, lead the Troop as if breastplate and backplate and pot helmet were armour against all dangers: he had been brave, he had been reckless. To start with he had not cared if he had lived or died. This is the sort of man who makes a reputation, if, as Hugh Malahide had, he'd cared if his men lived to fight another day.

The truth of what he'd become seemed some sort of breastplate now, a protection against the prim Manor House he journeyed to, the married life in which he'd refused to be Athalia's poodle.

The opened doors of memory showed him his return from some estate business, muddied from riding, coming in, as Athalia had complained, like a common desperado in leather jerkin and bucket-top boots, into a nest of good little women, her friends, all sewing and sticking needles into embroidery and looking down their noses at him. Of Athalia early on, before what she thought were his looks had deserted him, pursed and coy in newly married bed, complaining he was a coarse goat with his advances. "I don't care to tolerate that sort of thing," she'd informed him, buttoned her mouth, nightshift and all points south against that sort of thing – and on the evening he remembered – had pulled the curtains on the tester bed leaving him standing on the floorboards. His separate cell, after that, had been solitary as a vault, but preferable.

She should have married Fentiman, thought Hugh, that'd have been interesting.

Two overnight stops at flea-pit taverns and he was through into the heavy clay and trees, the Sussex Weed of broad, spreading oaktrees. Sussex, where the products of the iron works had threatened him and his men with iron peril. The roar and red blood of butchery originated here, from the clearings of the forest where the hammer-ponds sent their beat through the forest.

Wasn't it typical that not King Charles but the Parliament held the armament manufactury? Not a Cause, nor the Right the King held, but the iron-masters held, here in Sussex.

How different it looked now he'd been out in the wide world. Smaller, almost, as if his young-man's memory had been that of a child who returns to his old home. Hugh had been his two yards high then as now, though.

Here was the village, with weatherboarding. No brick and flint here. The old days beset him, the day he'd dismissed Athalia's bailiff for having his barn full of her grain, and the man had tried and failed, to crack his jaw.

The miserable Puritans had a hold here, of course, there'd be no jolly maypole any more. Three men in sober hats looked curiously at Hugh walking Bonny along, their heads and the hats rotating as one. Not so much as a jolly goose girl crossed the green. O, for the Jack-in-the-Green and the mummers; O for discovering what Athalia wanted, and riding away.

She'd see a down-and-out in him already, of course; riding a down-and-out horse. Poor Bonny! But he'd not weaken. He wasn't here to let the past ride him.

He settled his collar, set his straight back and straight shoulders, and trotted Bonny vigorously between the manor gates, up the neater than neat drive, a contrast to his uncle's dandelions, to the stone-faced box of the house.

A rattle and dash cut Hugh's thought threads as if with shears. Behind him, between the tall gateposts, came a horseman riding hard on a cob, saddlebags flapping.

This was one race where Hugh was happy to finish second, but as he reined Bonny aside and the cob and man rattled by in a spray of gravel, he was puzzled. Athalia's was not a house often favoured by unseemly arrival, and yet he saw this man hopping off his piebald, clapping his hat on his head, and bursting in ahead of Hugh, saddlebag clasped in one hand. The door actually slammed behind him. Athalia wouldn't stand for that!

Well, let her send down old Treliffe to give her visitor a flea in his ear, divert her attention from her other caller, Hugh now decently arrived and dismounting.

Hugh supposed at this hour Athalia would be closeted with some crony-of-the-day, some lesser female; imported to be good to Athalia, simper with her at Hugh's masculine intrusions, amid the nest of little women he would interrupt sewing or playing with a wee dog or stuffing little cakes into their mouths, good little women together, so cosy and intimate. Hugh detested good little women, particularly Athalia.

He trod into the ebb of passage of that traveller, just in time to behold the swirl of his coat-tails rushing upstairs, followed by two female servants in full-sail skirts, all vanishing.

This brought a temporary vacuum behind it all, stranding Hugh there in the hall looking after the stampede. Doors on the landing were as shut left and right as closed mouths.

The hall was precisely tidy, formal chairs their two yards apart to the inch; great jars exhaled too pungent a dose of pot-pourri, like stepping too close to a perfumed woman. No welcome from a sporting dog, no untidy, ransacked jumble of easy life, only the chairs nobody sat on and the glassy floor.

Footsteps? He braced himself to turn and be recognised, if, indeed, he was recognisable at all, these days.

The left-hand doorway slid and out came a refined, mimsy young lady, like a smaller version of Athalia. This must be the confidant of the day, thought Hugh: what an unbecoming, great nose... his wife had always selected a lesser looker, to show her up favourably. Hugh did not know her, nor she him. A new comer... perhaps this was easier, first of all, than having Athalia look him up and down and sniff.

But the young woman hardly seemed to notice his arrival, left him standing there hand on hip about to accost her, because she drew up her skirts and also pelted upstairs.

What was going on?

Then a pair of stick legs, a stouter torso, a stern linen collar and lastly a turtle-bald old face came progressively into view, descending the stairs. Here was the steward, someone who must know Hugh, he thought at last.

Old Treliffe got three parts down the flight before identifying Hugh, appearing unimpressed by his former master standing there; as if his mind was elsewhere.

"Bless me," said he in his old nanny-goat's voice, "bless me."

Well, thought Hugh, hath he forgot he wrote to fetch me?

Treliffe left three stair treads between him and the flat lands of the floor and halted to focus better. Hugh, unwilling to burst into conversation with the old party, waited, fiddling with the glove in his hand. Did he need a ginger wig, two heads, before he caught the attention of these dullards?

But it wasn't that.

"Come with me, sir," quavered Treliffe, hand to his domed

old brow. Hugh walked up the stairs behind him, beginning to realise the scenario was not one he had painted. Where was Athalia, and who was the sudden arrival before him?

"Here, sir," bleated Treliffe, thrusting inwardly at the door fronting him. "Here—"

What he saw was a shadowed sickroom, the centre of it the prone figure of Athalia as if on her tomb, drawn and sunken on the bed.

He took three steps forward, grasped the bed-pole, dumb. To the unprepared Hugh she was an effigy, both faraway and close. He had tightened his grip on the bed-post until his nails drove back upon his fingers. On either side, he began to be aware of the physician who had arrived so soon before him, now putting something away in his leathern case, and on his other side servants, one holding a bowl, and the other with hands-to-head in the time-honoured gesture.

The confidante's contribution was to utilise that nose for loud snuffling into a handkerchief.

Treliffe was saying something in his dry nasal half-tone when Hugh was distracted by the arrival of a third newcomer, with limp auburn hair and a folder of papers under his arm. Hugh watched him creep through the door, recoil at the sight of the sickbed, and clutch much as Hugh had done, at a spare bed post.

Athalia opened her eyes, twin leaden sockets. These shifted from one to another there present, then back to Hugh standing at the foot of the bed.

He recognised extremity, he'd seen it before, men dragged aside on hurdles, wounded soldiers crammed into hovels, poor souls in twilight before darkness claimed them.

Athalia knew him, as if satisfied she held the power to bring him. She gasped, breathed twice, and died.

He actually observed the passage from spark in the leaden eyes, to blank.

He turned from the corpse and found the door, fumbled it, walked out on to the landing. He left them to shut her eyes, do what people do.

The sickroom smell turned his stomach. So did the death of someone he couldn't mourn. But yet, the passage of Athalia made a pang. How dreadful there had been no comforts of love shared.

He shook himself.

Freedom whistled in his ears.

There was no trap to keep him here. He had been summoned and yet released. It was sentence and reprieve.

Hugh walked straight down the staircase, strode the black and white squares of the hall. He threw the front door, and fresh air on his face was welcome.

He would be straightaways gone.

What had happened, though? Athalia had the health of ten men. But lying there, was reduced to a half of what she'd been – a pear-shaped woman with big knees. The difference was pathetic.

He thought, if he thought at all, that the household would see to things and he need not concern himself. It wasn't going to trap him.

He reached, out of comforting habit, to smooth Bonny's nose. All he really attended to was the swelling crescendo telling him he could grasp the reins here to his hand, mount, and go away.

He had his booted toe into her stirrup, poised to swing up, when he was distracted by the red-haired stranger who had come upstairs, now running out after him and restraining him by tugging at his sleeve.

"Sir, sir, you surely are not leaving?"

Hugh, still dazed, shook his arm to throw him off; but in so doing dislodged papers in a folder from under the other's arm onto the gravel of the drive. His bad manners brought him back to reality with a jerk, he looped up Bonny's rein hastily again and began darting about collecting the papers. "Here," he said, handing them back, "and I apologise, I've been discourteous."

"Nay, sir, you must be distracted, don't apologise. You would be, er, the husband?"

"I am," said Hugh, then stopping short. "I was."

"Thought so, thought so."

"What was it with her? What brought her to this? I had no idea."

"I understand it was a growth, poor lady. But only a fortnight since did the great decline come upon her, when, I believing there was yet time, I prevailed upon her she should have a line sent to you. But this very morning as you saw, a crisis came upon her, and Treliffe scarce had time to send for the physician out of town. He came hot on your heels, I hot upon yours."

"And you are, sir?"

"The lawyer, sir, Enoch Whitlock, your servant."

"Thank you, then, for your trouble in the business."

Hugh nodded civilly at him, thinking his surname inaccurate, turned to mount Bonny so he might get on his way. The mare responded to his boot heel and he turned her head for the gateway. Only to find Whitlock, ginger hair tossing like a dishmop, still hanging on to the rein, digging his buckled shoes into the gravel and generally preventing his departure. An unlikely staghound, an unwilling quarry. "Would you hinder me? Let go! I'd be away."

"But, sir, you can't go—"

"That's your opinion. Watch me and see!" exclaimed Hugh, set upon it. "I shall not stay here, nor shall you hinder me."

"Hold, hold, I must speak further!"

That the unfit pen-pusher should go to these lengths of personal exertion finally brought it home to Hugh that he was in earnest and that he, Hugh Malahide, was being most unreasonable.

"What then? But be brief!"

"I told you I'm the lawyer, sir. You really cannot rush off like this, I declare it. You don't seem to realise…"

"Realise what?"

"Sir, that what your wife summoned me to do and I came in haste too late to accomplish, was to see about the terms of her Will, her papers. She had not acknowledged the mortal nature of her illness, you see. Whatever it was she was minded to alter, to change, I cannot know, I came too late."

"What exactly are you telling me this for?"

The lawyer, orange mop subsiding, declined to offer up his folder to the breeze, but pointed emphatically at its closed cover. "I'm telling you, sir, that as your wife has died, you have, in due form, inherited."

Chapter XV

A hundred miles away the disguised voice of Fentiman had been making the offer Josiah's household thought they had been waiting for: under the name of Fentiman's agent, Henry Platt, and in his pinched London tones, the offer Fentiman had considered they couldn't refuse.

Josiah, of course, could refuse anything. Blinking and feeble, he sat up a little and growled quietly at this Master Platt for presuming he might want to sell at all.

"Do pray understand me," quoth Platt, anxious they should do no such thing. "I'm wishing to settle in the area, liked the look of it—"(he waved his hand airily in the direction of the window, the derelict bowling green and the further horizon, impartially). "All this. I am attracted to living out of Town. The easing of the Conflict turns one's thoughts to peaceful prospects."

He delivered the latter part of the speech rather better, as it happened to be his own sentiment: though he would prefer somewhere nearer to, like Hammersmith.

Josiah, his pulse fluttering like a private bird, felt the quandary of having his bluff called. He'd said, Wouldn't sell to old Fentiman, the reptile. Said it many a time.

Sure in his own mind noone else would offer.

Now it wasn't Fentiman, but this London creature. Platt with his lack-lustre chin dropping its little paunch upon his neck linen; who'd passed through Stonebury and been struck with the area.

Luisa would often chide him that he wouldn't face up to

facts. Facing them did not make them palatable. But it was a good offer. It'd set him up in decent rooms in Stonebury with Luisa, wouldn't it? Perhaps it would be a relief?

"… you'd keep my tenants in?"

"I can't say which way to that," answered Platt, unprepared, "I'll have to go into that later."

Josiah, focussing unevenly on his visitor, conceived a mislike of the dapper person nursing his knees on the edge of the chair in front of him. In front, indeed, of Josiah's bright, cheery fire, in his, Josiah's little retreat as personal with him as his favourite suit of clothes… a migrant, Platt, thinking he would become a colonist, was he? Settle here? He didn't look the part, the indoor cheese complexion, the neat furry dead-mouse moustache hiding the ends of his smile so one could not tell whether to smile back (always supposing, growled Josiah inwardly, that one wished to go to those lengths) – and the air, so difficult to pin down, of determined crawling.

He didn't want to believe in this man Platt, but – here was the rub – he was not his enemy Fentiman. Fentiman's tone, as he knew from those hated letters, was 'naturally I am doing you a favour.'

This Platt was oiling round with 'please do me a favour.'

It would have been better judged, thought Josiah, if I cared for soft soap.

It was a good offer. He did know that.

But he'd used up his strength. He felt a little tired and clasped one claw hand over the other to keep shaking to a minimum.

Why didn't he sign and be done with it? Luisa wanted him to sign.

But Josiah wasn't that tired.

He wouldn't capitulate. Not he. He glared like Vesuvius at the disconcerted Platt. "Don't expect an answer," he said, "until my nephew returns."

"And how long will that be?" enquired Platt, hoping the nephew was merely gone to market. His moustache did not quite hide his regret that the stay in this area he admired so much was come upon him quicker than he anticipated.

He called each day for the next three days, but the nephew was slow coming.

On the fourth day, Isabella saw him.

She had a memory for faces.

Anxious about the old gentleman, she and John Block stepped down the meadow, crossed the plank bridge and came up the slope to Josiah's house, now bowered in sweet-smelling gillyflowers. At the porch they nearly collided with the outward going Henry Platt as he bundled forth; for a moment they were eyeball to eyeball, she perhaps half an inch the taller.

"That's strange," she murmured to Block, "strange."

"What is, my girl?"

"I know that man. He is that master Henry something who did business off and on with Father."

Block fixed his little eyes on his charge. Isabella knowing things he didn't? "Are you certain?"

"He looked to me the very man father had to dine, I was allowed in after the meal to get a sugar violet, and just as I came in the room he spilled his wine down father. It caused a wonderful uproar, that's why I remember."

"That's the effect you had on him," said Block kindly, "you are not to be trusted."

"Nay, be serious. What's he doing here, of all places? Whatever does he want?"

"He's your father's man. He was coming out of Josiah's."

Block clumped through the kitchen, ignoring the maids chopping at the tarragon and the new oregano. "This is beyond coincidence."

Brownie raised his domed head from his forepaws and watched them pass.

Block was putting two and two together, as was Isabella, and they consulted Luisa, readily made four. Luisa had been tending the bees in the kitchen garden when they found her. "They've had a bad winter," she greeted them. "They'll like these warm days."

"Is it true that you tell them births and deaths?"

"Or events, yes."

"Then." Isabella had led for an opening. "It maybe I bring something for the bees. Did you know that gentleman who has just left, is a man of my father's?"

Luisa sat down on the bench by the new mint spears, dismayed. "Oh no. That's the lie of the land, then. A go-between, to buy us up so Josiah wouldn't know and say his Nay the tenth time to your father. That's what it is." She swatted at the mint. "So you recognised the man, this Platt?"

"I did: whereas he didn't know me, I have grown six inches since we encountered. He is a man does business with father off and on."

"Doesn't hanker after country life?"

"I think not for an instant. What's he been saying? But – you are not selling up? Please say Nay!"

"Do I tell you all?" asked Luisa gravely. She made a choice, for what could they do, if not allied? But trust Fentiman's daughter? Isabella had hardly been acting like a Parliamentarian daughter, and her brother was of no such persuasion, after all.

251

It was a treaty as in warfare. Here, the Parliamentarian household and the Royalists were making terms. They had united on two fronts. To rescue Josiah from the schemers, and, to accept Hugh had embroiled with the young lady.

Luisa clear as day, had seen the target of Hugh's attention, Hugh who she'd known all the years he'd come a-visiting, now grown out of his breathtaking looks into wrecked handsomeness. He'd held them all together over the winter – and had evidently felt the blind boy's arrow with all its complications over Isabella.

She, Isabella, had a right to know what Luisa was finding it painful to tell her. "The farms have failed till we cannot pay our way," said she reluctantly. "Josiah won't sell to your father. We thought, noone else would want us. Then this man came to lead us to believe we'd netted an offer to avoid him."

"But this is Father using a device. I know him."

Isabella crushed the sprigs of new mint she'd picked into an inhalation; she added up Hugh's strained face, the fear she'd carried of something amiss he couldn't bear to tell her. She sat down as if told of a death.

Lose the game old gentleman in his lovely muddled house, lose the people who'd saved Tom and befriended her. Lose Hugh, lose him.

"Tell me you haven't agreed a sale."

"Josiah refuses to do aught about the sale till Hugh returns. Praise be, that he stuck on that. This has been a near run race, has it not…" Luisa's expression lifted. "We'll tell Josiah you've seen through this Platt. 'Twill cheer him mightily to learn he has outsmarted your father."

"Ah," sighed Isabella. "All this when I had considered Father reconciling with Tom, not a monster, but now I learn this."

"Without you," began Luisa cautiously, "Josiah would never

have known the nature of this caller of his. I urged him the wrong way and we'd have sold to this enemy. Hugh will be back directly, never fear. Then we will together find some solution, God knows what, that Josiah can bear."

They stepped towards the house, shadowed by Block in his black clothes, he concluding that the old lady and his young one had likely allied rather better than had King Charles with all his Scots and French and Irish, yet the old gentleman in his run-down private castle might be beleaguered Oxford at its last ditch, for all the hope he could discern.

Hugh had to remain where he was, then, all amazed. He saw his wife into the ground. He grieved for her pain, but could not for her life, during which she had not softened, nor kissed back. Not that after a fair trial, he had wanted her to.

Standing at the graveside trying to steer between duty and false pretence, he realised he'd never know what it was she intended with the lawyer, had the time remained for her to do it. Her Will... had remained as it was, untouched since whenever. It seemed she'd had second thoughts by her very action in sending for Whitlock, when she knew how matters ran with her.

But he was her wedded spouse.

...What had he said, ages back, to Isabella? "That which the wife hath is the husband's." He'd been no charge on that. He'd left, and been poor in the world, been self-sufficient, and sometimes been paid by the army.

The clergyman was eyeing him sideways. Had he to throw soil now? He hadn't been attending. This grisly business had to be gone through. He wouldn't ape tears. Let him stand here impassively, eyes on the tussocks and the gravestones encrusted like old grey cheese with lichens.

The red haired lawyer at his side tugged his sleeve, like the pilot fish in charge of a brooding shark.

The lawyer was indicating they'd done, could come away. Leading the way back to the house, back to the papers Hugh must see, he felt Hugh needed an ally. He hadn't seemed quite the masculine brute he had expected from the scenario given out at the Manor. He couldn't have lived with Athalia, himself. She gave him the quivers.

Two days' business and a compact between them was established.

Hugh finally grasped it wasn't too good to be true. He was of worth in the world. The estate he had masterminded ran in the tracks he'd set.

"The sum of it?" repeated Whitlock, the pen behind his ear wagging as he shrugged. "I need more time to be precise, but the sum of it is prosperity, if I may say so."

"Can I leave it under your hand to look at it for me? No, no! I will be back to see to it—" (the lawyer's ginger prawn eyebrows hopped up and down) "Let me explain. I must, must, get me home to my uncle. He is very old indeed. And hath been in such straits. What has happened is wonderful for me because I can save him. By circumstances he's been forced to the brink of selling up the sweetest of acres, the fairest house. I cannot hang here, I simply cannot."

"You'll be moving down here, though, I take it?" asked Whitlock, his prawns drawing together for company over his nose.

"Good God!" cried Hugh, leaping up; papers flapped like seagulls round the tabletop. "Don't you see I hate the place?"

"In that case," murmured Whitlock, "you will need a man in your stead. Until you decide what suits. I could shut my office for a while. Business has been…"

He never completed. Hugh was round the table shaking his hand.

In the morning he was away at the daybreak.

Journeying home, whether in the best inn in Marychurch, never mind the Puritan vultures praying in the church, impervious to the long extempore sermon – (they were still in there when Hugh remounted Bonny in the cobbled square) – he pulled Bonny's ear affectionately, and they trotted off.

He'd gone out so poor if his saddlegirth had given way, he couldn't have replaced it.

He could put money in the farms, hearten the dispirited men who worked them; he could – blessed thought – ride in to his uncle's waving his hat for joy that he could save him. No nightmare of strangers coming in to oust the fusty cornucopia of treasures. No last-ditch Naseby for his uncle. Josiah could stay put.

Josiah had given him a sanctuary. Now he could tell the good old Trojan he, Hugh, in his turn, could do the good deed.

Hugh's tearing spirits ran like a bolting horse before him: the shackles fell away, his uncle, Isabella; all he hadn't been able to do, couldn't lawfully offer. Now, now …

The bolting horse ran all the way with him up to The Red Lion crouching with its cat-slide roof against the slope of the valley, the valley he was coming to save.

He wasn't for stopping, he was riding Bonny by, dazzled by the whitethorn and serenaded by every bird whose egg had hatched that morning, when out of The Red Lion came voices hailing him.

He whoa-ed Bonny and half turned in the saddle, hand on her quarters, to see his friend the landlord, in his apron, signalling to him, and at his elbow the broad flat face of the horse doctor, Ebenezer.

"Friends, good day..."

Hugh sat at ease relaxed and happy, mane of hair blowing, the smoothing of anxiety leaving his face younger, eyes a-spark.

"Sir, glad we caught you," called the landlord in a queer tone, whereupon the bolting horse of Hugh's glad spirits dug its feet in and threw him.

"What is it?"

"You'd best come in a minute," suggested Ebenezer, and he stood at Bonny's head until Hugh swung down. Evidently dodging whatever it was, Ebenezer began to lead Bonny round the back, to the dismay of the landlord, deserting him.

"Benezer – now then!"

"I'll be right with ee," allowed Benezer, caught.

Puzzled, disturbed, and unseated from euphoria, Hugh had to watch whilst Bonny's hooves rang a muted march away in the horse doctor' charge, to wait while the landlord, embarrassed and dumb, armed him physically indoors and refused to say a word until he'd given him a dose of brandy and Ebenezer had come back.

"Well, tell me what's to-do."

The pair eyed each other.

"Look, I hates to bring this." Ebenezer actually took his hat off and sat staring down at it on his lap, stroking it absently as if petting the cat. The landlord hemmed and tried to regain speech.

"Ebenezer's come up from your place, he's got news, I'm afraid."

"Do you start, Olly," said Benezer faintly. "Tell yours."

"Is it true you been sold up, sir?"

"By, Jehovah, no! What is all this?" Had Josiah run mad in

his absence? Had Danae appeared in a shower of Fentiman gold? Not now, when I'm arrived to save the day! Not now!

"I've had this gentleman staying, see," Olly began, unhappily, "an 'every day this last week he's gone down to your uncle an' come back as if, as if he were warming something up there."

"I know naught of this." Hugh shook his head.

"We all knows what a struggle you been having, begging your pardon, sir – Hayman's boy and them others, they all been saying, these past months. It ain't true, then?"

"Not to my knowledge, no, no. I pray not in my absence."

"Only that, my guest, sir, kept saying he meant to settle in these parts, see, that's why he came. And seeing as you'd gone, sir, an' people wondered if 'twere for good, an' yesterday my visitor, he, he—"

"He what?"

"We none of us want it, sir, that we don't. All regard for you and yours."

"For God's sake, what happened?"

"He gone down again to your place all smiles, that' the burden of it."

"And—"

"We were afraid he must'a concluded, sir, because he were hanging around for a purpose, like. 'Sfunny, we all believed ol' master Fentiman were after the purchase, but 'tweren't he. This person paid our reckoning, an' said his business here was all done an' he was very glad the matter was settled."

"That's no proof!"

"He looked most noticeably pleased with himself."

Hugh had heard supposition and gossip, would be off in haste to discover the substance of all this, if any; dimly glad his friends should care so much, but their faces opposite him were still as long as fiddles.

"Right. I'll be off to discover what this nonsense is." Hugh, only a little disquieted, swung himself out of the corner seat where they'd thrust him, thinking it really wasn't worth them standing him a brandy unless – no, his uncle wouldn't sell up, ever.

"Sir, sit down again," begged Ebenezer. "There's more."

Josiah had full measure of the information Isabella brought and once he'd understood Fentiman had sent his man to do the dirty work he growled and sparked and cackled with the sense of vanquishing his enemy. Seen through him, had the last laugh.

He wrought himself up to see off Master Platt. This'll be ripe to tell Hugh, he thought. Pity he wasn't back to share it. But it was good to feel that old as he was, he had the reins in his hands, and he'd allow himself the pleasure of the little interview.

So he was tucked up in his rug with the sun coming in the windowpanes of his best chamber, dust-motes dancing in the light; he'd had Harry wheel him in especially, from the little room where he had parked for the winter.

Let Fentiman's creature see what he, Josiah, was about to deny him! What he wouldn't be getting his hands (concealed by the gloves of pretence) upon!

See this handsome room with the carvings on the panelling.

He'd be the match for guile.

"I have decided not to sell," he quavered, watching the Platt moustache rise, "O," and chins fall.

"You will consult your nephew, first, of course?" parried Platt, surprised. He'd thought he was coming on nicely, water wore stones away and even this old flint was prey to natural causes. If he needed the money as rumour said he did.

"My nephew's views are as mine own."

"Sir, you cannot know this until he be home to tell us so. We, um, could decide to keep those tenants in…"

"Nay," quoth Josiah, "I am loath to waste your time further, well knowing that The Red Lion hath its fleas aplenty. My house hath its watchdog. Between fleas and dog, I fear you must be mighty pricked by bites."

Platt twitched. He'd never liked this assignation. Had the old man spies? What did he know? It wasn't his idea to be here under false colours.

"You, sir, have the look of a London man about you, no true protester of a love of ricks and meads and our country muds," the old man asserted. "I am happy to lessen the shock for your town-bred nature. Your place is among the sea-coal smoke, if ever sea-coal be restored to you. I only am glad to do you a favour, Master, er, what was your name?"

Platt, thinking he was well rid of the whole horrid pretence, rejoiced all the way back to The Red Lion, and thence, to familiar, bustling London.

Josiah wanted to tell Isabella he was indebted she had a memory for faces, and called her in. By then he was tired and a little muddled. He held her hand, reflecting that she must favour her dam, not old Fentiman. He just restrained himself from a favourite saying, for it was possibly not appropriate to mention enemies when talking to his enemy's daughter. But, inwardly, he ran it through:

"Stand long enough by the bank of the river and sooner or later, you will see the body of your enemy floating past." Fentiman, outmanoeuvred.

Fentiman hadn't bought him out, not by fair means, not by

any means. Here was Fentiman's daughter, who had tipped them off. Bless her for it. Wasn't her fault, her father. "Saved the day, lady," he was telling her, "'Tis still my hearth and home, as ever was."

"I wished you to be able to say so."

"Hugh won't be long returning, say, tomorrow. Slip down to us to see."

The room swam a little, but he hadn't finished. "Glad we saved Tom," he said, and then, inconsequentially, "I never liked Athalia."

That night he thought Luisa a girl again, bending over him to tie his broad ribbon sash, her hair brushing his face as she straightened. Then her dark eyes changed, and became full of light, amethysts, as Isabella took her place, elusive, far and near. He couldn't catch her. Then a fallow deer ran into the springtime woods, as green and new as lettuce. Something beautiful passed by.

The real Luisa came, and he knew her. It grew dark. She was holding his hand. Time went by in fits and starts until at last in the black night, his spirit felt the cage of his body, like a trapped bird; the bars beat upon him, the cage opened, released him and he died.

Within ten minutes, everything was perfect, then nothing perfect. Hugh Malahide, beset with demons, could only rattle down the valley as fast as Bonny could go, feeling the air thick with mocking, jeering companions. The gargoyles off the church roof, the cruelty in the doom picture, all these.

The whitethorn drooped, the birds had fled. He couldn't bear it – that, with tidings to make the church bells peal, prosperity within reach – he was about to face that he had no home, and, that his uncle was no more.

He wouldn't be able to tell Josiah, "All's well!"

The old man had given him hope and he had been about to return it.

The waterweed trailed its flowers in the brook, so lovely, the ford eddied, shallow now, and the meadow was starred with every constellation, white and blue and yellow.

Why must his homecoming mock him? To find he'd lost it all, the meadow was a wasteland and the house showing its summer face to the evening, derelict. He flung himself from Bonny to walk up the last stretch, not wanting to face reaching the door.

He beheld Luisa coming from the kitchen garden, her skirt sweeping the daisies. Her hands were hidden in a muff of pansies.

"I have been telling the bees," said she, "and here are my strewing-flowers. I needn't ask if you've heard."

She showed a more serene face than he. He read the sorrow in hers, but not, however, desperation. What she saw in his, was that of King Tantalus when all he desired receded.

"I met Ebenezer and Olly at the Lion. Oh, Luisa, I was nearly here – why couldn't he wait?"

"He tried to," she told him, "he said you'd be home tomorrow, and, see, here you stand. He faded away, that's what it was. I held his hand."

"Thank you for that. But, Luisa, the – other?"

He couldn't say it, for the moment, and she was puzzled. "What other?"

"The landlord said his visitor, Fentiman's creature, had – dear God, Luisa, tell me, tell me, is all sold up and lost? Olly thinks it was all signed while I was away?"

"My dear, no, no." With her gesture to comfort him as his

face worked with emotion, she spilled the strewing-flowers around their feet and around Bonny's hooves. "We are hard-pressed, broke and failing, but that is not news. And yes, we did have an offer. We didn't accept it."

Can one believe good news? Luisa, uncomprehending as yet of all it was with him, tried to explain how Fentiman's agent, under a false flag, had tried to buy them out, indeed he had. "Your uncle died happy because he'd seen off his adversary."

Bonny was eating the strewing-flowers.

Hugh hadn't said a word of his news yet.

"You'll trust me with the mare?" He heard Luisa's quizzical voice behind his shoulder. "For sure, I've led a horse before this. By the way, it is your lady that recognised the purchaser as your father's agent: Josiah was delighted."

Hugh, reviving, now awaited the living Isabella, attempting calm. He considered what entry into Heaven Josiah would have made, trusting the other enemies that had gone before might be cordoned off so as not to aggravate him, much as if when Hugh's time came, he found himself next to Colonel Cromwell, Ireton his son-in-law, and... Athalia.

He anticipated then heard Isabella's footfall, soft as she came near, aware he had become a free man.

"Now, Isabella," he commenced, "I am home now you are come." Thus declaring himself in front of the others, unaware of the strength of his charm-the-birds smile but all aware of her pull upon him.

This now was his house, the special Kingdom. Aware of the first time he could do so, he bid the others, even Block, to leave them be. The door shut.

Now, this mattered more than all the rest.

"Isabella, you've held the perfect excuse not to have me

hitherto, seeing as we aren't Anabaptists, with women in common (I did think of changing) – until now, I was tied to Athalia. Now, your excuse is removed you..."

It was only now he was free to take the words, offer them.

"Marry me?"

She saw his parted lips, that he was strong and tender. The depths of the blue of his eyes overwhelmed her response. He felt the hand he had taken tensed, that she shivered, and he feared his faun became the wary long-lashed doe and would run from him.

But he was mistaken. Isabella took one step and clasped him fast in her arms, told him the truth in his ear.

"I love you beyond words."

Ah, the moment. A blur of triumph (where were the trumpets? Where was Block at the keyhole?) dulled the battleground ahead, that of persuading her father not to have him thrown forth on his enquiry for Isabella's hand. Perhaps the weathervane had shifted in his favour. The rescue from the mutineers had to have helped, he hoped.

Let me not discourage the moment: I am embracing this gentle creature. Let me call up Isabella's smile.

"Let me call up Isabella's smile."

He flourished bravado. "I intend to buy myself the most sober suit and hat in the world, in which disguise to entreat your father most sedulously that I may pay court to his daughter. A black hat and a black suit... and when my hat is in my hand, I shall show him a fine hatful, of acres. I shall be irresistible."

"Please resort to bribery, but you are not surely going to renounce Josiah's lands?"

There came the place of pitfall. He had more to tell. First, "Could you live in this rackety house?"

"In heaven's name! It is a happy Kingdom." Isabella's eyes gave the dowry to the stern man before he so much as got near to ask her father for her.

Hugh was visited by a helpful vision of the bait to offer. As good as had he been the bride with a dowry. "I have it!" he cried. "I have the very thing to charm him." I have blandishments. I have the very house, and, aha, fine acres – the very inducements! He can live in a fine, well-ordered establishment, in style."

"Athalia's!"

"Oh yes," affirmed Hugh, eyes sapphires. "I do think Sussex will suit him."

He'd refuse to visit, of course. He'd compromise, and allow Fentiman a little trip up here occasionally.

Tom could come, on different days.

"I can bear the pompous creature, if you're the reward and I need not see him too often."

And Isabella would be led to him in church on strings, not unwillingly, just the show; and this disordered treasure house here would welcome them.

"Do we tell John Block first, or the bees?" asked Isabella. He saw the crescents in her smile and delight.

"Ask both to keep our secret while I commence with your

father," sighed Hugh, wanting a trumpeter to tell the valley, the world. To think he'd believed the house sold and all lost.

"We would have told Josiah," Isabella regretted.

"Oh, yes," the thought brought back the whirligig of these days, but he rode it, because she looked up at him, amethysts.

"We live here and now, this is our turn. We shall be clay, but oh, not now—"

When he felt her embrace through his thin shirt he wasn't clay in the least.

It was strange, with the dark coming down, the royalists routed, King Charles held by the ear by the Scots, that he could feel light and hope rush in, that now, in the Puritan dark days, with his darling he could live in his hole, and sing.